# A NEW
# PILGRIM'S PROGRESS

# A NEW PILGRIM'S PROGRESS

*John Bunyan's Classic imagined in a
contemporary setting*

*by*

GEOFFREY T. BULL

HODDER AND STOUGHTON

*Printed in Great Britain*
*for Hodder and Stoughton Limited,*
*St. Paul's House, Warwick Lane, London, E.C.4,*
*by Richard Clay (The Chaucer Press), Ltd.,*
*Bungay, Suffolk*

# CONTENTS

Prologue                                    *page* 9

Chapter 1    The Bones and the Book                17

2    Mishap on the Mudflats                        23

3    The Menace of the Mountain                    33

4    Mansion of Mystery                            45

5    Searched by The Symbols                       50

6    The Horror that Heals                         62

7    The Skull-faced Summit                        67

8    Sleeping Sickness                             71

9    The Voice of the Virgins                      81

10    Motel Magnificent                            88

11    Trail of Terror                              100

12    Walking and Talking                          105

13    The Fun of the Fair                          113

14    The Judge and the Jury                       118

15    Gods of Gold                                 129

16    The Giant and the Gaol                       138

17    Hilltop and Sheer Drop                       148

18    Ignorance and Arrogance                      152

19    The World of Wolves                          156

20    Fall-out! Fall-in!                           161

21    Faith Fogbound                               165

22    The Road to the River                        170

23    The Crisis of the Crossing                   181

24    The Gulf at the Gate                         188

# ACKNOWLEDGEMENTS

THE author wishes to thank all those who assisted him and encouraged him in the completion of *A New Pilgrim's Progress*.

Especial thanks are due to:
Mr. F. T. Wells, curator of the Bunyan Museum, Bedford, for so willingly supplying data regarding John Bunyan's life and times.

Those specialists in the literary, theological and medical fields, who though they may wish to remain anonymous, submitted, on request, their assessment of this work in its preliminary stages.

Marshall, Morgan and Scott Ltd, Publishers, for the use of the stanzas on page 161, composed by Harriet B. Stowe.

# PROLOGUE

*I stood at the crossroads*
*in the heart of Bedford,*
*on a day of wan spring sunshine.*
*The traffic surged and stopped,*
*then surged again*
*before the red, green, amber eyes*
*of winking traffic lights.*

*I counted ten sets altogether,*
*plus a host of hostile signs.*
*No Entry! No Parking! No Left Turns!*
*No Loading! Not to speak of*
*the bus-stop and the firm reminder,*
*Dogs must be kept on lead!*

*All around me*
*stared sundry symbols of human need;*
*a men's clothiers, a women's clothiers,*
*a chemist's shop,*
*two insurance firms,*
*a solicitor's office,*
*a departmental store*
*and four bright telephone kiosks,*
*painted red.*

*Hither and thither on the bare road,*
*criss-crossed a multitude*
*of yellow lines*
*and sharp white arrows.*
*Then, as if to clarify the situation,*
*there stood three metal hoardings,*
*each like a preacher in his pulpit,*
*each like a judge on his bench,*
*strong in their set high places,*
*warning the unwary,*
*exhorting the populace,*
*DO NOT ENTER THE BOX*
*UNLESS YOUR EXIT*
*IS CLEAR.*

9

### A New Pilgrim's Progress

*At my feet on the pavement*
*shone brazen letters.*
*They formed a plaque,*
*the memory of a single man*
*forgotten in the footsteps*
*of the many men.*
*It read:*

*ON THIS SITE STOOD*
*THE*
*BEDFORD COUNTY GAOL*
*WHERE*
*JOHN BUNYAN*
*WAS IMPRISONED*
*1660–1672*

*The gears were changing*
*but a voice came through the gears,*
*equally metallic.*
*The cars were fuming*
*but the stale blood*
*reeked from the flag-stones,*
*equally pungent.*

> *'Hear your judgement.*
> *You must be had*
> *back again to prison*
> *and there to lie*
> *three months following;*
> *and at the three months' end,*
> *if you do not submit*
> *to go to church*
> *to hear divine service*
> *and leave your preaching,*
> *you must be banished the realm;*
> *and if after such a day*
> *as shall be appointed you*
> *to be gone, ye shall be found*
> *in this realm;*
> *or be found to come over again*
> *without special license*
> *from the king,*

*you must stretch*
*by the neck*
*for it.*
*I tell you plainly.'* *

*John Bunyan entered the box.*
*The light was red but*
*none could stop him.*
*There was a fatal collision.*
*Justice died, but*
*Truth survived.*

*'As to this matter,' he said,*
*'I am not at a point with you,*
*for if I were out of prison*
*today,*
*I would preach the Gospel*
*tomorrow.'†*

*Now the lights have changed*
*and we all drive on;*
*but we don't make history any more;*
*only noises,*
*ugly, faceless noises*
*in our endless,*
*graceless streets. . . .*

I went from the crossroads to the river, where the massive foliage of the horse-chestnuts, alive with a myriad fresh pink blooms, bowed heavily towards the placid waters of The Great Ouse. Beneath its quiet flow the foundations of an earlier bridge lay unperceived, whilst on its banks the fourteen stories of a new hotel surveyed with glassy eyes the bustle of the ancient town. A parapet attracted attention, and I gleaned another piece of history from its clear inscription.

On the shallow, east of the third pier,
stood the stone house, wherein Bunyan,
imprisoned from 1675–1676, wrote the
first part of *Pilgrim's Progress*.

It was not too far, I found, through the fields to Elstow, hamlet

* Justice Keelin's pronouncement.
† John Bunyan's historic reply.

of Bunyan's birth and scene of his youthful years. On the way I peered briefly through the rustic windows of the rectory of St. John the Baptist's. The cedar tree was still growing in the garden and the centuries-old mansion, though crumbling, had kept its character since Bunyan's day. It was here he came, for spiritual counsel, to the 'holy Mr. Gifford' and was so helped in his pilgrimage that he later immortalised it as 'The House of the Interpreter'. Not far from the village, amidst the hedgerows bright with the mayflower, stood a simple memorial to mark his birthplace; and on the green, covered with the fresh spring grass, were remnants of the village cross, where as a youth he played his 'Tip-Cat', and the words of God rang in his conscience,

Wilt thou leave thy sins and go to Heaven or have thy sins and go to Hell?

Just a stone's throw away from the green towered the Norman Church of St. Helena, a landmark of a thousand years. There Bunyan heard 'many a good sermon' and culled his thought of the wicket-gate from the narrow entrance constructed in the larger door. I visited also The Mort Hall, a fine old Tudor market-house nearby. It was restored for the Festival of Britain in 1951 and today its fiery brick and ancient timbers still add their warmth to the tiny community. It was within these walls the humble origins of the tinker-evangelist were best portrayed. A reconstructed fireside, with the barest furnishings, gave meaning to his own remark that at his marriage, his bride and he had 'neither dish nor spoon betwixt them'. Despised in his village as an inveterate liar and habitual blasphemer, who could have imagined that this ignorant and uncouth peasant of the English countryside would have authored a spiritual allegory, which under the hand of God was destined to lead a countless throng from many nations to the feet of Christ. Such is the transforming power of the God who saves. It is nothing short of a miracle that one hundred thousand copies of *Pilgrim's Progress* were published within ten years of its writing, and that well nigh three hundred years later it is being read, in part or in whole, in no less than two hundred and eighty languages.

Beyond the village of Elstow, the landscape stretched away through broad flat fields, a parade ground for rank on rank of brick-kiln chimney-stacks. Like sentinels they stood, stiffly alert to challenge all intruders, and as I passed, their long white plumes of smoke were lifting lazily in the meagre breeze. The car now bore me swiftly to the wooded ridge that circles Bedford. 'Hill

Difficulty' is quickly climbed at fifty miles per hour. It is our ease
we find so insurmountable. Alighting at a cattle grid I took the
path through the quiet lush pastures, leading to the ruins of 'The
House Beautiful'. Before my eyes its gaunt yet stately walls rose
strangely magnificent, commanding, as in a bygone day, the distant vistas of the meadowland below. I wondered, as I paced the
sequestered drive, how fierce those watch-dogs must have been
when Bunyan passed that way. His frightened Pilgrim all but
fled, he tells us, and would have done so had not 'the lions' been
chained!

At Harlington I found the bridge over the main line under
repair but there was an improvised footway and I crossed over
into the village to find its streets almost deserted. Taking my
stance by the war-memorial, I looked across to the manor-house,
once the country seat of Justice Wingate. Although largely hidden behind the trees, I could see its new white facing through the
leaves, crowned with soft brown tiling and matched with neat
and tidy windows. The careful renovation had removed much of
the old austerity, and more than that, it was lilac time. The tall
mature bushes, in fullest fettle, protruded their white and purple spikes in gay profusion across the wall. It was here, I learned,
the accusing finger of a lifeless orthodoxy first made its allegations
against John Bunyan. He was in a neighbouring village at the
time, called Lower Samsell. Folk from the farms had gathered,
and as he opened his Bible, a constable stepped in, arrested him
and brought him to this very house where now I stood. There he
was kept overnight pending the return of Justice Wingate. After
an ill-tempered interrogation by the magistrate, he was finally
marched to the county gaol. But God admits of no defeat. Three
granddaughters of this judge were later won for Christ and
worshipped at 'The Bunyan Meeting' in Bedford. I lingered a
moment but found it hard in the peaceful atmosphere of that
sunny afternoon to capture the drama of those far-off days. All I
could ponder was the beauty around me; the buttercups in the
fields, apple blossom in the gardens and cow parsley nodding a
thousand white heads all down the lane. Is this where men fought
for their faith? But now, perhaps, they have no faith to fight
for!

I came back into Bedford and gazed once more at the river. On
the site of the Duck Millstream a group of schoolgirls, complete
with life-jackets, were preparing their canoes. Then, from under
the bridge swept two hard-rowing crews of boys, watched by their
coach with a critical eye, from a raised seat aft. Where were they
going? Nowhere, I suppose, in particular. It was for the sport of

the thing and such fun for the moment. But soon they must grow up. Then they will need another answer. 'On the shallow, east of the third pier' they may still find it, in the words of a man to whom Christ was everything, and a prison his pulpit.

As I talked to Mr. F. T. Wells, one of the old pilgrims in Bedford, and curator of The Bunyan Museum for many years, he told me of some visitors from the Soviet Union whom he had shown the relics and documents of the Bunyan story. They looked with interest on the anvil bearing his name, the metal violin exquisitely fashioned by his own hand, and the little round jug used by his blind daughter, Mary, to bring him his soup in the cell every night. Then suddenly they saw the model of the old prison-house spanning the river. This moved them as nothing else. Maybe the hearts of many in Eastern Europe beat nearer to Bunyan's than our own. From time to time I receive long lists of people who even now, in Soviet Russia, are being sent to restrictive camps for preaching Christ from an open Bible; and some, the reports indicate, have already been robbed of their children. Is it not true that the battle of Bunyan's day must be fought afresh in every generation?

What then shall we do? Our land fills up with dark persuaders. A seeping anarchy erodes the liberties our forbears won. The lust for loathsome things makes monsters of us all and tottering nations wrestle on the brink of hell! Is there no answer?

John Bunyan's 'Pilgrim' stirred the world! The varied characters his pen portrayed, mirrored mankind to men and showed them God. Next to the Bible, his book became most widely read. Born in 'a den' and laughed to scorn, it grew to unimagined fame. But that was yesterday. Its vast appeal has largely waned. Though ranked a classic in its field, it sadly moulders now upon our shelves. Can Bunyan's 'Pilgrim', faced with all our so-called progress, walk again?

Then came the challenge. Why not revive his ageing figures, give them our dress and speech, sit them in cars, in capsules and in planes and see what they would say today? 'A gimmick and a parody,' someone will carp. 'Why tinker with the tinker's tale?' Yet if the vessel serves again is not such tinkering well worth while?

So in my travels of the last twelve months, in Canadian cold and Caribbean heat, the modern allegory emerged, until amidst the Scottish hills this book was born. If, thus conceived and brought to birth, the story shocks you or disturbs, count it not puerile or profane. The naked truth of Bunyan's work was never pleasing, but here at least, 'the swaddling clothes' are fresh and new; and still a sign, I trust, to lead men to the Saviour of the world.

And now, maybe, you've had enough. You feel quite sure that this is not your line. But wait and see; who knows, the wave-length after all, might still be yours.*

---

* The Scripture quotations embodied in the text of this New Pilgrim's Progress are drawn from various editions, though chiefly from The Revised Standard Version.

The quotations from Bunyan's verse are occasionally re-phrased to achieve cadence in the new context. Those wishing to ascertain the original text should refer to his own works in their earlier editions.

CHAPTER ONE

# THE BONES AND THE BOOK

As I staggered on through the grey death of the post-Hiroshima era, I was suddenly aware of a ragged rubble crater at my feet. Being nervously exhausted, I took shelter in it, and yielding to my ever-present fatigue (neurasthenia the doctor called it), I quickly slipped into oblivion.

In my traumatic state, I witnessed what one might call a tableau of torment. A human being festooned with rags was standing, as if on a set location. From his tired sunken eyes seeped an unspeakable sadness. His limpid posture bespoke a total despair. Crippled with crisis he looked vacantly future-ward; a product of the shrivelled generation; a man outward bound from his home.

From behind a Stonehenge complex of multi-storied flats built on a reclaimed bomb-site, the setting sun shone through, turning his furrowed face to gold. Was he a refugee, a hitch-hiker or just some vagrant beatnik? His category eluded me, but one thing was certain, he was literate, for he held a book in his hand. As I scrutinised him, the shadow of this solitary figure stretched backward and away, growing ever broader and less defined, until it merged into the sombre backdrop of the past from which he came. Then in one brief moment the sun was gone and a chill swept through the concrete wastes. Like a child's penny in a slot machine, the copper disc slipped ominously between earth and heaven. 'Man's splendour is always borrowed,' I thought. 'How cheaply we evaluate our days!'

Through my reverie I still could glimpse him, hunched and gaunt in his silent stance, his cavernous shoulders so grossly arched, as might suggest an octopus around his neck. Quietly I edged towards him, anxious to learn the proper nature of his dread condition. Nausea took hold of me. A monstrous rucksack, stuffed full of putrid bones, clawed cruelly at his back. Bent like a hairpin beneath its weight, he found lifting his head almost more than he could do.

At last the man showed movement and I stiffened expectantly. With pitiful exertion, out of all proportion to the task, he struggled to open his book, and as he began to read, I gained the impression he was racing against time. He was out to capture the

B                 17

final glimmers of the day and, if it were possible, cheat the very night of its quarry. The longer he read the more affected he became, until his whole body was shaking convulsively; then breaking into hysterical sobbing, he screamed the words, 'What shall I do? What shall I do?' In the stillness of the evening his cries echoed eerily from building to building, and one might well have imagined that all the adjacent flats and offices housed persons similarly afflicted.

Once darkness had fallen and the man could no longer see the pages, he quickly quietened, and to my surprise retraced his steps towards what must have been his own front door. His home was a basement, half below pavement level and situated at the foot of an old tenement due for demolition, it was said, some twenty years before. During half that period his name had been 'down for a house', but as far as he was concerned, it mattered little now. From the low-set kitchen window the yellow light filtered obliquely along the dishevelled flagstones. Assisted by the soft glow, he shuffled towards the cellar steps and descended them heavily, one by one, like an infant child. Ignoring the big old-fashioned knocker, he thrust his free hand through the letter-box and pulled a string. He gave the door a rough kick with his left foot. It yielded and he stepped inside. He made no announcement of his arrival, but dodging the washing hung low from the ceiling, he lurched over to his wife and kissed her work-worn hand. It was as high as he could reach since the business of the bones had doubled him in two.

Without a word, he put his book down on the T.V., slumped into a chair and buried himself in yesterday's newspaper. With genuine restraint he sought to hide his agony of mind, but as he considered the world of riots, strikes, stabbings, bottle-throwings, race meetings, unemployment, births, deaths, rapes, murders, earthquakes, famines, floods, plane disasters, road casualties, wars and bomb-tests, not to speak of the recent tax increases, the news of the past only confirmed him in his fears for the future. He reached for his book again, gripped it firmly, then blurted out in a loud voice, 'Mankind is finished and so am I! We've got to get out of here!' His wife turned and looked fearfully at her husband, but in spite of the outburst she sensed only his tenderness towards her and a haunting look of heart-break glistening in his eyes. It was this that hurt her most of all. Was there nothing she could do to make him happy, or was happiness just something you read about in women's magazines?

'Don't get me wrong, Christiana, it's just that I feel so frantic at times; and I love you so much, just the same as I always did. And as for the children, I daren't think of them. How could I ever leave you all? If we go, we must go together. Don't say you won't come! You always say that and it just tears me to pieces.'

'Will you stop talking that way, Chris! It sounds as if something's wrong with you. It's just ridiculous to expect me and the children to pack up everything and come with you on a mystery tour to your Celestial City. We don't even know where it is, much less the way to get there. In fact I doubt whether such a place exists. Why can't you spend a night with the boys and forget the whole thing. They've been pestering you to play Monopoly for weeks.' Her attempt to humour him failed abysmally.

'It's this filthy sack of bones that gets me down. You've got no idea what it means carrying a load like this about, day in and day out, everywhere I go. I tell you, if I don't get shot of it somehow, I'll go stark raving mad! It wouldn't be so bad if I could get my sleep, but you know yourself how I lie awake at night, thinking and thinking.'

'I don't know what you find to think about,' interrupted Christiana with growing exasperation. 'If you'd only do a good day's work like you used to, before you got this bee in your bonnet, you'd sleep all right!'

'But it's the fire that haunts me. Always the fire.' And the terror began to distort his voice. 'Believe me, when it comes they'll be saying the H-Bomb was a Christmas cracker!'

By this time a few neighbours and relatives, alarmed at Christian's ravings, had slipped through the doorway and were listening to what he was saying.

'Crackers,' the old lady from next door piped up in a rasping, audible whisper. 'It's 'im what's crackers! And to think she's got to sit there and stomach that lot. I'd soon tell him where 'e got off! Off 'is rocker! that's what 'e is!' And she turned to the others for some measure of confirmation for her uncompromising diagnosis.

The sight of people in the room made Christian more aggressive. He knew he was the subject of discussion, and felt he must challenge them directly. 'You can see what's wrong with me all right! It's this thing on my back! But is there a single one of you who can do anything about it?' At this his young nephew, who had gained a place at the university and was now in his third year, offered an explanation to all present.

'This is what is commonly known as a fixation,' he explained. 'What my uncle needs, of course, is a visit to a competent psychiatrist. A few skilful interviews may be all that's necessary, but failing that, there's always the electric shock treatment which, I

**19**

understand, will do a lot for people in this condition. In the more drastic cases'—and he eyed his uncle rather critically as he said it—'the mere cutting of a little brain tissue can transform the entire personality.'

'Will you stop talking such downright wicked nonsense!' his aunt intruded angrily. 'No one's touching *my* husband's brain! The trouble with you young people is you think you know everything and the truth is you know nothing! You bring up four kids on ten pounds a week and see what you know! That's life, that is! Grants for university? Money for jam I call it, and all you can do is talk about cutting people's brains out. All very nice for young gents like you, but someone's got to get their hands dirty!'

Her line of argument was not immediately apparent to the student, but before he could defend his proposals all eyes turned towards Christian. He had opened his book and was speaking with remarkable composure and obvious sanity.

'Listen to me,' he said, 'You simply *must* face it. I have here indisputable proof that this city will be scorched to a cinder in the very near future. Like hot breath out of the sky, God's blazing presence will engulf us, and without an escape route, every one of us is doomed!'

'Sounds quite frightening, I must say,' chipped in one of the neighbours sarcastically. 'Been reading the latest science fiction, or else watching too much of that space stuff on T.V. Anyhow it's not my idea of a bedtime story. I'm off!' And with that, he unceremoniously left the room. No sooner had he gone than someone else took up the analysis.

'To me it seems more like he's got hooked by one of those religious fellows who come knocking at the houses. There's a different lot every week. Once let them get their foot in and they'll hardly let you shut your own front door.' Then turning to Christian he said, 'I can't for the life of me imagine how a down-to-earth chap like you ever got mixed up with them. Leaves me standing, it does!'

'Nobody here's got hooked on anything! Get that into your head will you!' said Christiana, her face flushed with indignation. She would stand so much interference, but no more; but then, quite oblivious to the rising tension, a more affluent friend, who had been silent up till now, began to speak.

'My suggestion is that our esteemed neighbour, Christian, should just drop everything and get right away for a while. A month's cruise to the Canary Islands would be the very thing! He'd come back a new man.'

'And bankrupt into the bargain!' Christiana flung back. 'Who in the world do you think would pay for that? Do you want me to pass the hat round? No! I've got a cheaper cure than the whole lot of you; a couple of aspirins and off to bed! Who knows, he might be a great deal better in the morning?' The relations and friends, relieved at the postponement of the collection, responded with a will. Gathering around Christian, they lifted him bodily from the room and propelling him up the narrow stair saw him safely between the sheets...

Gradually the clatter of feet and the raucous sound of the neighbours' voices died away and Christian lay alone in the bedroom. It was a long tedious night. His mind was a railway junction and trains of thought were being shunted to and fro by mysterious phantoms. In his near delirium, the marshalling yards just down the road became part of his mind. The green and red signals flickered incessantly. One minute it was 'Go'. Yes, he would leave first thing in the morning. The next minute it was 'Stop'. He would stay with the family.

It must have been about one a.m. when Christiana came to bed. Normally he would have been so glad and felt such comfort in her warmth and nearness, but he turned boorishly away and hung over the side of the mattress. If only he could be sick he would feel better, he thought. 'Quieten yourself, Chris,' his wife whispered, and he felt her hand feel softly for him. He lay back again for a while, more relaxed, and pulled the crumpled bedclothes into position. 'Sorry,' he said, and as he spoke something hot and wet trickled slowly across his cheek, gathered momentum and dropped swiftly and silently on to the pillow. He thought of the little orb of water soaking down through the cotton threads. It was thirty years since he cried.

By the time they got to sleep it was at least half past four and the first thing Christiana knew was the eight o'clock hooter 'blowing its head off' (as she was prone to say), across the road. But there was worse than that. Somebody who ought to have known better was hammering the front door with that brute of a knocker. She hastily slipped on her dressing-gown, glanced in the old cracked mirror (seven years' bad luck was the least of it), and realised to her dismay that she still had her curlers in from the night before. 'Well,' she said, 'if people will call at this time in the morning they'll have to take "her royal highness" as they find her!' By the time she had reached the foot of the stair she was all set for a 'blast off'. Opening the door on the chain, she peered through the slit into the bleak foggy morning. To her surprise it was little Mrs. 'What's-her-name' from next door. 'And how's the patient this morning?' she asked cheerily. She was going to say,

'How's the Christmas cracker?' but had second thoughts when she saw Christiana's face. 'None the better for your hammering the door! That's for sure,' she replied curtly. 'Do you mind handing me them two milk bottles before the birds peck the tops in.' 'Don't let it get you down, deary,' her neighbour said in a softer tone. 'A bad night, eh?' 'He's in a shocking state, that's all you can say. Now I'll have to go in, I'm not even dressed yet and it's cold standing here.'

'Oh, that's all right. I just wanted to know how 'e was. You've got no idea 'ow interested my old man is in your Chris. So long for now!'

Christiana shut to the door, ruefully rubbing her cold bare feet one upon the other in quick succession. 'Funny thing,' she thought to herself, 'when anything goes wrong everybody's *so* interested but they'd cross the very street another time rather than waste their breath talking to you!' She turned to go upstairs when a young voice greeted her. 'Hello, Mum! What's for breakfast?' 'Cornflakes, I guess,' she said, 'And you can put an egg on if you like.' Then she passed into the bedroom and closed the door behind her.

# CHAPTER TWO

# MISHAP ON THE MUDFLATS

CHRISTIAN'S condition tended to deteriorate rather than improve. A deep melancholia settled over him, and if anyone were rash enough to enquire of his health, he would reply, but tersely and with great depression, 'Worse and worse!' There were odd times, however, when he became more loquacious and tried to persuade the passsers-by that they stood in hourly danger of their lives. Some ignored him completely whilst others, being a little more courteous, would pause a moment or two, thinking he was asking them the way; but in the end, all would hurry on, for there was so much for everyone to do, and so little time in which to do it; and they simply had to get it done, otherwise they would not be able to do the next thing, and that would never do in a world of action and achievement. The very idea that time would end and God would do something was, in the minds of most, quite an absurdity. 'Don't you realise,' ranted the rudest, 'God never does anything!' 'Get out of my way, you silly old fool, and let me get on!' So on they all went crissing and crossing, coming and going, until Christian's eyes swam, and they looked like so many blades of grass tossed in the wind.

Christian now became more and more isolated. His friends and acquaintances kept conveniently out of the way. Behind his back they nicknamed him, 'Old Firewatcher', so little respect had they for his sombre forebodings; but then, few had heard of Sodom and Gomorrah and the name Nagasaki meant nothing to the younger generation. Such was the cruel rebuttal accosting Christian's concern.

The persistent indifference of the people, whether they were local residents or daily commuters, drove Christian more and more to prayer. Sometimes they deemed him mentally affected, oppressed as he was with a sense of guilt and an imminence of judgement, but nevertheless he bore a nobility of expression in his sad face that was infinitely preferable to the debauched appearance of the sex-drunk riff-raff littering the clubs and pubs of the city.

In his loneliness he began to wander further and further from home. This caused considerable anxiety to his wife, and even his older children became perturbed. They themselves could be wanderers too, especially at night when there was so much fun to be had, but of course it was different with 'dad'. He wasn't quite right in his head and could easily get run over. He might even commit suicide. That's why they'd given him 'The Samaritan's' phone number, in case he had a bad turn and felt desperate.

The time came when Christian would be away most of the day and they began to fear that one night he might not return. This led to their organising a party with some of the neighbours, to shadow him and find out just where his haunts were. The agreed morning came. One or two sat in cars at either end of the street. Others were on bikes and some of the young people had their motor-scooters at the ready. From various windows, faces peeped surreptitiously from behind the curtains. At the first sight of Christian, bowed low beneath his sack, the alert was on. Down street and alley they followed him, through subways and arcades, over vacant sites, along broad boulevards, across the public parks, then out from the shopping centres to the distant suburbs. Now and again the cars lost him in the crowds but as he reached the city's dormitory areas, he was clearly visible all the way.

Gradually the drab urban expanse petered out into the more rural environs of the metropolis but still Christian went walking on. Finally he turned quite deliberately from The Broad Freeway, which was the main trunk road out of the City of Destruction, and took a narrow bridle-path across the moors. He tramped several hundred yards through the rough grass, then stopped abruptly in his tracks. The wide expanse of country surged to meet him. He was so small; just a fragment of humanity, pathetic and alone beneath the open heaven. He cast his eyes around but there was nowhere to go in all the tangled growth that tore at his trousers and scratched his legs. Lost in the wilderness, he opened his book, now moist and clammy in his hand. No sooner did he glimpse its message than fresh agonies swept through him, and from his lips broke the old familiar cry, 'What shall I do? What shall I do?'

Crouched low behind the bushes just off The Freeway, the tracking party watched carefully the turn of events. They were utterly mystified at Christian's behaviour. Straining their ears they tried to catch what he said. There seemed to be another word this time. There it came again. 'What must I do to be *saved*?' For a long time they focussed their binoculars on him. They saw him turn his face, with no little effort, towards the sun-filled sky. They could tell he was talking to Someone, and so intensely that surely He must answer if He were real. But one of the party, more bored than the rest, broke in on the tension,

'Strange how it's so clear out here yet so foggy in town!' 'Not at all,' answered Christian's nephew. 'Just think of the industry we have; what else could you expect?'

As Christian's voice rang out in the still air of the untrammelled countryside, a vehicle pulled in quickly from The Freeway to a lay-by on the edge of the moor. A man got out who was evidently aware of Christian's plight, for he tried at once to attract his attention. 'What's the matter over there?' he called to him. 'You can't stand in the middle of nowhere shouting away like that! Hold on a minute. I'm coming right over to where you are!' When the two men met, they took each other by the hand and the stranger pulled out his wallet and handed Christian one of his visiting cards. 'That's by way of introduction,' he said. Christian seemed reassured and began to pour out his story to the stranger. 'What concerns me is the information I have in this book. It tells me I'm doomed to die and that after death I shall be judged by Him who knows my every secret. This simply terrifies me. For one thing, I don't want to die; and as for facing prosecution at "God's Great Assize", the whole prospect is just unthinkable!' To this the stranger replied quite unexpectedly, 'I would have thought you'd have been glad to die. Isn't life in this world miserable enough? Fancy wanting to stay here longer than necessary!'

'But you don't understand,' remonstrated Christian. 'Surely you can see my rucksack and don't you smell the bones? They get more putrid every day. And they're human bones! "*Dead* men's bones", the Book calls them. I only have to die with this lot round my neck and my grave won't be deep enough. I'll drop like a stone into the depths of Hell! If it were a question of prison here on earth, I could face it, but to stand naked before my Maker, it makes my flesh creep. After all I *know* what I've done and this Book says, "He is able to destroy both soul and body in Hell!" Do you wonder I'm crying out here on the moor, "What must I do to be saved?"'

The reaction of the stranger was immediate. 'Man,' he said, 'if this is the state you're in, whatever are you doing standing here?' 'For the simple reason,' replied Christian, 'I haven't a clue what to do next.' At that the stranger drew out his wallet once again and wrote something on a piece of paper. 'Read that!' he said, handing it to Christian. The words were cryptic. 'The Anger falls! Run for your life!' As Christian glanced downward, he also spotted the name on the visiting card. It was 'Evangelist'. Looking at the man very intently Christian asked him, 'And where do you want me to run?' The stranger stretched out his arm across the landscape and pointed to where a drystone wall ran over a rise. 'Do you see that small white gate in the wall?' he said. 'No, I can't say I do,' answered Christian. 'Well, do you see a glow out there beyond the heather, a kind of light on the crest of the hills?' Christian turned his eyes to where the rugged earth reached out to the windswept sky. 'Yes, I think I can,' he ventured with some hesitation. 'That's your direction then. Keep that light before you all the way and you'll come to the gate. The wall will be high there and the gate's in solid wood, but don't be deterred; give a knock and someone will open it and tell you what to do next.'

Evangelist took his leave of Christian and came again to his mobile preaching-unit, parked in the lay-by. For a few moments he sat praying at the wheel, then turning the ignition key, he prepared to continue his patrol on The Broad Freeway looking for other folk in need. As his eye scanned the oncoming traffic, he could just see Christian in the mirror, running as fast as his load would allow, on towards the light. 'Another pilgrim secured,' he mused with deepest satisfaction; yet not for himself did he think it, but for his war-scarred Director of Service. 'How glad He will be,' he whispered, 'my Lord of the Hill.'

At this unexpected development, Christiana and her children, together with the other members of the tracking party, leapt out from behind the bushes and careered madly across the open heath. 'Go on! After him!' bellowed one of the more outraged neighbours, known as Obstinate. 'Don't let him get away at the last!'

'Chris! Chris! Come back! Come back!' cried his wife. 'Dad ... dee...!' shouted the children in long drawn out syllables. 'Don't run away!' 'Come back! Come back!' It was a full-scale hue and cry, and like a pack of hounds with the fox in sight, they strained every nerve to close the distance between them and their prey. For one brief instant it appeared as if Christian had heard their entreaties, for they saw him put his fingers to his ears; but whatever the case, he never looked back. As he drew away, there were wafted on the wind, like a message from another world, those last words which his loved ones would always remember. 'Life! Life! Eternal Life!' And with that cry he ran on and on through the bracken.

Christiana, breathless and exhausted, eventually gave up the chase. She dropped to the ground quite overcome by all that had happened, and her children gathered round her stunned and amazed at the loss of their father and the collapse of their mother. Her nephew now came to the rescue. He picked her up and giving her his arm, escorted her back into the City of Destruction. Somehow she began to feel differently towards him and was glad of his company, not realising that the intellectual is so frequently the one who leads the bewildered soul back into unbelief.

Meanwhile Obstinate, and another acquaintance of the family, called Pliable, were pursuing Christian for all they were worth, until they were lost to view in the undulations of the moors. Noted, as they were, for their remarkable stamina and length of wind, Obstinate and Pliable eventually caught up with Christian. More like wolves than hounds, they panted and snapped at his heels until they forced him to stop. Then with looks that would kill if they could, they brutally harangued him, demanding that he return at once to his own house.

'What!' expostulated Christian, 'Go back to the City of Destruction and be caught sooner or later in the Conflagration of the Almighty? The shoe is on the other foot. You ought to come with me!' 'Not on your life,' scowled Obstinate, 'Imagine walking out on all our friends and leaving the amenities, entertainments and every other mod. con. we have in the city, to traipse around the countryside going who knows where.' 'That's your own perverted outlook,' said Christian. 'The truth remains that all you let go here is nothing to what God gives you there. He has enough and more besides to satisfy your empty heart: if once you grasped that fact you'd walk with me towards my Father's house.'

'I haven't the ghost of an idea what you're talking about!' rebuffed Obstinate, with downright annoyance. 'Whatever you're after baffles me, for you've left just about everything to get it. It's so ridiculous. You're anti-social, that's what you are!'

Christian answered him in a voice that already seemed far away, 'Mine is an inheritance, imperishable, undefiled and unfading. It is kept in heaven for those who seek it with all their hearts. It is safe and sure, and will be given at the time appointed. You can read about it in my book.'

'You can cut that talk out, Christian! We don't want any "pie in the sky when we die" and I might as well tell you, we haven't the slightest interest in your book so we won't be referring to it. Are you coming back with us or not?'

'Never!' said Christian. 'I've put my hand to the plough and I'm not turning back.'

'Well, if that's the case, Pliable, we'll make tracks for the town. The whole afternoon's already up the stick. I'd thought of going to the match before I was raked out on this wild goose chase. I might have known the whole thing was a waste of time. It makes me sick when I come across these kind of people. They're just plain bigoted fools! There's no other word for them. They get an

idea into their heads and then they'll listen to no one but themselves. You're as well talking to a brick wall.'

All this while Pliable had stood looking first at Christian and
then at Obstinate. Now he was looking again at Christian. It was
their eyes that spoke to him. Obstinate's eyes seemed so beady and
greedy but Christian's eyes were liquid with the light towards
which he looked. Jolted from his thoughts, Pliable suddenly
spoke. 'I don't think you ought to be so abusive, Obstinate. Only
fools are personal. Supposing there were some truth in what
Christian says. Couldn't his outlook prove better than ours? To be
honest with you, I've half a mind to go with him. There is something that fascinates me about this call of the Unseen.'

'Oh, not another one,' groaned Obstinate despairingly. 'You
mean, go with a down-at-heel good-for-nothing like that. Look at
him. No home, no clothes, no job, no sense! Pliable, for the sake
of Beelzebub, take a grip of yourself and let's get back to the
city!'

'No, you come with me,' pleaded Christian, 'for I tell you, Pliable, instead of your room and kitchen, there's a mansion with
my Father; for your worn-out clothes, you'll have robes of salvation; for occupation, labour in the vineyard of our Lord; and for
wisdom, the counsels of the Most High. All God's best is before
us. I have shown you but little. Look in my book for the rest. You
can trust what it says. Its contents are sealed by the blood of Him,
of whom it speaks.'

'Yes, I'll come,' said Pliable, although his voice wavered just a
little. 'But do you know the way?'

'I certainly do,' continued Christian confidently. 'A man called
Evangelist, driving a loudspeaker-van along The Broad Freeway
came to me on the moor. You must have seen him park in the lay-
by near where you were hiding. He told me to go first to the gate
in the wall that lies there across the hill. Once we get to that
point, he said, we shall be told the next step to take.'

At these remarks Obstinate exploded like an intercepted mis-
sile! 'I'm finished with you both!' he snorted, and turning
abruptly strode angrily towards the city which, for all its glitter
and redevelopment programme, was destined to God's everlasting
contempt.

Once he was gone, the two men walked on together towards the
light. Feeling more at ease, Pliable began to question Christian
concerning the nature of their destination. As he answered him
slowly and thoughtfully, Pliable began to feel he had seriously
misjudged him. He had always felt Christian's words were sancti-
monious and divorced from reality. In fact, all that Christian had

previously said had seemed thoroughly distasteful to him; but now, tramping together across the heather with an iridescent sky above and a cool wind freshening his cheek, he felt he was breathing in a new dimension. There seemed to be another Presence and another World not very far away; and in the solitude, the things that Christian said began to be so logical, and even wonderful to his ears.

'Naturally,' said Christian, 'these matters are more easily conceived in the mind than audibly expressed, but seeing you are so interested to know where we are going, I'll read you some extracts from my book, for it will state the truth much better than I can remember it; and need I emphasise that these words have been written by Him who cannot lie.' Pliable's expectations being heightened, Christian went on, 'First it tells how there's an endless kingdom waiting to be inhabited, and life eternal for those that enter it. Then to the citizens are given crowns, or, if you like, insignia of authority, for it's not a place of indolence but of responsible activity, and to every subject is awarded clothing and equipment excelling the sun in glory, to fit him for his task.'

'But tell me, Christian, who exactly makes up the population of so fabulous a kingdom?'

'Oh, there are seraphim and cherubim, which, in the scientific language of our city are known as "supra-spatial beings". Their persons are of such dazzling brilliance that only reconditioned sight can register their movement. We shall see also, the myriads of fellow-pilgrims preceding us, each filled with the love of God and standing in His presence. We shall see the elders, each with a golden tiara, prostrate in worship before The Throne. We shall have fellowship with every soul of virgin-heart and converse with the martyrs of this world's history, who for the love of Christ were cut in pieces, burnt at the stake, mauled by the lions, staked in the tide, and of later years, murdered in gas-chambers, shot by the firing squads, hanged and guillotined, who in the slave camps of this so-called civilised age were sent like sheep to the slaughter, being mutilated, tortured and starved to extinction.' At this description Pliable became quite animated, naïvely thinking that such a paradise was just over the hill!

'Can we be sure of inclusion in this unheard-of society,' he earnestly asked.

'Yes, for the Lord of that country has decreed in His book that all who would enter it shall have opportunity.'

'Let's go a bit faster then,' urged Pliable.

'I'd like to be able to,' replied Christian, 'but this rucksack is so heavy and its contents are digging into my back.'

Then in my dream I saw that whilst they talked, they entered, quite unconsciously, a part of the moors skirting a desolate area of mudflats. At one time it must have been an inlet of the sea, but now was no more than a stagnant depression; a kind of peat-bog, into which drained all the brackish waters of the marshlands that stretched for miles around the City of Destruction. One end of the basin was utilised as a waste disposal site for the whole urban area, and although a blot on the landscape, it was, notwithstanding, tolerated, being situated on lower terrain and largely hidden from public view. The tip did, however, increase the stench of the place, and on occasion the acrid smoke of the smouldering refuse would blow back across the city. This was of considerable annoyance to the ratepayers, who had already had to finance several unsuccessful projects to make the city-centre a smoke-free zone. Occasionally representation was made to the municipal authorities, and sometimes even to higher authority, but in spite of all the paperwork, and the frequent memoranda issued for the improvement of the place, two milleniums had done nothing to abolish the eyesore, or to reduce the hazard presented to travellers. The immense dump grew bigger and bigger each year, and was, undoubtedly, a pitiful commentary on the superficial and transient nature of the city's preoccupations. Everything spoke of the aftermath of pleasure, of creeping obsolescence and incipient decay. In the conglomerate heap could be seen the wrecks of cars, empty tins, smashed crockery, forgotten newspapers, threadbare tyres, old clothing, jagged glass, broken toys, dead cats and dogs and, not infrequently, the corpse of some newborn babe. Various factories also used the dump for industrial waste products and lurid sulphurous colours snaked out into the slime, right up to the peat side of the bog where the pilgrims passed.

So taken up with 'the theological mysteries of the Eternal State' were Christian and Pliable that they had now strayed unwittingly amongst the tufts of reedy grass. Before they knew where they were, their heavenly dreams were rudely shattered and they fell simultaneously into the mire and filth. As if to mock them, the first thing that caught their eye, after the initial shock, was a little white notice raised for the safety of the pilgrims. The words, painted in bold black print, read quite clearly, 'BEWARE! —THE SLOUGH OF DESPOND'. With grunts of disgust and disillusionment, Pliable immediately began to castigate Christian. 'And what have you got to say now?' he taunted. 'Don't ask me,' spluttered Christian, trying to rid his mouth of dirty water, 'I honestly don't know.' This only enraged Pliable the more. 'A fat lot of good speaking like that, after landing me in this sewer of a place. Talk about no more tears and no more sorrow! If this is what it's like to start with, I wouldn't like to think where we'll end. If ever I get out of this cesspool alive, I'll be back to my own fireside as fast as my legs will carry me.' With that, he managed to grasp one of the tussocks, and heaving himself up with an effort only a drowning man could exert, he stood once more, begrimed and crestfallen, on the footpath that led back to his own house. 'From now on you'll go it alone,' he shouted at Christian with venomous anger and he was off like a shot from a gun.

Weighed down by his heavy burden, Christian sank lower and lower, until he doubted whether he would ever extricate himself from his fearful dilemma. Yet even in the throes of such a nightmare, he was struggling all the time to reach the footpath on that side of the marsh which led to the gate in the wall. Slowly the evil-smelling ooze crept higher and higher. He could feel it penetrating between his ragged clothes and his bare skin. It was cold and took his breath away, the nearer it came to his heart. A host of memories began to throng his mind. Like a studio ticker-tape, his words and deeds ran helter-skelter before him and all he could see was sin, sin, sin, day after day. His bag of bones seemed suddenly heavier, a thousand times. He sensed the blackness of darkness closing in. Then a voice rang clearly in his ears. 'Come on now! Give me your hand!' How he ever managed to grasp that hand, to this day Christian hardly knows, but grasp it he did and with one mighty wrench of quite astonishing strength, he was snatched from the very jaws of death. His newly-found friend proved to be none other than 'Help', a powerful ally to all the pilgrims on the King's Highway. The secret of his phenomenal vitality lay in the Sanctuary of God, which had been his residence as long as any could remember. Christian stood at first, shivering with cold and fright, whilst two black pools of water formed around his feet. 'Thank you with all my heart,' said Christian. 'You have saved my life.' 'Thank rather Him, who is the Source of all my strength,' replied Help reverently. 'Now you must be on your way as Evangelist instructed you.' 'There's just one question I'd like to ask before I leave you,' Christian said. 'Speak your mind then,' answered Help. 'Seeing how dangerous this Slough of Despond is to people like myself, why has something more not been done to ensure the safety of the public?' 'This desperate stretch of marsh-land,' replied Help, 'if you only knew it, is quite impossible of improvement. This area has defied every attempt at reclamation. Not only is it the catchment area for the whole of this vast wilderness, but, as you see, the entire garbage of the City of Destruction is emptied into it. In addition to that, all the scum exuding from man's conviction of sin runs to the place, so that what you have just experienced only reflects the condition of your own individual conscience at this critical time. That is why we have the notice up and why the place supports the name, The Slough of Despond. Mind you, by the direction of the Lawgiver, there are certain stepping stones set at intervals through the bog but with the conflicting winds of doctrine blowing so violently these days, and the moral climate of our country so variable, there are periods when the level of the slime rises exceptionally high, and the stones become submerged. This means that pilgrims tend to miss their way and arrive at the gate even more soiled than when they set out from their native cities; but the ground is better, the nearer the gate you get.'

At this moment I saw in my dream that Pliable had reached his home and the neighbours were already calling to see him. Some slapped him on the back and said how wise he was to return. Others maintained he was a fool for going in the first place, whilst others called him a coward for turning back so soon.

Nevertheless it was only a little while before they were all good friends again, laughing together at the thought of their crackpot neighbour floundering in the mire. 'He always was an old stick-in-the-mud;' they roared. 'Hell-fire fizzles out in local swamp! There you are, a first-class headline for the local rag!' Washed and changed Pliable was really enjoying himself once more. 'Let's have a sherry all round,' he said, and as the drinks began to flow he wondered how ever he forsook such splendid company for the silence of the moors.

# CHAPTER THREE

# THE MENACE OF THE MOUNTAIN

As Christian trudged on, he was puzzled to see another main road cutting across the common in front of him. Even in his youth he had never been a boy for hiking or 'biking'. Born and bred in the city, he knew little beyond its boundaries, and this accounted for his bewilderment now. If his children had only accompanied him, they would have known immediately where the road came from and where it led. They could read an ordnance survey map before they were any age, and often visited the country places situated around the City of Destruction. But all this was mere wishful thinking. Christian was alone and must make his own decision. The strange thing was, Evangelist had never breathed a word about another highway existing between the moors and the gate. Far in the distance, the bright glow in the hills still beckoned him.

'If I go towards the light surely there can be no mistake,' he thought. Just as he came to the tarmacadam, a big limousine, chauffeur-driven, swerved in sharply from the right. If he had not drawn back at once, he would have been under it. As it came to a halt, he fully expected some high and mighty industrialist to grind him verbally into the dust for being a stupid working-class pedestrian, but what ensued was quite to the contrary. An affluent well-groomed gentleman alighted from the car, and addressing him with meticulous courtesy, said, 'Allow me to introduce myself. My name is Mr. Worldly Wiseman and I live in the City of Carnal Policy. We were coming down here to try out my new Gehenna on The Broad Freeway, when we saw you step on to the road.' Christian listened, fascinated by the soft lilt of the man's voice and the unexpected attention from such an imposing personality. At least he knew where he was now. *Carnal Policy was the twin-city of his own native municipality and the road before him was obviously a connecting link with the main freeway leading to Hell's End. All this time Mr. Worldly Wiseman had eyed Christian with a penetrating scrutiny . . .

No, he was not mistaken. It had been a near thing, but the phone call had been in time and now he'd just caught him before

* A designation chosen by Bunyan to describe a community catering solely for man's natural appetites and baser desires.

he disappeared through the gate and beyond the wall ... 'Intelligent young boy, that,' he thought to himself, 'to inform me so promptly. It's a good job nephews don't always listen to their uncles. Once he's graduated I must try and find him a place in the Company...'

'My dear good fellow,' Mr. Worldly Wiseman began again. 'It was when I saw your pitiful condition that I said to my chauffeur, "Caiaphas, stop the car, I simply must do something for that man there, crossing the road." Tell me now, what's happened to you? You're covered in mud. Did you meet with an accident?' He paused a moment and then added. 'And that fearful sack on your back? What's the meaning of that?'

'Well might you ask, sir. The biggest concern in my life is how to get rid of it. In fact that's why I'm here just now. I'm on my way towards that light over the hill. I've been told I shall eventually come to a stone wall and a small white gate. I'll only have to knock there, and someone will tell me how I can lose it for ever.'

'You seem to be all on your own. Have you any wife or children?' he asked with seeming kindness.

'Oh yes,' he said, 'I've a wife and four children, but ever since I've been carrying this burden, I've found I can hardly think of them, or look after them as I should. Until I get this matter settled, all other considerations must go by the board. I wonder sometimes if life will ever be the same again.'

'It's really imperative that something be done about it,' agreed Mr. Worldly Wiseman, 'God has given us so much to enjoy but I guess *you'll* never enjoy anything until this problem finds a solution.'

'But there's not a man on earth who has a solution,' groaned Christian despairingly, for it seemed now as if a reaction from the mishap in the Slough was setting in. The slime of Despond still clung to his person and made him utterly miserable. 'My only hope,' he whimpered, 'lies in that grand estate beyond the wall.'

'And who, may I ask, told you that?' enquired Mr. Worldly Wiseman rather imperiously.

'A person I met just two or three hours ago. His name was Evangelist. A man, I would judge, of the highest integrity.'

'Would you believe it!' Mr Worldly Wiseman exclaimed, evidently irritated at the very thought that such persons existed. 'These preacher types really are a scourge, always trying to hoodwink people into "being saved" as they call it, as if burdens like yours can be lifted at the drop of a hat. Believe me, the advice he's given you will lead you into no end of trouble and by the look of you, you've met some of it already. Well I can tell you, that's only the beginning. You go on like you're doing and you'll be facing "the high jump" at every turn of the road! You'll be worn out, dog tired, footsore and hungry. You'll encounter violence and bloodshed, prison and death, and who knows what else. History is full of unfortunates who've listened to that kind of evangelist. Just imagine it. You never met this man till this afternoon yet you're ready to risk your whole life, and family too, on what he says.'

'If you were as desperate as I am,' Christian blurted out, 'You'd do anything to get rid of this load. Have you never felt the weight of your sins or smelt them either? I'd be ready to face all that you've said and a lot more, if only it could fall from my back.' Seeing his approach did nothing to dissuade Christian from his pilgrimage, Mr. Worldly Wiseman slightly shifted his ground.

'Tell me,' he asked sympathetically, 'how did you first become like this?'

'By reading this book,' Christian replied, holding up the volume he treasured so much.

'I thought as much,' grunted Mr. Worldly Wiseman. 'That's the trouble. When ordinary people like yourself start investigating things they don't understand, they become unbalanced. I've always maintained a little knowledge is a dangerous thing. Once get the average man involved in religion, or politics for that matter, and he becomes a fanatic. If only they'd leave such things to those who've been intellectually trained for them, they'd be all right, but they put their thumbs in the church puddings and the party pies, and expect to pull out all sorts of plums to their own satisfaction. The trouble is they don't know what to be after.'

'But I know exactly what I'm after,' remonstrated Christian, 'I want my burden lifted.'

'Of course, you do, but there's no need to go chasing some "will-of-the-wisp" out in the wilds to get it. If you'll listen to me, I'll direct you right now to the place and the person where the whole thing can be dealt with, and I can guarantee that instead of meeting all the hazards I've mentioned, the outcome will not only be a new happiness, but the making of new friends as well.'

At this, Christian pricked up his ears. Could it be true? He looked again at the big car parked by the roadside and the fine appearance of the man before him. Such prosperity was surely an evidence of God's blessing. He must be trustworthy. On the back window of the Gehenna, Christian could see a sticker-poster, depicting an emaciated Asian child. 'Give liberally this flag-day to the starving millions!' the words ran. His interest in good causes could not be doubted. In fact, when he came to think of it, he half remembered hearing about this gentleman in connection with the renovation fund for the cathedral in Carnal Policy. Advice with such a record behind it could not be lightly set aside. Mr. Worldly Wiseman watched Christian carefully. He had long experience in the handling of men, and he soon sensed that Christian's will to go on was beginning to waver.

'Do you see that village down there just below the hill?' he continued, pointing to where the present highway joined the trunk road. 'Well, that's the village of Morality. It's a highly respectable place where everyone owns their own house, runs an extra car if they can, keeps a poodle, plays golf and has a wide range of interests in all sorts of social matters. If you want to describe it in a nutshell, it's a place where everyone is as good as his neighbour; and that's saying something these days, when in most places one person's as bad as another. The man you must ask for is a well-known resident held in high repute. His name is Mr. Legality. He's a specialist in burden lifting, and very able, I'm told, to relieve people who are tormented by their conscience, although I've never been to him personally, being happily free from that complaint. His secret, I might say, lies in the right application of the Oil of Conformity. Taken internally as a stimulant, it liberates the natural energies of good intention, and this gives immediate relief to people like yourself, oppressed with an over-sense of sin. Quite quickly after the first dose, you will realise your burden and feeling of wretchedness was, all along, just a figment of your morbid imagination. You, like anyone else, have sufficient resources within you to meet the demands, not only of God but of life in general. They need release, that's all. Then you'll forget what you failed to do, and be delighted with all you are able to do. Some people, of course, need the Oil of Conformity applied externally, that is as a linament, because they carry a false burden of responsibility and feel a religious duty to put the whole world to rights. The result is they get chafed shoulders and aching "complexes" into the bargain, but Mr. Legality's Oil is excellent for relieving these conditions. Many who have felt their beliefs totally incompatible with the requirements of the State Law have, after only one application, been able to continue living as normal citizens in our twin-cities. After all, if the powers that be are ordained of God, surely our religion should be able to operate within the fabric of constituted authority?

'So I suggest, if it's a sense of well-being you want and some measure of self-satisfaction, then you should get to Mr. Legality as fast as you can. Naturally it's just possible he won't be available and in that case you should see his son, a man equally gifted in the same profession. He is known in the village as Mr. Civility, to distinguish him from his father. After you're cured, you may want to return to the city but I would strongly advise you against it; not that I feel such a course would be dangerous, as far as the future is concerned, but really, it is very nice out here and it would be lovely for your wife and the children to settle in this kind of place. There are still a few houses lying vacant. No doubt you could obtain one at a modest rent. Being out of town will mean cheaper living, of course, and the neighbours are such honest and upright people; a great advantage, I must say, when one thinks of the vandalism and gang warfare in the more built-up areas.'

Christian was quite taken aback to think that, after all, there was relief so near at hand, and without giving the matter another thought, he eagerly asked for the exact address of Mr. Legality. Mr. Worldly Wiseman gladly complied and gave him the necessary directions.

'Do you see that hill over there?' he said. 'Yes, quite clearly,' answered Christian. 'Go to the foot of the hill then, and the first house on the road will be his.' With these words Mr. Worldly Wiseman returned to his car, very pleased with his successful interception of Christian.

'I really must have that young nephew of his to a meal in Carnal Policy,' he murmured to himself. 'We shall need someone of his calibre on the computer side and he's the type that could be a director before he's thirty. And what's more, judging by his attitudes to his uncle's religion, there shouldn't be too many scruples when the crunch comes and we attempt the take-over.'

Christian watched the car go on its way downhill towards The Freeway, then he followed on foot into what proved to be a kind of gorge. It was not long before he was walking close under the hill, taking a keen interest in all around him. To his amazement, the green slopes proved very patchy. The hill was really a dumping ground for slag. Over the years the waste of many workings had all but obscured the original mountain. Vegetation had encroached to some extent but the crags were still very menacing above the village of Morality. The road to The Broad Freeway on which Christian was walking had been cut right across the nether slopes of the big slag-heap and the sides of the cutting were buttressed with blocks of granite, providing as impressive a symbol of human resolve as you will find this side of the City of Destruction. In spite of all precautions, however, it still looked exceedingly unsafe and the more under the shadow of the hill Christian went, the more apprehensive he became. As he rounded the bend in the road that brought Mr. Legality's house in view, Christian looked up, and to his consternation realised that the tip was still in use. Against a dark storm-laden sky, he could see wisps of smoke away near the summit, rising uneasily in the growing breeze. Here and there was a burst of flame, yet Mr. Legality's house looked so prim and serene. Everything about the building and the garden was immaculate. In fact it was hardly possible to see a tile out of place or a weed amongst the flowers. 'Most commendable,' muttered Christian and then came a clap of thunder so violent that he nearly jumped out of his skin. As the lightning flashed and the reverberations echoed round the hill, the clouds literally burst at the seams. The rain was torrential and floods of water poured down the mountain. Then Christian heard a stupendous roar above the hiss of the downpour. The mountain shuddered and the slag, like lava from a volcano, slid relentlessly across the road. With the agility and speed that only fear can give, Christian ran for his life. He took tremendous punishment as he hurried with his heavy load back up the valley. A hundred yards was enough to bring him to safety. Blinded with perspiration and trembling from head to foot, he blundered straight into the arms of a man standing in the middle of the highway. He looked up, intending to apologise, but found to his chagrin he was face to face with Evangelist. At the roadside stood his loudspeaker-van. In fact, he had been warning the people of Morality that very afternoon of the dangers of living in the shadow of Mount Sinai.

At the sight of Evangelist, Christian felt thoroughly ashamed. Already he deeply regretted listening to Mr. Worldly Wiseman and began to feel how very credulous he had been. What could he say to Evangelist, who had given him such straightforward directions? Two narrow escapes from death in one afternoon were quite enough for anyone. The whole situation made him feel ill, as well as spiritually disturbed.

'Whatever are you doing here,' Evangelist exclaimed in astonishment. 'Aren't you the man I found on the moors outside the City of Destruction earlier this afternoon?'

'Yes, I'm the same man,' acknowledged Christian lamely.

'But didn't I tell you to go to the little white gate in the wall?'

'You certainly did but I met a well dressed gentleman who stopped his car and spoke to me kindly. He looked one of the aristocracy and assured me I would get relief down here in the village of Morality. That's why I ventured along the road beneath the hill but when the storm broke and the slag shifted, I fled for my life and here I am. If I'd stayed a moment longer I feel the mountain would have swept me away.'

Evangelist gradually drew from Christian the whole story, until he knew every word Mr. Worldly Wiseman had said. He saw at once through the whole plot, and felt it was high time to clear away the dangerous impressions imbedded in Christian's mind. Taking up quotations from the book Christian held in his hand, he thrust his points home, like a skilled swordsman, to their mark. 'The things I say to you now, Christian, are not my own words but the words of God,' he began. 'See to it, you refuse not Him who is speaking, for if they who refused Moses escaped not when he spoke on earth, how shall we escape if we refuse God Himself, warning us from heaven? If you want to be right with God and live in His presence then you *must believe*, but if you shrink back from believing, you will die in your sins. God will have no time for you whatever.' At this Christian began to tremble and the terror of God's holy, unseen presence came over him.

'You!' said Evangelist, his eyes aflame, 'are heading straight for disaster, for you're turning against God's truth, you're spurning the offer of His peace; in a word, you're inviting your own ever-lasting perdition. This is your precise position as you face me on this road, and remember, this road is nothing less than a short cut to Hell's End!' No sooner had Evangelist uttered these words than Christian fainted and lay for some seconds like a dead man. Slowly he regained consciousness and all he could say was, 'It's hopeless, hopeless! I'm lost! I'm lost!' But Evangelist caught hold of his right hand and assured him, 'Every sin shall be for-given a man. Don't be faithless! You must begin to believe!' Then Christian seemed to rally a little and stood to his feet although he was still shaking all over.

'Now listen carefully, if you can, to what I'm telling you,' con-tinued Evangelist, with great earnestness. 'I want you to realise the exact nature and the true identity of the man who deluded you. His name is Mr. Worldly Wiseman and it suits him down to the ground, because he is of the world, what he says is of the world, and the world is quite content to listen to him. That is to say, he is part and parcel of our present evil society which con-ducts its personal life, its business, its politics and religion in a spirit completely alien to, and independent of the Living God. He is self-sufficient, self-complacent and completely at home in this self-centred world. Though feeding on the slime of a profiteering commerce, he is the essence of respectability. For this reason, when he is not attending the Cathedral in Carnal Policy, he goes down to Morality to church. This man's teaching is summed up in the concept of expediency. He'll do only what suits him and what suits the occasion. He insists on this outlook to spare him the Cross. His own opinions are his sole criterion. He consequently opposes me in all I preach, for "the unspiritual man does not receive the things of the Spirit because they are foolishness to him. He is impervious to them, they being spiritually discerned." Now there are three things in this man's advice you must reject out of hand.

'Firstly, you must recognise that his influence over you is thoroughly evil, in that he diverted you from the way that leads to Life. What's more, you need to censure yourself most drastically for ever listening to him. It means you turned from the truth of the All-Wise God, to accept the useless chatter of a mere charlatan. How could you forget the words of the Lord who said, "Strive to enter by the narrow door, for the gate is narrow and the way is hard that leads to life and few are those who find it."

'Secondly, his advice must be shunned like the plague, for it despises the way of the Cross. Did not our Master say, "Whoever would save his life will lose it"? And what about Moses? "He chose rather to share ill-treatment with the people of God, than to enjoy the fleeting pleasures of sin; and all the abuse he suffered for Christ was of greater wealth than the treasures of Egypt." Let this word be like salt in your wounded conscience. "If anyone comes to Me and does not hate his own father and mother and wife and children and brothers and sisters, yes and even his own life, he cannot be my disciple." Do you hear that Christian? "He cannot be my disciple."

'In the third place, you must abandon the whole idea of aligning yourself with so fatal an administration, for what is the gist of Mr. Worldly Wiseman's patter? No more than this, that Mr. Legality will lift your burden and then you can live in peace in old Morality. Well, it's a lie and I'll brand it for what it is. Don't you realise that Mr. Legality is the son of that slave-girl, Hagar,* and that everyone in Morality, in spite of their affluence and moral standing, is still head over heels in debt. There's not a community in all this part of the country that boasts of greater independence, and yet is more desperately in the red. When their leases run out and they have to reckon with the Lord of Sinai, they will be left without a thing to bless themselves. If the residents of Morality are up to the neck in debt, do you think they can lift your burden? Why, they can't even lift their own. And as for Mr. Legality, he's never lifted a burden yet! He speaks about the

* See Galatians 4:21–31.

honour of his profession but he's just a quack. His son, Civility, is no better. Remember, it's not what we look like that counts, but what we are. This idea of doing the best you can and being a "Sunday-go-to-meeting" type, all with a view to so impressing God that one day He'll let you into heaven, leads only to eternal death. Trying to be what we call good can never of itself fit us for heaven. Our sins remain. That is the force of the words, "Man is not justified by the works of the Law". Believe me, Mr. Worldly Wiseman is just an interloper and these so-called specialist burden-lifters are all impostors, robbing you of God's means of deliverance.' Evangelist paused and then said pointedly, 'Do you know that Christ died for our sins according to the Scriptures?'

'I read that somewhere once in my Book,' replied Christian 'but fail as yet to grasp its meaning.'

'Then what you need to do,' said Evangelist, 'is to get back to the narrow bridle path across the moors and go on towards the light that shines beyond the little white gate.' Then looking upward, Evangelist cried to God for a sign from heaven to confirm his words. No sooner had he done so than great tongues of flame burst through the slag on the mountain, making Christian's hair stand on end. Like thunder the words echoed in his heart. 'All who rely on works of law are under a curse, for it is written, "Cursed be everyone who does not abide by all things written in the book of the Law and do them."'

Christian felt now under the very sentence of death and so distressed in mind was he that he cried like a child, bitterly reproaching himself for his sinful stupidity that had allowed him to be so beguiled by Mr. Worldly Wiseman. Overwhelmed with shame he could only seek Evangelist's help once more and trust it might be possible, even yet, to get back into the right way.

'Is there any hope?' he asked almost pitifully. 'Can my sin still be forgiven? Can I yet get to the gate? And if I do, will the man at the Lodge give me access to the estate beyond the wall?'

'Your sin is great!' reiterated Evangelist, 'for you not only forsook what you knew to be the right road, but deliberately chose what was obviously the wrong road. Nevertheless, the man at the gate will receive you for his name is Good-will. Now you must go forward, but whatever you do, take care! Don't try any more short cuts. Keep on the narrow path right up to the gate then you'll be safe all the way.' The two men warmly clasped each other and Evangelist set Christian forward with the blessing of God.

This time as he went, he turned neither to the right hand nor to the left, nor would he greet a soul along the road, but made a bee-line for the place where he had first left the bridle-path at the subtle suggestion of Mr. Worldly Wiseman. So anxious was he, as he went along, he looked for all the world as if he were crossing thin ice expecting any moment to be engulfed in the depths below. Then at long last he came to a drystone wall where he saw the small white gate. The light was failing but still sufficient for him to read the words engraved about it. 'Knock and it will be opened to you.' Encouraged by this invitation, and the remembrance of the words of Evangelist, he knocked once, twice and then again, and as he did so he hopefully hummed to himself a little song that formed in his mind.

> *May I now enter here? Will He within*
> *Open to sorry me, though I have been*
> *An undeserving rebel? Then shall I*
> *Not fail to sing His lasting praise on high.*

After some time a person of serious demeanour came to the gate, asking who was there, from whence he came and what he wanted. That must be Good-will thought Christian and plucking up his courage he said, 'I am a sinful man bent double with guilt. I come from the City of Destruction and am travelling to Mount Zion hoping to escape the final burning. I flee from the wrath to come and believing the way to safety lies through these portals, knock now for admission. Will you let me in?'

'With all my heart,' replied Good-will and with that he swung back the door. As Christian entered the narrow aperture and stooped low beneath the lintel, Good-will suddenly gripped him and pulled him quickly through to the further side. 'And why did you do that?' asked Christian, baffled by the abruptness of the action. 'The reason we do this is because only a short distance from here lies Fort Lust. In the military barracks over there, the young recruits from the City of Destruction receive a basic training under a commanding officer called General Beelzebub. The first month they are allowed to do what they like, although by the time their General has finished with them, there's not one can do what he would. They are taught how to kill and to destroy, and to "shoot in the dark at the upright in heart". As pilgrims come to the gate, especially at this time in the evening, they are not averse to using people like yourself for target practice. Whatever the representations made to the authorities of the City of Destruction, they always reply that no incident of this nature has been brought to their notice. Yet this kind of thing has been going on from antiquity. So you see now why I pulled you in so roughly. General Beelzebub's men would like to have picked you off before you passed through the gate.'

'It makes me both hope and fear,' exclaimed Christian with relief. 'And who pointed you to the gate?' Good-will asked. 'A man call Evangelist. He told me to come here and knock at the gate, and that you, Mr. Good-will, would tell me what to do next.' 'An open door is set before you and no man can shut it,' encouraged Good-will and Christian began to feel all his troubles had been worthwhile.

Good-will now enquired about his adventures along the way and Christian related his story, telling him how he had left home in great distress and how his family and neighbours had sought to restrain him. He told him, too, about Obstinate and Pliable and the near-disaster on the mudflats in the Slough of Despond. 'But,' said Christian, 'when it came to it, I really was no better than Pliable for I listened to Mr. Worldly Wiseman and took the wrong road.' 'I suppose you were directed to Mr. Legality,' Goodwill surmised. 'That's right,' rejoined Christian 'and I would have been in his house had it not been for the terror of the mountain.' 'Yes, that mountain has been the death of many, and will, I expect, be the death of many more. It is wonderful to think you escaped with your life.' 'It was only the mercy of God, for not only did I escape but I met Evangelist again, and it is through his help that I now stand here before you. It's amazing to me how you could ever let me in.' 'We never refuse anyone who knocks,' replied Good-will. "All those what come to me," says the Father, "I will not cast out." '

Now the time had come for Christian to go further and Goodwill pointed the way to a magnificent mansion set in its own grounds. Christian could see its regal towers standing high in the twilight. How he longed to press on to his God. 'The way before you,' said Good-will, 'has been paved for present-day pilgrims by patriarchs, prophets and apostles but, pre-eminently, by Christ Himself. It is the only route to the Celestial City and goes right through without the slightest deviation.' 'But surely there are ups and downs,' queried Christian, 'and side roads too?' 'Yes you will meet many but you will be able to distinguish between the right and the wrong direction because the route to the Celestial City is always straight ahead. That is your rule for the road. Let nothing turn you aside.'

'And what about my burden?' asked Christian anxiously. 'Is it not possible to remove it now?' To which Good-will answered, 'If you'll be patient, all will be well. When you come to the place of

deliverance, it will fall from your back of its own accord.' And
with this promise ringing in his ears, Christian walked through
the gloaming, towards The Great House, silhouetted against the
sunset sky.

# CHAPTER FOUR

# MANSION OF MYSTERY

THE approaches to The Great House were quite unguarded and as Christian passed through the open gateway, he wondered at there being no lodge, no office and no turnstile. All was silent and deserted, not even a watch dog barked as he entered. Quite a few persons, it should be said, had applied for the post of lodge-keeper but had been told that both the grounds and the contents of the Great House were in some mysterious way capable of their own defence and perpetuation. This was discounted by the pundits in the City of Destruction as superstitious nonsense, but in view of the numerous thieves, robbers, poachers and other trespassers that had maliciously marauded the place over the years, its present prosperous condition attested the fact beyond question. When a vandal tore down a tree, or pulled up a shrub, it immediately took root again and flourished more vigorously. When an article was purloined by some ideological kleptomaniac, it slipped from his hands and remained where it was. The most serious attempts down history to break up The Great House had been by parties of commandos, dispatched on exercises from Fort Lust. In these operations, intelligence units supported by pioneer squads staged bitter attacks, in which the elements of intrigue and brute force combined to pillage the property. These onslaughts, needless to say, were termed 'unofficial' by the authorities at Fort Lust, who from time to time vociferously disclaimed any responsibility for lawlessness outside the area of their jurisdiction. Despite this wanton aggression, fires started by these terrorist bands either failed to spread as planned, or else turned in the wind to their great disadvantage. They would then retire in confusion, many being caught in the dense growth of the forest or burned by the very flames their hands had kindled.

In view of such happenings, it is understandable how many extraordinary tales have grown up around The Great House of the Interpreter. In fact, the time came when the hearsay reached such proportions that the Critical Faculty of the Universities, both in Carnal Policy and the City of Destruction, inaugurated a joint venture to determine the origin and functions of The Great House standing beyond the wall. A number of committees have been in session now for several decades, but up till the time of writing have failed to issue a common statement of their findings. This is due largely to fresh evidence coming in, which not infrequently discredits earlier conclusions. Meanwhile there remain several schools of thought on the matter.

Some say The Great House is an old feudal dwelling, which for no other reason than its age has drawn to itself a mass of legend. Hence all the talk about the place being haunted by spirits and demons. The party in question, however, categorically denies there is anything supernatural about it. The Great House, they say, is no more than a crumbling edifice, archaic and anachronistic, which should really be bulldozed to allow for the extension of the motorway network across the whole of the estate grounds.

Others, again, view the mansion as a building of outstanding historical importance and feel it should be preserved as an ancient monument; a kind of witness to the culture and religion of earlier civilisations. It houses, they say, an incomparable collection of literary documents containing quite unique data on the pattern of life in the Middle East both prior to and immediately following the appearance of Jesus in history. They hold the opinion that, whilst many of the works are steeped in mythology, some of the material is, on the contrary, historically reliable. The application of the Jewish ethic to society as a whole, they insist, has great interest for the contemporary sociologist studying the emergence of the 'almighty' state and its formulation of fresh codes of conduct for the 'true' citizen. It is suggested that a permanent commission be set up at The Great House to deal firstly with the question of de-mythologising, and secondly, to interpret that which is of genuine moral import, in the idiom of our times.

Another school of thought, less academic in some ways but more religio-commercial in others, view The Great House as a shrine, or museum displaying various religious relics, to which pilgrimage should be encouraged. Whilst a certain measure of criticism and misunderstanding is envisaged, with charges such as idolatry, bibliolatry and even tourism being levelled in current periodicals, yet they consider the policy of popularisation is preferable to sheer neglect. The Association of Spiritual Guides has long suggested that living quarters be built in the grounds and a qualified staff be employed, firstly to maintain the appearance of the place and secondly to escort the public round the property and inform them of the true significance of the objects of veneration. The expense involved could be defrayed by the charge of a moderate entrance fee. It is appreciated that not everyone would be able to sustain interest in the guided tours, but the open lawns would be ideal for fêtes, side shows, jumble sales, or for stalls selling souvenirs and literature. Even if people had only sight-seeing in view, as long as they took home some pamphlets, some good would have been achieved. Then, of course, the main fore-court would be ideal for alfresco bingo on fine afternoons, and when it rained, the vast foyer with its polished floor could be made available for dancing. Once running costs and staff wages had been met, all funds accruing from the booths, the bingo and the entrance fees could be expended on the embellishment of the fabric.

Before leaving this rehearsal of ideas confronting the present generation, it should be mentioned that a most menacing move-ment has been gathering momentum in recent days. Quite a number occupying seats on the City of Destruction Town Council have been agitating for legislation to make The Great House, together with its grounds, a prohibited area for any citizen under forty-five, and furthermore are insisting that reference to it should be deleted from all school text-books and government sponsored literature. The reason for this, they say, is that The Great House represents the philosophy which inspires all reaction-ary thinking. It blunts the political awareness of the masses and in-hibits the innocent enjoyment of the ordinary citizen. To inflict such medieval concepts on the present generation is nothing less than an outrage. What such people forget, of course, is that The Great House has at no time in its history been subject to the Town Council, a fact which the Council has never been willing to acknowledge.

Such absurd malignments of The Great House, and Inter-preter, its Lord, had undoubtedly influenced Christian and made it difficult for him to ever consider travelling to The Celestial City. In fact everything in his wholly secularised society had been directed against the proper appreciation of what existed beyond the wall. Now, however, he was on his way and at the very approaches of the Mansion of Mystery, he found his doubts and misgivings falling from him and in their place came a sense of awe and wonder at all that lay ahead.

This afternoon had seemed very long to him, for much had happened, but now the sun dipped low behind the hills and a last ray of light streamed down the long leafy avenue. In the spacious grounds stood stately cedars, myrtles and sycamores together with oaks, firs, and even the apple tree, amongst the trees of the wood. In sheltered areas grew the fig, the vine and the olive. There was also a garden of herbs, and hyssop growing out of the wall; and somewhere amidst all this luxuriant growth, Christian knew there was the tree of life, which one day would bring God's healing to the nations. A fresh, invigorating wind came sweeping through the branches above him, and as the leaves flapped one against another, it sounded like the distant applause of a multitude no man could number. Then it was that he remembered the words from his book.

> *All the trees of the field shall clap their hands*
> *Instead of the thorn shall come up the cypress*
> *Instead of the brier shall come up the myrtle*
> *And it shall be to the Lord for a memorial*
> *For an everlasting sign which shall not be cut off.*

The peace of the garden in the cool of the day was a foretaste of paradise itself. Once at the house, Christian knocked at the door and in a little while was received into the presence of Interpreter, the Lord of the mansion. Seeing his great fatigue, Interpreter ordered that Christian be given a good meal of milk, bread and such meat as he could take. He was then ushered to one of the many guestrooms kept in readiness for the refreshment of pilgrims. 'Tomorrow we will meet again,' said Interpreter, 'and I will begin to show you the wonders and mysteries of this house, which have so great a bearing on the new life you have been called to live. Yours is a great privilege. Many before you have desired to see the things that you will see but have not seen them. It will be good for you to spend time in the precincts of this place, to take in its atmosphere and to assimilate its perspectives. The more you learn here, the easier it will be for you.'

As Christian lay down, he noticed on the wall of his bedroom a quotation. It read 'In all thy ways acknowledge Him, and He will direct your paths.' This surely, he felt, is the key to the heavenly highway code.

Next morning Christian awoke with the sunlight flooding his room and the sound of music in his ears. The song immediately caught at his heart and made him want to get up and press on.

> *Arise, my love, my fair one*
> *and come away;*
> *For lo, the winter is past,*
> *the rain is over and gone.*
> *The flowers appear on the earth,*
> *the time of singing has come,*
> *And the voice of the turtle dove*
> *is heard in our land.*

After another meal, with Interpreter as his host, he felt ready for the day. The only regret was that he could hardly face the meat, so a little broiled fish and a piece of honeycomb were brought to him.

During the succeeding days Interpreter went over many matters necessary for a man to know on the threshold of his pilgrimage. Before he eventually departed, Christian spent a whole day in prayer, writing down what he had seen and heard, that the testimony of Interpreter might remain in his mind and lodge in his heart. It is from this personal document the following extracts are now quoted. They should be of special interest to the public, who in this question of The Great House have been exposed so long to the conjectures and speculations of unscrupulous and prejudiced persons.

# CHAPTER FIVE

## SEARCHED BY THE SYMBOLS

THE first place to which I was escorted that morning after breakfast was the extensive foyer at the front entrance. There, on the
open face of the wall, and opposite the door, was a work of art,
sublime in conception. The floor was so highly polished, and the
mural reflected with such startling accuracy, that in comparing
the mirrored picture with the original, fresh facets of beauty continually caught the eye. For a long while I stood with Interpreter,
pondering the figures before me. The central motif showed a man
of solemn, yet inspiring countenance. His eyes looked upward, as
if to God Himself; and although his feet were on the ground, he
seemed to belong more to heaven than to earth. In the background were Roman galleys, Greek amphitheatres, and Israel's
temple at Jerusalem. In the foreground were skyscrapers, atomic
reactors and a whole range of inter-continental missiles. Skilful
lighting, constantly varied by unseen hands, alternated the em-
phases of the picture, between the distant past and the immediate
present. In his hand, the man held the Book of all books, and
from it, rays of light struck hither and thither, to illumine the
things both before and behind him. The meaning was clear. The
Book was relevant to ancient empires, yet still held good for
nuclear fears. I looked more closely. As he stood, he pleaded with
men and on his head was a crown of gold—an emblem, I deemed,
of his heavenly mandate. I sought intently to evaluate these de-
tails, then Interpreter said, 'I have shown you this picture now,
because this man depicts the apostles' witness to Jesus Christ.
They alone are authorised to be your guide and to expound the
teachings of the book, which you and this man both hold in your
hands. Listen carefully to what I'm saying! You'll meet many who
think they excel the apostles, but do not be deluded; their words
lead only to the gates of death.'

The next place we visited was the first floor balcony, which
looked out to the farther side of the property. At our approach
the long glass windows opened of their own accord, and we stood
together at a stone parapet, surveying a broad expanse of
ploughed fields. A harvest had just been gathered and prepara-
tions were now in progress for a fresh sowing. Whatever the recent return, the ground held little promise of a further crop. Hay

and stubble littered the furrows, and the mounds of earth seemed hard and unyielding. Beneath the blazing sun, even the soil just turned looked starved of moisture. Only an optimist could have 'ploughed in hope' and most, I think, would have 'sown in tears'. Then I glimpsed a giant tractor, trailing behind it a fierce looking harrow. Its ruthless strength broke up the clods and thrashed them to powder. As it rumbled over the field, brown, billowing clouds of dust rose high in the air, obscuring the sun itself. They caught in the wind and fanned out menacingly across the empty flats to where I stood. I began to cough and splutter, but Interpreter, quite unaffected, continued talking in his clear cut tones. 'To you,' he said, 'a human being of the twentieth century, The Great House tends to look very old and outmoded. Maybe you wonder, in this world where men raise concrete fingers skyward, and toss their satellites far out in space, if it can be of use at all. Should this be so, then you are terribly mistaken. Within these walls we have the means to counter all the chaos of this age; and more than that, to satisfy the hopes of everyone who yearns for God. To search out "matter", that is one thing; to know your Maker, quite another. Look in your Book. You'll find a realm there, described in multi-dimensional terms, where one experiences in breadth and length, in depth and height, a love surpassing all mankind has known. This is God's fulness; but what can wordlings say? Earth's highest wisdom falters still at Heaven's alphabet. How can your planet's meagre symbols hope to show the Alpha and the Omega of God?'

A sense of awe came over me; but so violent was my coughing, I had to speak to Interpreter about the dust. 'Do you wish to have it laid?' he asked. 'Seeing it's everywhere around us, I don't see how it's possible,' I replied. To which Interpreter answered with quiet strength, 'The things which are impossible with men are possible with God.' Then he showed me a small control-panel installed in a weather-proof enclosure on the balcony. We went inside and he said to me. 'Do you see the little push-button there?' It was situated so near the floor that one had to kneel to operate it, but Interpreter assured me that this was no technical oversight, but was so designed for the protection of the operator. 'Can you see the word inscribed on it?' he asked. 'Yes,' I answered, 'it says PRAYER.' 'That's right, but lest you deem this apparatus merely a mechanical device, let me say at once that this button of prayer achieves nothing on a mechanical principle. It simply provides the opportunity of contact with the Controller. Push it now and hold it down!' I sought to comply but found it too difficult to maintain in position. Interpreter, sensing my dilemma, came to my assistance and brought the strength of his finger to bear upon it. We were now in contact, and Interpreter, using a language I could not understand, spoke into a kind of microphone in the cubicle. I was astonished at the result. A giant pillar of cloud began to form over the layer of dust, and a soft dew-like rain started to fall. 'This is the early rain,' said Interpreter. 'There is also another rain later.' The effect was immediate. In a matter of moments the dust was laid. 'The ground is now ready for the seed,' said Interpreter. In utter amazement, I exclaimed, 'But how did it happen and what does it mean?'

'The giant tractor,' explained Interpreter, 'with the big harrow trailing behind it, speaks of the action of God's Law on the heart. It does not cleanse, but on the contrary fills the conscience with a sense of sin, until the whole being "chokes and splutters" to the point of death. Nevertheless the effect of the Law is beneficial, for by it man's heart is prepared to receive God's Christ, the Living Seed. The Law breaks to pieces the self-sufficiency of man, and proves conclusively that such ground can never bear fruit of itself. The gentle rain tells of the work of the Spirit in the Gospel. It was released when prayer became active under the prompting and enabling of the Comforter. Harrowed by the Law and watered by the Spirit, men gladly receive the Saviour. So the Seed takes root and yields much fruit for the Lord of this place.' The Interpreter paused, giving me a chance to assimilate what he had said; then confident I was still listening, he continued his instruction.

'The world talks about things *historical*, but you can see from our first picture in the entrance hall, how superior are the concepts of The Great House in relation to history. We not only show how the sequence of the past, present and future hinges on one unfolding plan; but we show the relation of things temporal *to* things eternal; and more than that, the effect the eternal has *on* the temporal. Man is imprisoned in his present. The past to him is only a deduction, not an experience. Whilst he can prove from today's facts that yesterday was real, he cannot recapture or relive what once he enjoyed or endured. Memory's index can turn up true impressions, but to re-experience days gone by is something quite beyond his powers. Man's future life is equally illusive. Fear and elation may prognosticate consequence, but future's facts lie ambushed still. To us in The Great House, "that which has been is now; and that which is to be, has already been". We are able, therefore, to direct a man from his helpless drifting into highest destiny; we make him taste today, the powers of the world to come. Man's fairest future lies in the "Eternal Present" of the Living God. Who does His will today, invests his moments with eternal relevance.'

Interpreter paused, then said with feeling, 'I do so want you to grasp this, Christian—to do with God what He is doing, this is the dawn of fulfilment; to become in Christ what He chose you to be, this is the ultimate of all realisation. So in that blissful eternal sphere, the past and future meet, to bring you to the moral likeness of The Great I AM whose grace you own. Yet many would be strong without Him, or try for ideal manhood through merely natural powers. We are dismissed, who most could help them. They petulantly demand an independence their puny powers are unable to sustain. They stage a tantrum at the small white gate. *They* are "too big". *It* is "too small". The word still stands, that only childlike can they enter, but they refuse to look "ridiculous". That's what they say. "We've grown up now!" And hence their tragedy. They are "adults", so cease to grow. They have "matured", and chances to develop fade away. Thus dwarfs in thousands walk your city streets. Have you not seen them Christion?' The form of Interpreter was suddenly immense beside me. 'I can't say I have,' I mumbled, quite dumbfounded. 'You'd notice them now!' said Interpreter decisively, and once again we stood in silence.

'As for today, you've watched "things *agricultural*" and "things *meteorological*",' Interpreter went on. 'That's how they say it, isn't it? To that which God has given existence, mankind so quickly gives his labels. Yet can man solve his self-made paradox? A law-ruled universe without a law-originating God? Since matter won't explain itself, must causes spiritual be made taboo? The natural laws, the fields will tell you, are not mere symbols of the spiritual. The laws in both these realms are one; a single set of principles that permeate the whole of God's creation, be it visible or not. Men reap the kind of seed they sow on either side the wall. It's true from whence you came; true where you go; and true of every step between. For angels, demons, men and things, there's no escaping the inexorable.

'Talking of labels—you need to recognise that man's distinctions are just stopgaps in the classifying of his scanty data. Here we do not make such pigeon-hole approximations. We are concerned with life itself, not only in its development and growth (although we authored that), but in terms of individuals, their mutual relationships and ultimate goals. The world has become so industrialised, systematised, computerised and even mesmerised, that human beings are quite de-personalised. The Great House is totally opposed to such a trend. Satan is the great depersonaliser. God made his creatures different. Satan would have them all the same. He is the arch-sponsor of mass-movement. Nazism, Fascism and Communism are all his evil mass-moving inventions. Since Satan first swept one third of stardom to his side, this has been the hallmark of his actions. Remember the raging mob that shouted Jesus to the Cross? By mass communication, the dangerous few who led the world in commerce, politics and faith can, through one telecast, inhibit or incite the nations. Yet in God's work, however wide the Sower's cast, each single grain alights on one location. Effective contact still implies, indeed demands "a person to person call"; and as you know, that always costs much more, Christian, even in your society!

'Now let us talk about the sky. World weather on your radio is just a background for people's breakfast. From outer space, the stratosphere and all the seven seas come bulletins that let you know what clothes to wear, what care to take; but in this House, the wind and whirlwind, peace and storm are all foreseen. World trends in nations, peoples, states and men are both discerned and then directed, for though man's wrath works not the righteousness of God, yet God still causes human wrath to praise Him. The progress of the Seed is all foreknown. No cataclysmic nuclear event can ultimately frustrate its harvest. Once reaped, the last great storms will burst to desolate the earth. God holds the times; God gives his signs; but men are weather conscious only. If they could really read the sky, they'd flee the hurricane of judgement.'

With this Interpreter concluded the day's instruction. It left me utterly exhausted, so the next morning I was allowed to stroll quietly about the grounds, breathing the fresh air of God's presence amongst the trees of the garden. What I had seen and heard, though it brought its own anxieties, gave me, nevertheless, fresh hope of losing my burden, the odour of which caused me much embarrassment whenever Interpreter approaches me.

On the third day, Interpreter told me we were to look at 'things *anthropological*'. All the time he used these classifications, I felt he despised them, and that he was only referring to them to show how narrow are the bounds of human conception. His opening words pointed to an order transcending merely earthly categories. With uncompromising seriousness, he began.

'The initial divisions of the divine fiat in creation give the real key to the understanding of man and his environment. You recall them? Light and darkness; Things above and Things below; The Visible and Invisible; The Temporal and the Eternal; Flesh and Spirit; Good and Evil; Male and Female.' Each time he spoke, I felt confronted with a standpoint wholly different from my own. One day, I thought, when my burden has gone, I shall stand with him in the truest sense. Then I shall see things as he sees them, and from where he stands. 'Man only graduates from childhood,' broke in Interpreter, 'when he stops pulling things to pieces and begins to use them for the purposes his God intended. Lusting and labelling will never do. Let's go to the nursery.'

We went upstairs to another landing where we approached a big glass panel. As I peered through it, I could see a most attractive room, beautifully equipped with miniature furniture. In two small chairs sat a little boy and girl, both about three years of age. There they were, facing each other, with nothing to play with and no one to amuse them. 'Now,' said Interpreter, 'by a very simple test I want to demonstrate the essential difference between these two children. They may look alike, but their natures are quite different.' At this, Interpreter lifted a telephone hanging on the wall and in a few moments, a kindergarten teacher entered the room, whispered something in the ear of each child and then withdrew. The effect was immediately apparent. One child became restless and irritable and kept looking at the door as if expecting the lady to return, but the other remained contented and undisturbed. 'Do you see the difference now?' interspersed Interpreter. 'The discontented one is called Passion, and the quieter one Patience. The whisper made all the difference in revealing just what they are. The kindergarten teacher told them that later today she will give them some toys. Passion cannot bear to wait, and so is quite unsettled, whilst Patience is happy at the thought of what she's going to receive and is actually enjoying her toys in anticipation.' As we watched the children, Passion began to get cross and started shouting for the teacher, but Patience still sat quietly. Interpreter picked up the phone once more and the lady reappeared carrying a number of big parcels. She entered the room and placed all of them in front of Passion. As she did so she looked at Patience and said, 'It's all right, your turn will come later.' Passion literally tore into the parcels, opening each one gleefully, then turning quickly to the next until all the toys were spread around him. He hardly knew which one to play with. He'd pick up one and then another, till having lost all interest, he fell to tormenting Patience. 'Look what I've got!' he cried. When at last the lady returned, Passion was back in his sullen mood. Some of his toys were broken and others thrown into the far corners of the room. As soon as he saw the teacher, Passion shouted rudely, 'Give me some more toys! I don't know what to do!' Completely ignoring him, she left Passion to shout himself hoarse and cope with his own bad temper; but beckoning to Patience, she said, 'Come along! I've got some really wonderful things for you. You've waited a long time and now you'll receive them.' So Patience went off happily down the corridor to realise her great expectations.

'Have you any idea what it all means?' asked Interpreter, but I could only confess how hazy I was as to the import of the incident. 'The thing is this,' he said, 'they are born of different fathers. Passion represents that attitude which is born of the Evil One, but Patience that attitude born of God. To be a person like Passion is to be a child of this present evil world. Passion, you notice, wants everything now. Passion is first "sick *for* a thing" but once he's received it, he's quickly "sick *of* the thing". Patience on the other hand exhibits the meekness and gentleness of Christ. She is content to forego many a good thing now, knowing that God has better things in store. The world says, "A bird in the hand is worth two in the bush", but the Christian believes in the promise "Go thy way and I will give you that which is right." '

From this I saw that Patience is possessed of superior wisdom, firstly because she waits for the best; and secondly because she will be enjoying the best when Passion has nothing but memories and regrets. To which Interpreter added the thought that the best things, which are always God's things, belong to the world to come and thus never wear out; whereas present things are the world's things, and in a state of continual decay. 'So you see,' he said, 'Passion has less reason to laugh at Patience than Patience has to laugh at Passion, for Patience will have the best things at the last. And remember, first always gives place to last, for the last things have to do with the time to come. He that receives his portion first must have a given time to spend it, but he that has his portion last shall enjoy it everlastingly. That is the meaning of the word spoken to the rich man by the Lord of this place. "Remember, you in your life time received goods things, but now Lazarus is comforted and you are in anguish." '

So I began to see how it is best not to grasp at things in this world but to wait for God and the time to come, and when I expressed this conclusion, Interpreter said it was a right one, for said he, 'The things which are seen are transient but the things that are unseen are eternal. Yet this is rarely appreciated because the "things that are seen" and our own natural urges are such near neighbours; and the "things eternal" and our natural appetites are so remote from one another, that the first two quickly flirt with each other to bring forth illegitimate children, whilst the latter two will never even catch the other's eye.'

Towards evening time, the same day, Interpreter came to me and said, 'Come with me, we are going to light the beacon. It's a breathtaking spectacle, and not every pilgrim sees it when passing through. I only light it for those who are vitally interested in what I have to say and who are willing to order their lives accordingly.' So we climbed a further flight of stairs until at last we stood on the rooftop of The Great House. I found it interesting, in the course of the days, to see what varied views there were of the territory, pertaining to the Authority under whose roof I was staying. One could look out from larger windows such as those in Room Three of 'The John Wing' or in Room Fifty-three of 'The Isaiah Wing'. All these commanded great vistas, but sometimes from the smaller windows of an unfrequented turret or a tiny prophet's chamber, one might get a glimpse of things from a fresh angle altogether. Now I stood on the roof, it was exhilarating to let my eyes range out to the great horizons. What an unfettered vision! I looked upward and a standard immediately broke from the flagpost, bearing the words,

> *Your eyes will see the King in His beauty*
> *They will behold a land that stretches afar.**

How my whole being yearned for liberty. 'That is the beacon,' said Interpreter, reading my thoughts, 'It is the truth that sets men free.' Before me I saw a great container supported on a single, metal stem of considerable height. Out of this reservoir protruded seven jets. 'You may be surprised to hear it, but the whole thing is fashioned in gold,' said Interpreter. 'This is the light you saw when Evangelist first pointed you towards the small, white gate. Now stand back behind this protective shield and I will commence the count down. Nine, eight, seven ... four, three, two, one, zero! Ignition!' Somewhere in the House a hidden power responded. There was a rush of fuel and seven sheets of blinding flame leapt seventy feet into the air. I stood, helplessly exposed in all my rags, yet fascinated beyond measure by the glare of the beacon. 'Now you will see the enemy hoses at work,' said Interpreter and even as he spoke, from somewhere outside the building came countless spurts of water interweaving through the flames. The hiss and roar was almost frightening but to my amazement the flames, far from diminishing in brilliance, increased in intensity. The surrounding countryside was thrown into sharp relief and Interpreter remarked that even the darkest

* Isaiah 33 : 17.

57

alleys of the City of Destruction are lit up when the beacon burns its brightest.

At this juncture I felt I simply had to ask a question. 'How is it that when the water cross-flow is increased the flames mount higher? I would have thought the opposite would have been the case.' 'Do you see the golden pipes,' he indicated, 'which run into the reservoir from which the jets protrude? Well, they are the connecting link with a concealed plant, which processes all the oil we receive from our perennial olive trees. The oil is of such quality and provided in such quantity that we are always able to feed the beacon with the fuel required, and whatever the volume of water cast across the screen of flame, we can exert the commensurate pressure necessary to maintain the supply. This is the inside story of what is happening. I would also like to point out to you that in the very subduing of the water, considerable amounts of steam are released, which, becoming luminous in the flames, diffuse the light over an even wider area.' 'And has all this some significance?' I asked, not a little astonished. 'Why, yes, of course, everything in The Great House has its own particular import. Let me explain this parable to you. The oil speaks of the grace of Christ supplied to the believer through God's Holy Spirit. The fierce counter-action of the hoses depicts the hostile work of Satan, who seeks to extinguish the Christian's witness. It is at such times, however, that "God supplies more grace", so that the opposition of Satan is not only overcome, but is made an occasion for the extension of the testimony. For instance, when Paul was imprisoned at Rome, he wrote, "the things that happened unto me have fallen out rather unto the furtherance of the Gospel", and in the same letter he declared with confidence, "I know that this situation will be to my spiritual advantage by reason of your prayer and the supply of the Spirit of Christ Jesus." '

So ended another instructive day. Under the skilful tuition of Interpreter, I had been led from one level to another until I stood now, in the light of the beacon under the open sky, on the rooftop of The Great House. But lest I should be over-elated at the abundance of the revelations, the bones on my back dug like thorns in my flesh, constraining me to seek with patience the deliverance promised of the Lord.

On the day following, my session with Interpreter proved quite different from the previous ones, for I was led into a very dark room. He at once sensed my foreboding and explained how I must be brought into this shadowy studio, to realise the condition of man's mind without the light of God. Far from being a negative experience, he said, it would prove of positive benefit to me, because in this very area, where man had nothing to offer, he would now bring into the open all the aspirations God was begetting in my heart. The content of the Book I held and all that I had so recently considered was having the desired effect. Apparently I needed to appreciate this development, and Interpreter summarised what was happening in the familiar quotation, 'Faith cometh by hearing and hearing by the Word of God'. He then outlined to me what was going to take place.

'You've heard of closed-circuit television?' he queried. 'Why, of course, they have it in the factories and stores, and even in cafés and churches in my old city,' I replied. 'Need I reiterate,' said Interpreter, 'that all we have here in The Great House exceeds the most advanced of human achievements. God's thoughts are not man's thoughts and the gulf between divine conception and human imagination is "measured" only by that infinitude existing between heaven and earth. Whereas, in closed-circuit television, a person speaking in one room is heard and seen in another; in our special process of "reflection, conviction, submission and transformation", you yourself are both telecaster and viewer, both speaker and listener. Away there in the shadows is a sheet of glass, a kind of mirror if you like, although quite different from either. It is highly sensitised. Whilst in one sense you could say it was composed of inanimate material, yet it has a living quality about it. If you sit in front of it, gaze into it, and begin to ponder over what you have so recently seen and heard, there will appear on the screen, in picture-form, a sequence which corresponds to your own state of mind. It will reflect this so perfectly that the picture will, as it changes, interpret to you, not only what you are but what you ought to be. This experience both corrects and stimulates. You see, the unit acts somewhat like a micro-computer, though the term is quite inadequate. In it there is tabled every conceivable aspect of human relationships, together with all that God intends for man, so whilst the unit reflects the viewer, it also directs his mind in an orderly sequence towards the highest and the best. Regular sessions with this unique little screen prove quite transforming. Paul of Tarsus, who helped to assemble it, described it in these remarkable words, "It is profitable for teaching, for reproof, for correction and for training in righteousness, that the man of God may be complete, equipped for every good work." The secret of its working is partially disclosed in his other statement. "We all, with unveiled face, beholding as in a glass, the glory of the Lord, are being changed into His likeness from one degree of glory to another; for this comes from the Lord, who is the Spirit." But there is one warning about the use of the screen,' Interpreter added. 'If anyone is a hearer of the Word and not a doer, he is like a man who observes his natural face in a mirror, for he observes himself and goes away and at once forgets what he is like. But he who looks into the perfect law, the law of liberty, and perseveres, being no hearer that forgets but a doer that acts, he shall be blest in his doing.'

Having spoken these words he said to me, 'Are you prepared to begin viewing? If so I will connect you.' Whereupon he brought two little pads which were wired to the unit. One he fastened to my head and the other above my heart. I waited a moment, then Interpreter cautioned me, 'Now is the acceptable time,' and with that, a picture began to focus gradually upon the screen. At first I saw a gleaming façade of glass, clear as crystal; then came into view the lines of a building, which for beauty and magnificence defied description. It was a vast administrative centre and made the Houses of Parliament in the City of Destruction look like slums waiting for clearance. At the windows and on the roof I could see human beings quite different from their jaded counterparts on earth. In fact they looked more divine than human, for they wore no masks and their faces were as the image and glory of God. On the road leading to this grand edifice congregated a large crowd of people all bent on gaining admittance to it. The procedure required each one to register at the kiosk by the turnstile. The picture changed now and I saw several car loads of men, armed to the teeth, drive up and take their stance at the gate determined to resist any who would enter the building. The mass of the people were astounded at their action and fell back, afraid to risk their lives—but suddenly out from the crowd stepped a man, ready at all costs to fight his way through. The gang of thugs let him reach the kiosk, where he registered unmolested. There he paused a moment and donned what I later learned was a 'Salvation-helmet'. Gripping a small, almost invisible weapon in his hand, he turned now upon the gangsters who bore down upon him with murderous intent. But a remarkable thing happened. He raised the little weapon and directed it pointblank at his attackers. One by one they collapsed before him, shot through by an unseen ray. Being only a single fighter, some struck him cruel blows before they fell but he stood his ground and when the fracas was over, I could see him there, still standing firm. He now walked on victoriously into the building and as he did so many shouted their welcome from the ramparts and the open windows. Then in a little while he appeared amongst them, his regalia as theirs, radiant in the glory of that other world.

It was with mixed feelings that I surveyed the screen. I felt so like the crowd that shrank back in fear and yet I yearned so much to conquer all obstacles and enter that shining palace. Inspired to go forward, I resolved that cost what it may, I would enter the Kingdom. 'Remember!' said Interpreter, 'this picture links with the first. The Book that you hold is both your light for the way and your weapon for war. It is a spiritual-laser. One thrust of that light will penetrate your persecutors so thoroughly, that the sharpest two-edged blade will seem like a paper-knife. This laser-beam is unique. It divides the soul from the spirit, the joints from the marrow and discerns the thoughts and intents of the heart!'

As he disconnected the pads from my heart and head, he told me his plans. 'We must go tomorrow to a part of The Great House which will distress you greatly.' It seemed almost too much to bear. 'But I would sooner continue my pilgrimage,' I pleaded. 'Surely I've seen enough for the present.' 'It is all too little,' said Interpreter. 'There are two more sessions, then you may go.' At this I felt weak in myself, but Interpreter spoke again to me and said, 'Be of good courage, and God shall strengthen thine heart.' So I went to my room and rested that night, wondering on all I had witnessed and fearing not a little, for all I was yet to see.

# CHAPTER SIX

# THE HORROR THAT HEALS

I was now led into what seemed a most sinister room. It was situated right under the house and was the chamber from which descents could be made into 'the lower parts of the earth'. I was immediately conscious of countless red, green and amber lights, flickering ominously along a massive bank of instruments lining the rear wall. In their eerie glow, I discerned a number of deep shafts, six to seven feet wide, in the central area of the concrete expanse. Within each socket stood suspended, for want of a better expression, a subterranean rocket, its long tail fins splaying up and out from the aperture, towards the ceiling high above. Nestling at the base of each set of fins was a small capsule of not more than five feet in diameter. I felt curious but apprehensive and would like to have found some reassurance in the face of Interpreter, but that was the strange thing, I never seemed to be able to catch him that way. It was always his voice, his movements, his demonstrations that transfixed me. His face, his nameless person, somehow escaped my grasp. He stood constantly beside me but always pointing beyond himself.

'Let's go over and talk to the terrestronauts,' he said, 'there's one, particularly, I would like you to see.' He directed me now across the floor of the secret underground hangar and for some reason I did not realise at the time, all the lights remained at red, casting a ghastly light upon the scene. As we approached the terrajets, (this was their technical name), Interpreter explained to me some of the problems of trans-strata penetration.

'In his exploration of the stellar field, man faces many hazards, not least of which is the possibility of a manned satellite breaking its orbit. It might be tracked for a hundred million miles, but only to become at last a wandering star, lost in the blackness of the vast unknown, bearing for ever, it's grisly reminder of humanity, into infinity. The hazards of the terrestronaut are naturally different from those of the astronauts, though not less fearful. Very simply, the danger is this. The deeper the terrestronaut penetrates into the under-world, the more deeply involved he becomes with oppressive and depressive atmospheres. However comprehensive the precautionary measures, and they are very considerable these days, it is still terribly possible for the terrestronaut, by reason of the change his whole system undergoes, to become quite incapacitated for normal respiration at terra-crust level. This means that, on resurfacing, a terrestronaut so affected cannot be extricated from his capsule without endangering his life; and yet to remain in the capsule also means certain death, though quite a time may elapse before the process is culminated. The decision to stay in the capsule, or to emerge, is left with the terrestronaut himself. It presents a heart-breaking predicament, which all human research has failed to overcome. Most terrestronauts faced with this dilemma elect to remain encased in their capsule, for after their "trip" they seem to lose their will power and be almost incapable of positive decision. We, at the Great House, have enabled some to emerge successfully, even from amongst those who have gone so deeply into "things below" as to have the smell of hell itself upon them.'

We were now standing at the edge of one of the shafts. The space between the casing of the terra-jet and the shaft-wall was minimal and left me baffled as to how this great machine could burrow through the earth. Subsequently, I learned it was to do with a screw-movement of immense power. The disadvantage, however, of this mode of projection, lay in the fact that it was virtually impossible for the terrestronauts to assume re-emergence, where their submergence in the under-world had been first achieved. 'Climb up on to the platform by the capsule,' suggested Interpreter, 'and look through one of the portholes.' I did so and to my horror saw a man sitting inside, his face drawn and ghostly in the crimson light.

'This,' explained Interpreter, 'is one of the terrestronauts, who is so maladjusted to life in normal atmospheres as to be faced with the dilemma of which I spoke. You can speak to him on the intercom if you like,' and he pointed to a little cup-like microphone close by. 'Hello there,' I began, 'can you explain your position to me?' 'Yes,' came the languid voice back over the intercom, 'I'm just the shadow of the man I used to be.' 'And what were you?' 'Someone like yourself, with high hopes of reaching the Celestial City until I got involved in the sub-terrestrial programme. I did not start the "dig-down" here; I did my first dive from Cape Deadbeat but I surfaced in this hangar, my craft completely out of control. The staff of The Great House, with their superior tracking-system, had my whole course mapped out from the moment of ignition.' 'Well what do you propose to do?' 'Nothing, for there is nothing that can be done. I'm like a mole in a trap. I can't stand the sunlight you see, or breathe the atmosphere you breathe. My whole person has undergone such a change through over exposure to the nether-world, that I'm now allergic to every God-given blessing you enjoy on earth. I have allowed my lusts free play. I have derided and spurned God's word. I have grieved the Holy Spirit and He speaks to me no more. I invited the devil to my heart and my guest became my master. I have been so provocative to God that He has left me to myself. I have so hardened my heart that I am now incapable of repentance.'

Then I turned to Interpreter and said, 'Is there no hope for this kind of terrestronaut?' 'Ask him yourself,' he replied. 'He appreciates his own predicament remarkably well, in spite of his declining faculties!' 'I can hardly speak to him again,' I said weakly. 'Won't you ask him?' At which, Interpreter said to the man 'Is there *really* no hope for you? Must you always be encaged in this capsule of despair?' 'There is no hope for me at all,' the man reiterated. 'But the Son of God is very merciful.' 'I know,' he said, 'But I have crucified Him to myself afresh. I have utterly despised Him. I have mocked His righteousness and counted His blood an unholy thing. I have done despite to the Spirit of His grace. Therefore I have shut myself completely out from the promises of God and now I can only ponder the threat of judgement and the whitehot flame of His indignation, for the Living God is "a consuming fire".'

'But how did you make such an error of judgement as to bring yourself to this pitiful condition?' 'What I did, I did for personal gain and self-gratification. I thought I was doing myself well but it was a course leading straight to ruin. Such thoughts gnaw at my conscience now and devour me like a virus, in my inner man.' 'But are you sure you cannot repent?' 'No, it's impossible,' he replied emphatically, 'God has denied me repentance. His word gives me no encouragement to believe I can. I believe it is God Himself who has shut me up in this capsule and there is not a man on earth who can extricate me alive.' He then relapsed into an incoherent babbling of words which sounded like 'Eternity! Eternity! Fire in the capsule! Fire down below! Oh Everlasting Fire!' At this I was profoundly affected. All my old fears returned and I cried out to Interpreter, 'Oh let me go! Let me go! I can't stand it!'

When I had calmed a little, Interpreter spoke again. 'Do you know how he spends his time in the capsule, during the short time he has to live?' 'I can't imagine,' I replied. 'Playing cards,' said Interpreter without the flicker of a smile or an indication of horror, 'and Snakes and Ladders. They're part of the diversional equipment on all the "digs" from Cape Deadbeat.' As he said it, he watched me carefully, weighing my reactions. 'Let the misery of this person be a warning to you!' he declared and with that we left the chamber.

My last night in The Great House was shared with another person. He was fast asleep when I retired and we must both have slept for several hours, when suddenly I awoke with a start. The occupant of the other bed was shaking and shouting in an alarming fashion. Up he jumped and began to pull on his clothes as if he must run for his life. At that particular moment, Interpreter entered and said to him, 'Tell Christian what's the matter with you.' The commanding voice seemed to steady him and once he was fully awake, he recounted the following experience in sepulchral tones. 'In my dream,' he began, 'I saw the sky grow black with a gathering storm. The lightning slit the clouds to ribbons and thunder rocked my eardrums, like gunfire when the battle's joined. Somehow I knew it was the climax of the years, the set-piece pageant of all our age-long history. Across the sky there scudded clouds, like refugees before invaders. It was a portent. There they came! Came in their thousands, Christian! A myriad vehicles rending the heavens; out from that other world into earth's atmosphere, each with their vaporous trails. Yet, even as the spectacle unfolded, I saw Him. The Man! Brighter than noonday-sun, blazoned in glory, coming with clouds. And Christian, we, who had pierced Him, saw Him, His face, that single face, scarred, yet magnificent. "Oh mountains, fall on us! Oh rocks destroy us!" we cried. "Hide us! Hide us! Hide us!" we screamed, "from the wrath of the Lamb. Oh Terror of meekness! White heat of righteousness!" Warmth of love would have saved us! Oh how He wanted to gather us. Now heat of His holiness slew us. Throughout the cities and across the lands, the millions curled into cinders. It was the flame of His mouth. We would not have Him. Therefore we could not stand Him. It was the consummation. His feet touched down on Olivet. The bedrock split. The living waters flowed. Then came a silence in the earth and man sat quiet, it seemed a thousand years. But at the last His voice, that mighty cataract of waters numberless! "Arise, Oh dead, and come to judgement!" It was the summons to the Last Assize. The graveyards stirred, the grassy aisles filled up with shadowy dead. The sea disgorged the many it had claimed and ash-filled urns fell empty to the ground, until before The Great White Throne stood small and great. Dread terror of the Lord! Dread books, dread works, Oh, total verdict. Guilty! Guilty! Guilty! Speechless, hopeless, helpless, I saw them. Filthy they died and filthy now they stood; leprous, diseased. Died in their sins they had, and dead in their sins they lived again to die. And so to the Lake, how large it loomed; strangely translucent, moving, rising; a swelling tide, surging, devouring, leaping to lick me from my slender place, down to the ceaseless burnings of the vast abyss. Hence, then, my terror in the night, my waking anguish at the eternal flame!'

And such, I tremblingly record, became the final sign The Great House gave.

'Have you considered all these things.' It was Interpreter who spoke. 'I have,' I answered. 'They cause me once again to hope and fear.' 'Then let them be God's spurs, to urge you onward to His City, and to your journey's end. The time has come for your departure.' Down the drive we walked until at last he bade me fond farewell. 'The Holy Spirit be always with you,' he said, 'and guide your footsteps in the way of peace.' A moment more and he was gone, but as I stood before the open road I seemed to sense his presence still and so it proved through all my pilgrimage.

*Written by me, Christian, in the year 1969 at the conclusion of my stay at The Great House beyond the wall. Should any portion of this diary fall into the hands of fellow-pilgrims, I only trust this record may prove the help to you that these experiences have been to me.*

# CHAPTER SEVEN

## THE SKULL-FACED SUMMIT

As Christian left The House of The Interpreter, he quickly found himself on a well-worn trail. The hard-packed clay left little doubt in his mind that many other pilgrims had already passed that way, heading for the Celestial City. This gave him fresh confidence to continue, and reassured him that he was not the odd-man-out his relatives so harshly maintained. In following the narrow track he was surprised to find that, on either side, high stone walls had been erected, impairing his view of what must have been an entrancing countryside. This irked him at first, for he had always been opposed to a restricted outlook, but as he scanned the walls, he was intrigued to find that there were numerous white stones dotted through the masonry and that they were set in the form of certain letters of the alphabet. Back in the City of Destruction he could recall many a wall and public building defaced with the crude scrawlings of hoodlums and rival gangs, but these letters were different. Such was the skill of the mosaic in the rough stone, that it seemed to him as the writing of God. The first letter Christian discerned was the letter 'S'. Then after a while, he came to the letter 'A'. So absorbed did he become, that in spite of the difficulty of carrying his load, he actually quickened his pace. It was only after he had been walking for some time, and the walls had ensured his arrival at the foot of a mountain, that he realised their builder had spelt out the word 'Salvation'. As the trail began to rise, it passed through some olive trees and a wind blowing through the branches whispered in Christian's ear:

> *We have a strong city.*
> *The Lord sets up salvation*
> *As walls and bulwarks.*
> *Open the gates that the righteous nation*
> *Which keeps faith may enter in.*
> *Thou dost keep him in perfect peace*
> *Whose mind is stayed on Thee*
> *Because he trusts in Thee.*

Gradually the path broke from the trees, and up through grassy slopes, until it led the traveller to a windswept summit. He paused for a moment, distressed by the weight on his back, which seemed to increase with every step. Without thinking, he turned instinctively to survey the trail he had covered. Like a cotton thread it ran out beneath him and his eye followed it, back beyond The House of The Interpreter, right to the great moor where he had first gained access to the territory of the Higher Authority. On the far horizon he could see the skyline of the City of Destruction blurred and confused under a great cloud of smog. 'Don't look back!' a voice called. Startled and condemned, Christian remembered Lot's wife, and turning quickly, pursued his upward way. The road now zig-zagged through a bluff of broken rock, and he could not help but notice the peculiar formation of the cliff face, as it dropped sheer into the gully below. There were dark cavities and one or two caves running into the hill, giving the clear impression of a human skull. Nightfall was quickly consuming the valley. Time was now short and as Christian clambered higher, he felt his heart pounding ever more fiercely against his ribs. A sense of unease came over him. What if he had a seizure in this isolated place. He would surely be attacked and devoured by the savage lion reputed to have his lair in the vicinity. Weaker and weaker he became and all the time his burden of bones stabbed cruelly at his flesh. Then the voice came again, 'It is hard for you to kick against the goads!' Christian looked up but saw no one. He was perplexed and unnerved. He found himself in the shadows now, for the sun had sunk lower and lower until it was eclipsed by the rim of the hill. At this stage Christian really felt he must lie down and die. 'And little wonder,' he moaned, 'for sin when it is full-grown brings forth death. Death, after all, is its wages and what more can a man expect!' So it was that he almost despaired of ever seeing the Celestial City. His eyes blinked back the beads of sweat but the salt water only made them smart the more. Blindly he stumbled on. Then suddenly, as he put his right foot forward, his toeless boot pawed at the air only to drop heavily to the earth. It was level ground. He had reached the summit. His eyes cleared rapidly and he found himself fighting for breath and looking away to yet another sunset sky.

The scene that met his gaze both calmed and inspired him. From the crown of the hill there stretched to the far horizons, a plain of prairie-like farmlands. With growing fascination he scanned the vast sea of ripening grain, golden in the evening sun and rippling gently in the night wind. The vault above was dark at its zenith but an expanse of eggshell blue, flecked with radiant cloud, lay low over the west. How the sight beckoned him. He could well imagine the Celestial City, away out yonder where the day still spurned to die. Then suddenly he saw it. In amongst the standing corn, there rose a pole with a crossbar. It was no more than a stone's throw away. On the pole was a turnip-face, like children make at Hallowe'en, and on the crossbar a tattered coat was fluttering in the wind. The scarecrow frame looked weird and stark against the distant sky, a lonely silhouette in the amber twilight. Then all at once something happened which rooted Christian to the spot. Directly behind the macabre pole and its single crossbar, a pencil of light was forming in the gathering clouds. It shot up first on the horizon, broadened a little, then extended upwards, until it reared, a pillar of splendour, touching heaven itself. Was it a natural phenomenon, a U.F.O., or a vision transcending the frontiers of sight? Christian could only wait. Soon from the brilliant column two arms of light shot forth to brand a luminous cross against the fast approaching night. He had never seen anything so breathtakingly beautiful. Then a gust of wind came eddying in across the ridge. The turnip toppled, and the ragged coat fell limply to the ground. Shivering and alone in his own poor garb he stared at the naked cross which found so great an answer in the skies, amazed that the thing despised should bring to him God's wisdom and His love. A whisper of wonder escaped his lips. 'It is the suffering and the glory!' he said, and, uncontrolled, the hot springs of emotion cast scalding tears all down his cheeks. In that one moment his heart was knit with the Crucified. His rucksack broke from his back, and there it went, bouncing and falling, all down the skull-faced rock. He fell to his knees wondering and listening, until at last the loosened stones were silent. It was an unimagined deliverance, for there beyond the edge of rock, a sepulchre of darkness had swallowed up his sin for ever. Words from his Book came freshly to him. 'The preaching of the cross is to them that perish foolishness but unto us who are saved, it is the power of God.' How sweet that understanding now! For hours he prayed; how long he could not tell; until the true light shone and all the east grew bright with God. Into the morning he set his face, fair as the moon, clear as the sun. 'Christ has given me rest through His sorrow, and life by His death,' he sang, and once again, to use his own quaint words, 'the water stood in his eyes.'

As he lingered in an ecstasy of weeping wonder, he became aware of three persons close at hand. Their noble features and splendid robes glistened in the dawning, wet with dew. Together they addressed him. 'Peace be to you, Christian.' Then one stepped forward and said, 'Your sins are forgiven.' 'And here are new clothes for your rags,' said the second. 'And your briefing for the road,' said the third, handing him a sealed document. Then they placed a brandmark on his person and declared, 'Now you are a Christian, not in name only, but in truth. You bear in your body the marks of the Lord Jesus. From this day forward let no man trouble you.' With this they wished him God's blessing, and Christian marched on, singing as he went:

> *O what a place! O what a moment this!*
> *Where I begin to taste all heaven's bliss,*
> *Here where the burden falls from off my back,*
> *Here where the straps that cruelly bound me crack.*
> *Blest Cross! Blest sepulchre! Blest ever be*
> *That Man, who there, was put to shame for me.*

# CHAPTER EIGHT

## SLEEPING SICKNESS

CHRISTIAN descended the further side of the hill as if he were walking on air. Who could have imagined he was the miserable wretch who so recently clambered to its summit with such agonising steps? He was a new man! Soon he came to a farmyard, where he saw three men lounging on bales of hay. They looked thoroughly down-and-out and he wondered who they might be. Pilgrims or tramps, hippies or hoboes? Entering the gate, he went over to talk with them but they were fast asleep. 'Rise and shine!' he shouted, surprised at his own temerity. Not one of them stirred. 'Come on, show a leg! You look like a bunch of drunken sailors, so dead to the world, at this time in the morning! Where do you think you are? At the top of the mast or down in the depths?' Encouraged by a few grunts, Christian changed his metaphor, 'Three fat beasts tethered in your stalls, that's what you are! Come on! I'll slip your chains for you, then out you go to graze! It's a wonder the devil hasn't got you. He's the lion that preys on all this country round the hill!'

One would have thought that any self-respecting person would have been roused by Christian's good-natured taunts, but self-respect had been sold for indolence and they could not be goaded. At last one of them, named Simple, turned lethargically and said in a plaintive voice, 'But guv'nor, there ain't no lion, so what's all the shoutin' about? Can't yer let an honest worker 'ave a good day's rest?' Then Sloth, his companion, opened one eye and chipped in 'What's up with yer?' he said. 'Looks like yer got less to do than we 'ave, comin' in 'ere and pokin' us around. I'm not "baling out" of 'ere this side of noon, so you'd better mind your own business!'

Christian was baffled at the lack of response. Had they taken him for the farmer? 'What yer want us to do anyway?' growled Sloth, as if confirming the thought. 'Work? Not on your life! A mug's game that!' Then looking blearily at Christian's abdomen, he pronounced with some deliberation, 'Your stomach's full but so is mine! You've got a bed but so have I!' He thumped the bales to emphasise his point, and then continued confidently. 'You'll have an overdraft but I'm a whole quid in credit!' and he waved a solitary pound note in Christian's face. 'Why should I

slave and other people grow fat on my blood and sweat. I've retired before I've got tired. That's what you call sense! You can
work to death if you want, but life's one long tea-break for me.
I'm going to sleep when I like; eat when I like; and have the
women I like; and what's more, I'll decide tomorrow what I'm
doing the day after, but one thing is certain, no one's going to tell
me what to do today! Do you get that, Mister whatever-your-
name-is?'

Christian had never heard anything so ridiculous in all his life
but before he could answer, Sloth, who was worn out by his
unintended exertion, slumped back on the hay. All this time
Presumption had been listening with his eyes shut but now he sat
up and joined in the conversation. He was obviously more intellectual than the others for his English was cultured in tone and
he sported a tousled mop of hair that had not been cut for
months. 'I don't know who you are,' he began imperiously, giving
every evidence he was not even faintly interested in finding out,
'but you need to realise that all men of leisure have their grounds
for inaction; and all men of pleasure their reasons for indulgence.
We are not philanderers but philosophers, the discoverers and
demonstrators of reality, long veiled behind the curtains of convention. We have withdrawn from the futile charade you call
society, not merely as a protest but as a project. We have shaken
off life as it is, to be the men that we are. We do our own thing, at
anytime and anywhere, that's the fun of living. Money completely
bores us. All we want is to look on the beautiful. Of course, we
shall never be understood and yet our following grows. Needless
to say, all who are truly great abandon society and in their turn,
are abandoned by it. Our practice is to use what nature provides
to discover what nature has put within us.'

'You mean drugs?' said Christian bluntly.

'Don't be so crude,' remonstrated Presumption. 'You only reveal your own out-moded thinking. I am a disciple of the psychedelic.'

'The psyche-a-what?' exclaimed Christian.

'The psychedelic,' replied Presumption blandly. 'It has to do
with a mental state in which all the perceptions are so heightened
as to bring one into an aesthetic entrancement altogether out of
this world. Through this magnificent release, we can attain to a
fresh creative impetus in this otherwise sterile society. If man
would only live naturally, he would learn to live socially!' As he
finished his speech, he lolled back into position and his rat-tail
hair splayed down over his sunken eyes and sallow face, as much
as to say, 'The last word in wisdom has been spoken and I need

neither to hear or see anything else. Just let me sleep on.' Of the three, Presumption had the loudest snore and was undoubtedly the most obnoxious.

Christian stood for a moment, many ideas thronging his mind and jostling for a chance of expression; but whichever took the platform, it mattered little, for the congregation was oblivious to all. He had come uninvited and he left unsung. The indifference appalled him and he decided he would go forward without delay. No sooner had his foot struck the road than he heard the sound of an approaching aircraft. He turned towards the increasing roar of the engines and he saw to his astonishment that a helicopter came in low over the wall. It hovered for a few seconds, then landed neatly in one of the nearby fields. The moment it touched down, out stepped a tall, handsome young man, dressed in black, brief case in hand and carrying a colourful saffron robe over his arm. He was followed clumsily by the ugliest woman imaginable. At first they hardly noticed him. The young man straightened his jacket, adjusted his glasses and combed back his sleek black hair. With a surreptitious air, he furtively polished his shoes on the back of his trouser-legs, then looking up took stock of his surroundings and advanced to where Christian stood. 'Excuse my intruding on your company without introduction,' he said, 'but I would be interested to make your acquaintance, as we may well be in these parts with a common purpose. My name is Formality, and this is Hypocrisy, my charming young bride. Actually, I hardly like to tell you, but we are on our honeymoon, and hope to visit some of the holy places. We were only married last week, although, of course, our families have been closely associated for centuries. But now you must tell me your name for I fear I am talking too much.'

Christian surveyed the extraordinary pair, completely dumbfounded. His first thought was, 'Whatever does he see in that repulsive woman?' but he held his tongue. Her hair was dyed, her face greasy with heavy make-up and her shifting eyes powdered, above and below, a hideous turquoise. Formality no sooner spoke than she nodded her head with great affectation, a movement that caused her large ear-rings to dance and twinkle in the sunlight. Each of these ornaments comprised a grotesque crescent clutching a star, and as if to complete the incongruity, from her broad fat neck hung a golden crucifix. Christian tried to think where he had seen her before. Then it came to him. At one of the shows in the City of Destruction he recalled a giant female puppet dangling on a string.

'I wonder,' began Formality again, 'if you could kindly direct us to a hotel in this vicinity, equipped with an aeroport. I would much sooner park our plane on private premises than leave it in the fields. One never knows what acts of sabotage the native population will do these days. Tell me, is the Martha Hospiz at Bethany as good as it's advertised? I was told it had an excellent tariff?' 'I doubt very much whether you'll find parking space for your helicopter there,' replied Christian, 'but my next stop is The House of the Virgins.' 'That sounds exciting,' said Formality with pedantic restraint. 'Nothing to do with Mary's birth place I suppose?' Christian began to view Formality, for all his courtesy, with growing distaste. He was something of an enigma, and the answer, Christian felt, would almost certainly be unpleasant. A cold wind began to blow from beyond the wall and Formality took his saffron robe and wrapped it round his shoulders. It gave him a distinctly Buddhist appearance, yet there beneath his clean shaven chin couched a big starched clerical collar. Christian looked more intently. No, he was not mistaken. Hanging from his waistcoat buttons were some small Hindu bells, whilst from his right hand drooped a rosary he was itching to twitch. Formality, growing sensitive to Christian's scrutiny, broke the silence and ventured, 'You might well wonder who I am, though you must have guessed. I am a priest.' 'But of what faith?' asked Christian. 'I am a priest of all religions,' he answered suavely, 'in fact I have an inter-credal and international ordination, that makes me equally acceptable in a Tibetan monastery, a Mohammedan mosque, a Christian Cathedral, or even a Communist Party Committee. You may not have appreciated it before, but there is not a faith in the world that can afford to do without the services of such a person as myself. I prevent philosophy and religion from becoming vulgarised. I preserve the interests of true analysis, and the proper application of ethical principles, by supporting the few who know what is best for the many. My task is to interpret and communicate "the truth" to the rank and file in that particular measure suited to the needs of the moment.' 'But whoever finances you?' Christian cut in, 'It's not everyone who can spend their honeymoon flitting about in a helicopter.' 'I'm financed out of remunerations for services rendered to sundry religious and political organisations. If you want the name of my sponsoring body, it is W.O.L.F., that is to say, "The World Organisation for Liaison between Faiths." No doubt you already realise that all religion and much of politics has to do with one basic ideal. They are all out to bring to fruition man's highest aspirations. They all want a better world. They all want to create one great brotherhood of nations and give mankind a society of peace and plenty.'

'Tell me,' said Christian, smelling an heretical rat, 'Where do you come from?' 'Oh, come from?' laughed Formality a little awkwardly. 'Both Hypocrisy and I come from that well-known city, Vain Glory. Everything that's said and done there is broadcast daily to the world in all languages. You must have heard of it. We grew up there, and now we are married, we are making a pilgrimage to Mount Zion to enhance our reputation, or perhaps I should say, to make us more acceptable amongst the varied religious communities we seek to serve across the world. On our engagement trip last year, we dropped in at Mecca but this year we thought we simply must get a glimpse of The New Jerusalem. How about yourself? Have you seen many of the holy places yet? I guess you've had a look at Mount Calvary just over there?'

The spirit of the question was so alien to his recent experience that it burned like blasphemy in Christian's soul. For a long time he stood silent and unable to speak. Then looking Formality between the eyes he said, 'How is it you didn't come to this place via the gate at the beginning of the road? As a priest, if that's what you are, you should know what the Word of God declares, "that whosoever cometh not in by the door but climbeth up some other way, the same is a thief and a robber."' Formality remained unruffled and replied politely, 'Christian, if that is your name, please don't view us uncharitably. After all, you cannot compare the present day with New Testament times. The many facilities and the increased knowledge we enjoy make it quite unnecessary for us to use the earlier circuitous and traditional routing. With our helicopter we are able to bypass all such out-moded obstacles as gates. With your own eyes, you have seen how we landed safely; and aren't we as far ahead on the journey as you yourself? It would be contrary to my nature to over-emphasise the fact, but it's fair to remind you that we've arrived where we are with a lot less trouble, too!'

'But surely,' remonstrated Christian, 'the Authority to whom we are all accountable will condemn your audacious entry as an illegal infiltration across His frontiers?'

'I don't wish to be rude, Christian, but your ignorance on these matters is really extraordinary. You view our incursion as something exceptional but in actual fact, it is *your* approach and *your* attitude which are exceptional. *Our* action is the rule. Whilst helicopters have only recently been introduced in our profession, giving us an unprecedented ideological manoeuvrability, yet there have been recognised routes traversing the boundaries of truth as long as man has been on the earth. We are not establishing a precedent, rather we are availing ourselves of it. Custom, once established, is ultimately legalised by authority. Surely, Christian, you do not view yourself superior to us, merely because you came in by the gate? Be reasonable. When all has been said and done, what mystical quality is there in a gate, provided one gets to one's destination along the same road? But as far as that is concerned, I personally believe there are many roads leading to the Celestial City. It is such a pity that sincere and zealous persons like yourself are always so utterly naïve and self-assured.'

At this Christian did not spare them. 'I take my pilgrimage on the authority of my Master,' he cried. 'You imagine you can do what you like, that you can come and go as you please, but you are greatly mistaken. You are nothing but trespassers. Do you think there is a tourist trade in the things of God? I tell you straightly, you've come in here without God's permission and you will be extradited without His mercy.' 'If it is a question of legal entry,' retorted Formality, struggling to retain his dignity, 'I have little doubt we are as capable as you, of meeting the requirements of the Lord of this place. At least we have earned, by our unceasing service, the position we occupy and the regalia we wear; but it looks very much to me as if you are no more than a beggar, and the coat on your back but an evidence of your neighbour's charity.'

Christian was not slow to reply. 'You may pride yourself in who you are and what you've done but God is no respecter of persons,' he said, 'and if you failed to cross the frontier at the prescribed point of entry, namely the gate, then nothing will preclude you from prosecution. And as for my coat, you are right. It was given me by the Lord of this place to cover my shame. I count this His kindness to me, for I had nothing before but my rags; and when I reach the gate of the City, He has said that by this coat He will acknowledge me. And what is more, His mark is on my forehead, the brandmark of my Lord, which I received when he loosed me from my burden. And in addition to these credentials, I have also my briefing for the road. I personally doubt very much whether you have any of these things. Without them, may I say, you will find no admittance to the City of God.'

A silence ensued and Christian noticed that Formality and Hypocrisy had clasped hands, and with evident affection were seeking strength in each other under the withering indictment. Christian left them standing in their strange honeymoon attire, a burlesque of fancy dress in the open countryside. 'Strange,' he thought, 'how they landed in The Aceldama Field.'*

These unexpected encounters gave to Christian a new sense of

* Acts 1 : 15–20.

urgency and he decided to go forward with all speed. In spite of the forthright conversation, Formality and Hypocrisy could be seen following at some distance, strolling along the road in the same general direction. No doubt they intended walking over to The House of the Virgins and booking in there for the night. They were careful, however, to keep well back from the pilgrim ahead of them, and at no time did they make contact again.

Not far from where the helicopter had landed there was an outcrop of rock that rose to a fair height. At the foot of this knoll, which was called Difficulty, the road divided into three. One path went straight over the hill, whilst the others skirted each side. Christian felt intuitively that the hardest road was more likely to be the right one and as it went straight forward, he chose it and began to mount the rock, but the honeymoon couple, following behind, had no such intention. Underestimating the terrain, they decided to go, one on this side and one on the other, and see who would be first to reach the farther side of the hill. From his point of vantage Christian could trace their progress below. Formality took the road marked Danger and after a while entered a dark and foreboding wood. An hour at least must have passed but he did not emerge from the trees, nor indeed has he to this day. Hypocrisy, his bride, took the other road, marked Destruction, only to be faced with a maze of boulders and ravines, where she fell headlong down a crevasse and was seen no more. Next day *The Vain-Glory Rumour* carried the news-headlines, 'Helicopter honeymooners missing in Holyland—City congregations mourn loss of progressive young priest.' It was said that the memorial service held in the great auditorium of the Unifaith Centre was attended by people drawn from all sections of the religious community. W.O.L.F.'s official organ, *'Sheep's Clothing'*, pointed out that whilst all mourned the loss of so promising a young leader in the movement, yet the occasion showed the growing tolerance amongst men of faith, the world over, and encouraged Christendom to work together with all men of goodwill for God's Kingdom on earth.

The higher Christian climbed, the rougher the track became; so when he found a shelter of cedarwood halfway up, he was delighted. Inside was a hearth where a fire could be lit in inclement weather, and in one corner rose a spring of crystal clear water, which bubbled up ceaselessly for the refreshment of any crossing the hill. On the fascia above the entrance was a small plaque on which were inscribed the words, 'Erected by the Lord of the Hill for the benefit of pilgrims'. Christian read the words with satisfaction, refreshed himself at the fountain and sat down

on one of the wooden benches to read his briefing. He also took a
more detailed look at his fine new clothes, received only that
morning from the hand of God. As he read, his fatigue began to
overcome him until he fell asleep. He had been up all night and
it was little wonder that he slept so soundly. Several hours slipped
by and as his hands relaxed, his precious briefing fell to the floor
and rolled away under the bench. Suddenly a voice rang in his
ears, whether in a dream or nor, he could not say. 'Go to the ant,
thou sluggard; consider her ways and be wise.' It pierced his conscience like a sword. Quickly he started up, dismayed at the
darkening sky. He could wait for nothing. As fast as his legs
could carry him, he ran to the top of the hill.

No sooner had he reached the highest point than he met a
young fellow and his girl friend, fleeing for their lives. There was
not an ounce of colour in their faces and Christian was somewhat
startled at the panic they exhibited. They were Timorous and
Miss-Trust. 'Turn back! Turn back!' they shouted. 'Two lions
have escaped from the circus down below. We saw them with our
own eyes. It's certain death if you go on.' Christian had heard of
this circus and had wondered how such entertainment was permitted this side of the wall, but such reflections were due to his
inexperience. Later on he was to find that very much contrary to
the Lord of the place was conducted in His Name; but it was
perplexing to him to find that lions should be allowed to escape
and molest those on the road to the Celestial City. He had heard
also of some of the acts put on under the big-top, as the tent was
called. The performance drew great crowds, as there were many
through all that area who had settled down rather than face the
rigours of pilgrimage. It was only right, they contended, that the
pilgrim should have his amusement and Jesus too. There were
tight-rope walkers, who could split hairs of doctrine and balance
on them for prolonged periods. There were people who were
specialists in fondling serpents and drinking deadly things. 'We
are the real believers,' they'd say. Some could eat fire and ex-
pectorate it. This was a fearful sight. Whilst other erstwhile pilgrims involved on the production side would, like the performers,
quote their biblical 'authority' for what they did. There were
noisy sessions of music and dancing, the pieces being taken from a
wide range of composers. You could have Beat and Beethoven,
with voices histrionic, and instruments electronic, and even some
'Christian' rock'n roll, which was no more than a riot. 'But all
things are ours,' they'd say, 'so why can't we use them? Must
Satan always have the best?' Many of the young pilgrims revelled
in these shows and constantly returned for more, counting them

better than secular revues in their former cities. 'Such lovely words,' some of the more 'spiritual' would simper but what they liked was the rhythm, and no one asked, 'How shall we sing the Lord's song in a strange land?' All manner of wild beasts were also paraded in this circus. Meek as lambs they were, and doing always as their masters willed, under the superb ring-management of the fund-raisers. At some matinée sessions, they had what certain called 'prophecy' and others clairvoyance. There were séances too, and even spiritist sketches performed in the Name of Christ. Sometimes under the big-top the crowd would become quite hysterical with people hooting and crying, clapping their hands and rolling in the aisles and some would shout, 'Jesus' and 'Hallelujah' at the top of their voices, like so many fans at a football match. At other times sick people would come from miles around because they thought some artist had the magic touch but they were fooled time without number. Then there were the preacher-clowns, who acted the goat, played to the gallery and so tickled the fancy of the audience that most forgot they had ever been pilgrims at all. This circus, with all its counterfeits of heavenly wisdom and divine power, was a standing joke in the City of Destruction, and such hollow performances, coupled with the fact that very often white and coloured people were not permitted to attend together or use the same amenities, hindered not a few from treading the appointed way to the Celestial City.

As for the lions Christian hardly knew what to think about them, but come what may, he was determined to advance. Looking at Timorous and his girl friend, he said, 'If I go back from where I came, I shall be destroyed, but if I go forward, even death can't rob me of my goal. Go back if you will but I must go on!' These were bold words and in order to strengthen his will to continue, he put his hand into his breast pocket to feel for his briefing. To his horror, it was not there. The loss of it made him feel physically weak. Where could it be? There was only one thing for it, he must go back and find it. Wearily he retraced his steps in the growing darkness, looking this way and that all along the trail. He could have wept, as time and again he stooped, only to find he had been deceived by a fragment of litter strewn by the way. So he came at last to the cedarwood refuge, and it was only when he looked under the bench where he had slept so long that he found it. Oh the downright sinfulness of it all! To let go those sacred words which gave him all his assurance now, and guaranteed his acceptance later, at the gate of the City. He thought of how he had scolded the beatniks and felt disgusted that he himself had slept in the daytime. How easy to fail on the very issue one preaches to others. In deep contrition he bowed before God, then with tears in his eyes but thankful at heart, he turned again to the road.

By the time he topped the hill the second time, it was nightfall. He remembered with what alarm Timorous and Miss-Trust had brushed past him. Now through his own default he must face those beasts in the darkness. As he turned a bend in the road he glimpsed the friendly lights of The House of the Virgins. 'Little wonder,' he thought, 'they call their hostelry "House Beautiful",' for the windows shone like stars to point the way Home.

At the foot of the hill, the path narrowed a short distance from the house; and just as he felt he had reached his destination, he suddenly saw the lions. Their appearance was so ferocious, crouching there in the half light, that the sight of them made his blood run cold. He would have fled in a moment but the porter whose name was Watchful shouted from the lodge 'Is your faith so small? Don't run away! We caught them half an hour ago. The lions are chained. Keep in the middle of the road and you'll be all right!'

In a few moments Christian was through to the gate of House Beautiful. 'May I put up here for the night?' he hopefully asked the porter. 'I've little doubt you can,' he replied, 'for this house was built by the Lord of the hill for the relief and security of pilgrims.' Once he had ascertained Christian's identity and the reason for his late arrival, he said, 'I will call one of the virgins of this place, who will, if she approves of your profession, bring you in to the rest of the family.' So Watchful put a call through to the house and in a little while a young lady appeared whose name was Discretion. As she came in view Christian was immediately held by her eyes. He thought instinctively of Christiana and how he had first loved her, but somehow in the young girl before him there was a beauty he had never seen before. Here was a woman so pure that he was drawn, not to her face or form, but to the God who made her so. Mature though he was, he felt unnerved in her presence and could only wait for her reassuring word.

# CHAPTER NINE

# THE VOICE OF THE VIRGINS

'AND why did you ring for me, Watchful?' asked Discretion.

'Because it's already very late and I had this man arrive, asking for overnight accommodation. He says he's en route for Mount Zion, but before admitting him, I felt you should see him, so that the order of the Household might be preserved. I did not think you would have me act on my own initiative.'

Discretion now turned to Christian, and with eyes that searched his own, she enquired about his journey, where it began, and how he had joined the road. Unreservedly, he told her. She listened carefully to his every word, after which she asked him his name. 'It is Christian,' he replied with the gladness of a true confession; then pausing briefly, he ventured his request. 'And may I spend the night beneath this roof? I ask this favour, not merely for my own convenience, but because I heard House Beautiful was specially designed to accommodate God's pilgrims.' 'Of course you may,' smiled Discretion, and her eyes grew moist as she thought of his resolve. 'I'm so glad you have come,' she said. 'Wait a minute and I'll call the other members of the family. They'll be so pleased to think you are safely through.'

Being light of foot, she ran swiftly down the corridor and Christian could hear her voice, like a song, echoing through the vast interior. In a little while, her three sisters, Prudence, Piety and Charity came into the hall. For Christian it was an indefinable experience. Men speak of natural charm, yet here was radiance, born solely from a quality of life within. While supper was preparing, they sat together, sipping water, clear as crystal, and speaking on such themes as might prepare them for their feasting with their Lord.

It was Piety who spoke first, for she longed to know how Christian left his home to become a pilgrim. 'I took leave of my native land,' he began, 'chiefly because I could not stay. To put it simply, I was driven out! Day after day, the voices of impending doom resounded in my ears, but God was good to me. No sooner had I fled than I met a man called Evangelist, who directed me to the little white gate. This brought me to the frontier, and once my entry had been granted, it was not so far to The House of The Interpreter.'

'And what, may I ask, did you see there?' continued Piety in genuine interest.

'Things I shall never forget,' said Christian with reverence. 'Three lessons, more particularly, stand out in my mind. First, that in spite of all Satan's efforts to quench the Spirit's work, Christ still supplies His grace and maintains His witness in the pilgrim's heart. Secondly, that a man who stubbornly refuses God's truth may ultimately find himself without hope of God's mercy. And thirdly, that a day is coming when Christ will descend with the armies of heaven to judge the nations.'

'But surely there were other important things to see?'

'Oh yes, wonders so numerous you would need eternity to view them, but one thing I *should* mention. I saw a man who, braving all opposition—and mark you, it was cruel—entered at last on Eternal Glory. His passionate zeal affected me profoundly. In fact I could have stayed a whole year in that place, it was all so fascinating; but the road to the City kept calling me on.'

'And what happened after that?' asked Piety.

'Well, it is hard to explain where I next came, but I clambered to the top of a hill and it was dark in the valley, though all before me was the sunset glow. It was then I saw it, a tattered scarecrow stuck in the fields, and would have dismissed it, an outworn symbol of derision and fear; but the wind was blowing and the rags were flapping, and I could see its bare wooden spars like the bones of a body. Then the wind blew fiercely, like a gale from God and the thing I despised was suddenly naked, one lonely cross in the pale night sky. Yet as I watched there mounted higher and higher a burning radiance that turned it to gold, till that which was foolishness a moment before became the emblem of the glory of God. Then all at once His love was in me and around me and that same moment I knew that Jesus Christ had died for me. With my whole being I embraced Him, and all I could do was weep and pray. So it was I trusted Him and my burden of guilt fell from my shoulders. The darkness swallowed it and I saw it no more. I awoke to a new day with the dew sparkling in the sunshine. My rags were gone and I stood in the finery you now see. This mark on my forehead tells the Name of my Master, and this brief that I hold is my guide for the road.'

At this Piety's face lit up and she said, 'You know now what He means. "My grace is sufficient *for thee*." Just one more question; tell me, whom did you meet today?'

'An odd collection of people to be sure,' replied Christian. 'No sooner had I started out than I met three ne'er-do-wells, lounging in a farmyard just off The King's Highway. After some words with them, I went on and met a honeymoon couple. An extraordinary pair, I must say! Believe it or not, they flew in across the wall, complete with helicopter! Formality and Hypocrisy, their names were, but sad to relate they came to a tragic end before the afternoon was out. I witnessed it with my own eyes. The last encounter of the day, I suppose, proved the worst. Meeting those lions in the dark just about finished me altogether. If it hadn't been for your porter I would have turned and fled. Still, the lions were chained and here I am, safe and sound, kept all the way by the power of God. How can I thank you enough, for receiving me as your guest tonight?'

Once Piety had received these answers to her questions, Prudence took up the conversation. Christian soon discerned that she enquired of his faith from a different angle. Whereas Piety was interested in the things that befell him, and people he met, Prudence asked more about his thoughts and motives.

'Don't you sometimes think about your old home,' she commenced very searchingly, 'You must be homesick sometimes for all your loved ones, and the things, too, which you left behind.'

'Yes,' replied Christian truthfully, 'but I reproach myself for harbouring such unstable emotions. There is little doubt if I had been thinking of the country I left, I might have had opportunity to return, but now my desire is for a better one; one that is heavenly.' But Prudence would probe him further.

'Without being unduly personal, Christian, don't you think that you still carry with you something that smacks of The City of Destruction?'

'If you mean my own self-centred desires, why yes; but the difference is, that whereas before I cherished and inflamed them, now I grieve that they are there at all. My own choice would be to have done with them completely but I've discovered that when I would do my best, my worst is most rampant within me.' 'Well,' said Prudence, 'if that's the case, do you mean there are no occasions when your lower nature is subdued?' 'Oh yes, there are moments of real triumph, but to my mind they are far too few.' 'When you *do* triumph, what do you feel are the factors that make for victory?' 'I would say that God's deliverance from my lustful urges is most real to me, when I relive my experience at the Cross; or for that matter, when I examine the quality of my God-given coat. Then also, when I ponder my briefing, or think on the bright prospect of my journey's end.' 'Your desire to reach the Celestial City is certainly a burning passion with you but why should this be, since you were reared in the City of Destruction with all its amenities?'

Christian answered with spontaneous abandon. 'Why,' he said, 'I hope to see there the living Christ, who died for me. I expect to be completely freed from all that hampers faith down here; to be within those walls where death has lost its sting; to mingle in that heavenly company, where angel throngs cry, "Holy, holy, holy!" at the Throne.' Prudence was overjoyed to hear his testimony and was content to let her sister Charity converse a while. Charity's emphasis proved different again. She wanted more particularly to know about his family life and the spiritual condition of his loved ones ere he left.

'Are you married?' she began, 'and if so, have you any children?' 'Oh yes,' said Christian. 'I have a wife and four very active youngsters.' 'But how is it they are not with you?' Charity enquired. Tears came to Christian's eyes. He struggled hard to maintain composure, then quietly said, 'I wanted them to come so much, but it was useless. They had no time for me and utterly opposed all thought of pilgrimage.'

'Surely, though, you could have persuaded them if you had been more earnest. Did you not tell them of their danger?'

'Why, yes, of course, but to them the whole thing was a kind of hoax. They would never listen to what I had to say.'

'But did you not pray for them, that God might save them through your witness?'

'Pray?' said Christian. 'I can hardly tell you how much I prayed. I wept before God and in their presence but they remained unmoved.'

'Did they ever tell you their reasons?'

'I guess so, in a way. The trouble with my wife was that she just couldn't bear to leave our home and all the knick-knacks we'd gathered through the years. She liked the city too, with its shops and amusements so close at hand, and of course, being a sociable person, she was deeply attached to her friends. As for the children, well you know what young people are! If it's not one craze it's another. They're already in their teens, and at night they were for ever wanting out to the cafés and their various haunts down town. I warned them, of course, about clandestine sex and the menace of drugs but I'd as well talk to a lamp-post. The more I applied my sensitive conscience to their doings, the more they resented me. Perhaps it was my fault, for in their earlier years I wasn't the father I should have been and the wild oats I sowed had their own sad results.'

'I know how you feel,' consoled Charity, 'but you are not alone in this. Why did Cain hate his brother? Wasn't it because his own works were evil and his brother's righteous? What you were is one

thing. What your children are is another. You had your responsibility and I believe you discharged it but they also have theirs.
The fact that your children spurned your pleading so wilfully
shows they themselves are intent to do evil.'

At this stage in the conversation supper was served and they all
drew their chairs to the table. The conversation had become
quite an interrogation but Christian was not averse to their penetrating questions, for he felt so at ease in their company. After the
rigours and terrors of the way, it was sheer joy to talk with people
of like mind about the things of his Lord. On the table before
them was the bread of heaven and the wine of the kingdom, and
ere they partook of the meal, they gave thanks to God for His
everlasting mercy. The four sisters talked much of the Lord of the
Hill, His mighty achievements and inscrutable purposes. They
told Christian how single-handed He had crushed the one who
held the power of death. 'It cost Him much blood,' they said, 'and
His glory was this, that for love of His own He went to the battle.
Indeed,' they said, 'such a Lover of pilgrims has never been
known in east or west. He would not dwell alone in Zion but
deigned to die, that from the scum of earth, the beggars of our
race might yet become His princes.'

Christian sat spellbound, his eyes alight with awe and wonder
and his heart's devotion kindled to a flame. But the night drew
on and the hour was late, so when they had worshipped a while,
the sisters retired to rest. As for their guest, they brought him to a
large upper room, named Peace, whose windows opened towards
the sun-rising. There he slept till break of day. 'How blue the
sky!' he exclaimed. 'How sweet the lark!' And so with joy he
greeted the dawn.

> *Where am I now? Is this the love and care*
> *Of Jesus, for the men who pilgrims are?*
> *Thus to provide! That I should be forgiven*
> *And have this place of rest next door to heaven?*

On the morrow the virgins insisted that Christian spend time
with them, viewing some of the unique treasures of the family.
They took him first to the study, where they showed to him the
pedigree of the Lord of the Hill. There Christian learned, first
hand, how He was the Son of the Father and the Ancient of Days
and came to the world with that eternal generation. Then he
scanned the register of those recruited to His service over the centuries and who, now, were asleep in Jesus until the resurrection
day. There were names also of men and women who in every age

had been true to their God; who through faith conquered king-doms, enforced justice, received promises, stopped the mouths of lions, quenched raging fire, escaped the edge of the sword, won strength out of weakness, became mighty in war, put foreign armies to flight, and, enduring all manner of martyrdom, had been steadfast to the end.

Amongst the many other records filed in that place, Christian found evidence of what he had already proved by experience, namely that even those who had insulted God's Person had known His acceptance through the Blood of Christ, once they had bowed to repent and believe.

The day following they took him to the armoury, where the divinely conceived equipment of the pilgrim was exhibited in very great detail. It was with no little satisfaction that Christian looked on The Sword of the Spirit, the Shield of Faith, the Hel-met of Salvation, The Breastplate of Righteousness, All-prayer and the Gospel-footgear that would never wear out. The armoury occupied an immense area beneath the house and Christian rightly concluded that this arsenal was adequate to arm and equip every soldier and pilgrim that would yet pass on their way to the Celestial City. In this area of the building, the Virgins also showed him some of the weapons of war used by God's servants in days gone by. There was Moses' rod; Jael's hammer and nail; and the pitchers, trumpets and lamps used by Gideon to rout the Midianites. They also showed him Shamgar's ox goad with which he slew six hundred men and the jaw-bone of an ass which Samson used when slaughtering the Philistines. Finally they brought him to the sling and stone which felled Goliath and Christian learned that even a pebble, used in faith, can achieve great things for God. Adjacent to these exhibits culled from antiquity was a collection of drawings and articles depicting the present day means whereby the devil is overthrown to the ends of the earth. They had chiefly to do with communications developed in the twentieth century and used in the spread of the Gospel. There were such things as tape-recorders, radio and T.V. installations, fountain pens, Biros, and typewriters; cameras, films and their projectors, gramophones and telephones, P.A. systems, office equipment, printing presses, newsprint, aeroplanes, automobiles, motor launches and even satellites! Finally he was given a look into the future and shown the ultimate in weaponry, that fiery breath by which the Lord would kill the 'man of sin'.

On the third day, Christian was escorted to the roof-top where, in the clearness of the morning, the virgins pointed to the Delect-able Mountains. This mighty range, lifting peak on peak into the cloudless sky, gave rise to deep longings in Christian's heart, to press on to the heavenly hills. Between House Beautiful and the distant ranges lay a vast stretch of country, unspeakably beautiful. Woodlands and well watered pasture lands reached out to the distance in soft undulating folds. 'And what territory is this,' enquired Christian. 'It is Immanuel's land,' they said, 'and once you reach the Delectable Mountains the Shepherds who live there will, when the weather's fine, show you the shining gates of that City to which you go.'

Before the Virgins bade their pilgrim-guest farewell, they took him to the armoury where, piece by piece, the equipment for the way was grafted to his mind and heart, in prayer. So they led him to the gate. 'Has any pilgrim passed today?' asked Christian of the porter. 'Yes there has,' he said, 'a man called Faithful.' 'I know him!' said Christian exultantly. 'I shall have company on the road. Is he far ahead of me?' 'No, just at the foot of the hill. He can't be more.' So Christian hurried, being anxious to proceed, but in so doing he slipped a little, and the virgins warned him that the Valley of Humiliation still lay between House Beautiful and Immanuel's Land. Their last service to Christian was to put in his pocket a packed lunch, filled with good things from the Master's table, together with a bottle of wine marked 'Salvation Vintage'.

For a moment he looked again at those incomparable women. They were a mystery. Each so fair, yet leaving flesh unmoved. Then came a phrase of his Book to enlighten him. 'Why, this is "the beauty of holiness",' he cried, 'and to think I had never seen it until now!'

# CHAPTER TEN

# MOTEL MAGNIFICENT

THE Valley of Humiliation descending from House Beautiful, was a sinister defile which dropped steeply into a dark ravine, where the light of the sun never shone. The waters that gathered there gurgled away beneath moss-covered stones to form an underground stream, which eventually emerged where an extension of The Broad Freeway cut through the mountains. The valley, by reason of its situation, acted as a kind of funnel for the acrid fumes of the many vehicles using the highway and as Christian went on, the air-pollution became so marked that he was obliged to cover his nose with his handkerchief. For one reason or another, he fondly imagined he had seen the last of these roads, but this notion was due, once again, to his inexperience. If he had thought for a moment, he would have realised how, from time to time, the way that leads above must, of necessity, cut across the way that leads below. With dogged steps he struggled on, clinging to the tortuous mountain track, fearing lest he should lose his foothold and plunge into the chasm below; but after some distance the cliffs broke away, allowing the path to go forward to a footbridge spanning the motorway. As Christian caught sight of the fleeting cars, he felt his old fascination for the world's mad rush rise up within him. Somehow the hurly-burly of his native city still caught at his heart, and it was only with the greatest of effort he could hold his eyes to the trail ahead. 'How can I yield to these worldly trends,' he religiously asked himself, 'after the holy fellowship of recent days. I must cultivate with more earnestness those virtues my friends exhibited, namely Discretion and Prudence, Piety and Love to God.' No sooner had he repudiated the call of The Freeway than he saw at the approaches of the footbridge a neon sign, in which an illuminated arrow jerked jauntily to and fro. 'To the Pilgrim's Rest', it flashed. He looked in the direction indicated and there, close to a massive motel that arched all sixteen lanes of The Freeway, was a welcome café. Outside was a board bearing the hackneyed announcement, 'Teas, Light Refreshments and Minerals'. Being thirsty, Christian walked towards the open doorway, glad of a break after the stiff descent of the valley. He slipped inside and quickly ordered a cup of tea. 'Just a few minutes,' he assured himself, 'and I'll be right on my way.' Whilst he waited, he picked up the menu. It was not without interest. There was fish served every Friday, and porkless meals on request. Vegetarian tastes were especially catered for. As for the beverages, there was dandelion tea, caffineless coffee, non-intoxicating liquors and even non-alcoholic wines. Against this item stood an asterisk, referring patrons to an advertisement at the foot of the card. 'Try "Timnath", the unfermented wine, especially suitable for communion services'. For those who wished for bigger meals, but better waistlines, there was starchless bread, unleavened rolls and cakes without calories. You could even buy cigarettes without nicotine, sweets without sugar, and pills without dope. In fact it was a café ideal for any pilgrim of tender conscience, where one might indulge without religious distaste.

Christian's tea was brought to him and it was really excellent. He would have said there was rum in it, had it not come straight from the pot! As he sat with his right elbow digging the table and his cup poised in hand, he found time to think. The days up at House Beautiful had been just great. There was no doubt about it. Yet life there, he felt, was a trifle unreal, a kind of back-water out of touch with the times; a bit strait-laced, too, for the average man. Not that he wanted to be critical of the hallowed atmosphere in that household of faith, but he felt, when all was said and done, that the sisters were somewhat extreme—'puritanical', that was the word, although he wasn't quite sure what it meant. He was anxious to be what people called 'a balanced pilgrim'. He had no time for the circus in the shadow of Hill Difficulty, but then to be monastic was no good either. One must be in touch with the world, if one were to win men from its ranks. He poured himself another cup of tea and his reflections deepened. In fact, he was finding much gratification in grappling with these spiritual problems, unaided. No, it would never do to go on willy-nilly with his pilgrimage. He would become a real thinker, analysing each step as he took it. He would cultivate a *conscious* commitment and seek to practise, in due proportion, both 'detachment' and 'involvement' in his daily walk. When the time came, he might even record his thoughts and write a book, say, on 'Pilgrim Psychology'. Not that he had any special qualifications, but then his personal insight might compensate for that. Analysis of the spiritual life would undoubtedly make him stronger ('superior' was the word he should have used), and enable him to help others along the way. He would refuse to be one of those self-centred pilgrims who thought only of his own salvation!

When at last he rose to go, he saw a woman, who had been sitting in a corner of the café, rise at the same time, and pass through the swing doors into a lounge-bar, which unbeknown to Christian linked 'The Pilgrim's Rest' with the motel restaurant over the motorway. At the sight of her, Christian stood stock still. The turn of the head, the style of her hair, the unbuttoned coat, the very pose—he could swear it was she. In a moment he was after her, through the swing doors, past a waitress laying tables, clear athwart a clump of musicians choosing their scores, and out to the corridor beyond. They all turned and gazed in amazement after the wild figure in pilgrim's habit, bolting through the lounge; but Christian could hardly think what he was doing or where he was going any more. On and on he blundered, down the long avenue of closed doors, with the endless carpet-runner racing beneath his feet. Abruptly he rounded a corner, just in time to see her entering a room. He gripped the handle, but the door clicked fast. 'Christiana!' he whispered, 'let me come in!' He waited anxiously, lest someone appear and question his action. 'Christiana!' he whispered yet again, but louder this time, and more vehemently. 'Do you hear me? It's Chris! Let me come in!' 'Do you really want me?' the familiar voice came back. 'There's a price to pay, you know.' 'Stop talking like that, Christiana, and open the door! I love you still! Do you hear me? Don't try to be different, just let me in! Quickly, or they'll hear me and wonder what I'm doing. Once we're together again, everything will be all right!'

Slowly the door swung open. Although still early in the afternoon, the room was in semi-darkness. He looked across to the Venetian blinds. They were tightly shut and the curtains partly drawn. Stepping stealthily inside, he closed the door behind him, then instinctively turned the key. She lay motionless on the bed with her face to the wall. He was breathless and trembling, and for a moment hardly knew what to do, as if he were a teenager again and alone with her for the first time. His eyes strained in the half-light to define her. Seconds slipped by, but neither of them moved. He could see her clearly now. Her left ear showed a little through her hair. Her shoes lay empty on the floor; her stockinged feet curled easily on the quilt. Something like an agony shot through him. He had missed her so much; more than he knew. For one passing moment he thought of the children, but then they were gone. How desperately he wanted her. Just to be close again; to hold her; to handle her; to have her completely; to know that release, that bliss of union, that nearest thing to heaven prior to his weeping at the cross. Yet how could this feeling be so like it? This oneness with her so like his oneness with Him? He found himself praying, even as he clasped her. 'Dear Lord, just this once, then I'll go on my pilgrimage. There's nothing wrong, is there, Lord? She's my wife. The fact that she's here must be your own overruling.' But the argument worried him and clogged his desire. Tighter and tighter he held her, almost beyond reason. 'Christiana!' he cried ... Then somehow his love was turned to lusting; and he knew it, too, whenever he shouted her name.

With a frightening slam, a gust of wind shut-to the window, thrusting the long metal handle through the Venetian blinds. For one split second a flash of sunshine lit up the room, then the blind buckled back and everything was plunged once again into shadow. In that brief instant he glimpsed her face and when he did so every pore in his body rose, frozen with horror. She was like her, yes, so like her, but he had never seen her before.

Suddenly a rasping male voice filled the room. It came from the T.V. 'Stay where you are, Christian, if that's what you call yourself! I've got you framed nicely on our closed-circuit two-way "tele"; a real scoop for my daily, *The City of Destruction Recorder*. Just imagine a photographic sequence of your activities, published with an appropriate write-up in tomorrow's papers. Your old cronies will enjoy that! They'll laugh their heads off! What do you think of my caption for the story. "Ex-citizen makes good on Holy Pilgrimage"?' A devilish guffaw followed; then the speaker chortled wickedly, 'that concludes our joke for the day!' Christian sat bolt upright, his blood rising. He couldn't decide whether others had fooled him, or if he'd just made a fool of himself. He didn't know whom to blame or with whom to be angry, the man, the woman, himself or the devil. On the dull grey screen, a grotesque figure was gradually focussing. As the image brightened, he saw what seemed to be a giant puppet miming back and forth. Its skin was a mass of slippery, slimy scales, like those of a fish. On its back flapped two bat-like wings. Its feet were the claws of a bear; and from its heaving abdomen, fire filled its leonine jaws, to be spewed out venomously wherever it turned.

'A bit of a monster, eh, Christian? A real live dragon if ever there was one! I'd take the novelty prize at a carnival anywhere! You know what they say? Poor old Mephistopheles! Just give his tail a tweak! I'm like God, you know, "dead and buried" these days, under the débris of reason. That's how Santa Claus and I keep company. We're all being debunked in the de-mythologising spree. But needless to say that was my own intention. I'm quite content for men to deride my image, or even deny my existence, so long as they serve me for ever. What do you think of my little Eve? Hardly in the same class as the original, you'll say, but then a man sees something of his wife in any woman. It wasn't hard to catch you, Pilgrim!'

'And who are you?' roared Christian in exasperation.

'Take it steady, Pilgrim, don't upset yourself. Since we've become more personally acquainted, I will tell you. I am Apollyon. For your information, my headquarters are situated in a subterranean bunker of great dimension beneath Fort Lust, although we operate, of course, at ground level and also in the supra-spatial spheres. In the immediate context, you will be interested to know that I'm the Chairman of The Pilgrim's Rest, and The Motel Magnificent Corporations, and also the Chief Controller of all the Fort Lust agencies combing the highways. Now I have been so courteous as to introduce myself, perhaps you would like to help me solve your problem. Let me put it to you this way. What would you say, Christian, should happen to you now that your plans for pilgrimage have fallen through?' Christian sat on the bed, his face almost purple with shame and anger. 'You can say what you like and print what you like but God knows, I never actually had intercourse with her!'

'Is that so?' said the voice sarcastically. 'For my present purpose that is quite irrelevant. *That you are compromised is quite enough.* The rest can come later. I think, Christian, it would be to your great advantage if you realised your true position. Seeing we are now conversing so happily, what about giving a little account of yourself. After all this *is* my motel.'

Christian braced himself like a wrestler rising from his corner. Maybe his character was tarnished but that was no reason to start serving the devil. He would dare to fight through. He was down, but not out by a long way. He'd resist to the end. As these resolves gained strength in his mind, there was a rustle of bed-clothes and before he could stop her, the strange woman had slipped her coat over her shoulders, snatched the key from the keyhole, nipped through the door and locked him in. 'Tricked again,' he thought. 'What wretched fighters!' Yet for all that, he was glad she had gone.

The suave tones of Apollyon's voice continued. 'Seeing you are my prisoner, Christian, I think you should relax a little. What's the good of battering your head against the brick wall of the situation. If you'll only accept it, we shall get on fine. You can view me in one of two ways, as a friend or fiend, serpent or angel. Angel, of course, is what I really am. It's only since that last affair, when I sought to expand my authority, that my name got blackened. Even so, a third of all heaven's forces stand with me yet. Now we have got to know each other, why not be friends and forget the fiend part of the story. Mind you, to those who are not my friends, I can be a fiend all right, and where is the fiend who is fouler than I? To withhold your friendship, Christian, would mean I would be obliged to harass you night and day till you submitted. After centuries of experience, we have a whole range of conscience-seering, mind-twisting techniques at our disposal. It would be a pity to put us, not to speak of yourself, to this trouble. In such cases, remember, there is a death to live before there is a death to die. But tell me now, where do you come from and where are you going?'

'You know already,' snapped Christian abruptly, 'so why do you ask me?'

'Because confession is good for the soul and out of your own mouth you will be condemned! Don't think I'm short of scripture. I make it up as I go along! One of my specialities!' he added cynically.

'And don't you think I'm afraid to answer you either,' flamed Christian. 'You'll get no chance to stab *me* in the back!'

'How very valiant, Mr. Pilgrim! A real credit to your Master, I must say! Come on now, let's have your reply.'

'All right then. You've asked for it and you'll get it! I come from that cesspool of iniquity, The City of Destruction and am going to that place of all glory, The City of God.'

'So you freely admit, then, you are one of my subjects. Why then, may I ask, did you abscond from my jurisdiction? This is nothing less than a capital offence; and were it not that I have hopes of putting you to work, your execution would be warranted right now.'

The pagan figure on the screen danced incessantly, lunging forward as if to attack every time Apollyon asked a question. Christian's eyes were drawn to it again and again, until he felt he was being hypnotised by its ridiculous, yet absorbing movements. Like some jitter-bugging devil-dancer, or prancing Chinese dragon, it was a medium of Satan to master the mind. The hurdy-gurdy of the background music dulled his senses. His mouth was filled with the taste of the tea. He must struggle with himself, as well as his accuser. Conscious of losing his grip, he found himself shouting as his voice seemed further and further away.

'I admit I was born in your country, but your policies exploited me and your regime oppressed me. I slaved to the bone, but what were your wages? Only death in the end! As I grew older, I perceived your whole despicable system and concluded, for good, I couldn't go on with you. Faced now with ruin, I decided for freedom. One day I fled and with Evangelist's help I got to the

gate and escaped through the wall.' Christian expected Apollyon
to react with a tirade of abuse but contrary to expectation he
continued his questioning with a studied 'forbearance'.

'What you say reflects, no doubt, your own feelings at the time.
Your decision, however, was made with a very limited understanding of the true state of affairs. Once we have acquainted you
with the full facts, you will realise just how mistaken you've been.
What you must realise is that no ruler can afford to lose his subjects. Our kingdom, thanks to the infinite opportunities for destruction our science affords, is not faced with a brain drain. Most
university types are, in any case, our loyal subjects but what we do
face is a "labour drain". Far too many of the rank and file desert
to the Other Side and this leakage must be stopped. You are just
one of the many we have caught, Christian, so don't think we
shall release you. Your present ideas will need to be wholly
erased, and our own thoroughly implanted, before we can do
that, so you can settle down to a good long spell in our company.'

On the screen, Christian glimpsed a hand with talon-tipped
fingers grasping a telephone. 'A-POL calling! A-POL calling!
Dragon Squad to Motel Magnificent. Dragon Squad to Motel
Magnificent! Over!' The strange words sounded ominous in his
ears.

'In a few minutes,' explained Apollyon, 'A-POL will have a
black maria draw in under this building. A-POL stands for The
Apollyon Police Auxiliary, one of the arms of my intelligence
services, and a long, strong arm it is, let me tell you! Few have
escaped their clutches. Once the vehicle arrives you'll be taken
back to The City of Destruction, not on your old status of course,
but as a defector awaiting trial. This is not because we need to try
you, or even give you a show of justice. It is for the education of
the people. As far as we are concerned, all that perpetuates the
Kingdom of Darkness is "light" to us. After your sentence, which I
will personally determine, you will be incarcerated in Fort Lust.
There you will be stimulated by professional agitators, until your
attitude towards us is adjusted. Later you will be allocated to a
rehabilitation centre, where you will have constant scope for
learning to distinguish between the wrong and the right. You will
then appreciate that the prohibitions and inhibitions to which
you succumbed beyond the wall strike a death blow at the very
pleasures you have the right to enjoy. You will see that your
defection is the kind of thing that weakens humanity in its
struggle to achieve real liberty and maturity under our leader-
ship. This, for you Christian, is a golden opportunity to expunge
from your thinking all the fables learned in such anachronistic

institutions as The House of The Interpreter. I hope you will be cooperative in your spiritual reform. If you make good progress, there is no reason why ultimately you should not enjoy all that our time-honoured society affords. As for the devil not keeping his word, you can forget all that stuff. If you'll co-operate reasonably, I can promise you nothing will be said or published about what's happened here today, although as far as we are concerned we don't care a hoot what women you sleep with—that's your private affair!'

The vicious cunning behind these words incensed Christian to such a degree that he could have put his boot clean through the T.V. screen. Feeling, however, that this could play into Apollyon's hands, he restrained himself and answered forthrightly, 'You might as well save your filthy breath, Apollyon. You are a liar from the beginning! I am totally committed to another, namely the King of all princes, so to side with you is quite out of the question.'

'That may be your outlook now,' he replied, 'but many pilgrims bearing a name as good, if not as bad, as yours have, after professing allegiance to your King, returned to us gladly. I could name a few and I think you would remember them. You'll only feel guilty if you still hanker after Him. Once back with us, your very desertion will be termed a virtue. Anyway you've already deserted Him, don't forget that! Would you like me to play back the film strip. Not necessary perhaps, in your case. We don't normally blackmail our friends, only our enemies!'

'Apollyon! I'm a man of one Master. The King of Kings is my King. The Lord of Lords is my Lord. My allegiance is to Him and to Him alone. I will not stoop to treachery. It would merit destruction.'

'You're a man of very fine sentiment, Christian,' carped Apollyon, 'but just remember the nature of your crime on our side of the wall. Everything you have, you owe to us in The City of Destruction. You were born and bred there, nursed in the bosom of our great society. But apparently it wasn't good enough for you. You left your homeland without passport or visa, you submitted no tax return; left your family a burden on the state and ever since your defection, have worked actively in the interests of our arch-enemy. It is nothing less than treason. One would wonder, sometimes, Christian, what kind of conscience people like you possess! You'll believe the very worst about the Satanic Kingdom, yet here am I, a top line official deigning to talk to you about your future and even offering you mercy, plus a rehabilitation course at government expense.'

'Yes, I was born and bred in your society,' said Christian, seizing on the words. 'You're right in that, so consequently my status with you was circumstantial and such service as I rendered was done in the folly and ignorance of my unregenerate mind. But now I've cut free from you, my new Master has received me and expunged from my record all complicity in your evil rebellion. He's set a period in which all who respond to His offer of pardon can obtain a reprieve. Knowing the fate of you rebels, can you blame me for making my getaway? In this short time of service with Jesus, my Lord, my peace and joy have known no bounds. His presence is real and His truth is freedom. I wouldn't forsake Him whatever you offer me, no, not for the weight of the world in gold!'

'I guess not, except for a drink at our Pilgrim's Rest and a girl friend in Motel Magnificent! You might as well quit talking, Christian!' said Apollyon with caustic sarcasm. 'No one's going to believe you now. Perhaps you've forgotten the fate of the traitors. But just you remember. We knife them and strangle them; shoot them and poison them, drown them and bomb them; crush them and gas them, we throw them from cliffs, under trains, into rivers. We tar them and feather them, blast them and maim them. Our techniques in the field of destruction and annihilation are now superb. Death can be swift or protracted, public or private, official or unofficial. Tell me, Christian, how many pilgrims has your King been able to deliver from the death-chambers and firing-squads of the twentieth century? Precious few! But we are for ever rescuing our people from *His* clutches whether it be by brute force or subtle intrigue.'

'You lie, Apollyon! The horrors are yours but death's keys are not! The Crucified has utterly annulled your power; and you know full well a physical escape is not a necessity for spiritual deliverance.'

The answer was right but he felt weak and compromised, and his words seemed useless. Then he remembered his girdle of truth. He had loosened it when lying on the bed, but he quickly tightened it now, and at once felt stronger in mind and body.

'Stand still, you worm, and stop sorting your clothes,' the voice roared. 'You're my prisoner! How dare you move!'

A sense of paralysis came over Christian; he stood rooted to the spot as if physically affected by the onslaught of his accuser; but then something happened.

'I believe God,' he shouted defiantly. 'He can and will deliver me and I trust Him to do it!'

This use of his faith as a shield from attack somewhat dismayed

Apollyon, and his prancing figure danced ever more violently.

'You, a believer?' he sneered. 'Then it's only you who think so! You failed Him on the mudflats and got a ducking in the Slough of Despond! You swallowed old Worldly Wiseman hook, line and sinker. You stuck out for short cuts and cheap methods to rid you of your "bones". You were so downright lazy that you were caught napping in broad daylight and when it came to the lions you were a complete washout. Faithful? You're nothing but a scared rabbit scuttling from one hole to another. And there's something else besides your movements you might think about and that's your motives. You so called Christians are all tarred with the same brush. You couldn't make a name for yourself in The City of Destruction. You were too working-class for that, so you become a Christian and start hob-nobbing with the toffs across the frontier. You couldn't be famous as a sinner so you're trying to be famous as a saint. You'll be famous all right and you won't have to wait a lifetime. I'll make you a celebrity by eight o'clock tomorrow morning!'

Instead of succumbing to dismay, Christian's resistance stiffened. His girdle braced him and his faith held high. The vicious words fell from him, checked still, by this hidden guard.

'You profess to know everything,' he parried, 'but your warped data has only scratched the surface. You're not the Most High, though you tried to be. Your superficial intelligence is useless before the omniscience of Jesus, my King. Regarding myself, I'm even worse than you say but as for my God, He's greater by far than you dare to concede. He knows my life, my sin, my heart's intent, yet notwithstanding, loves me still. He sees how you inveigled and corrupted me, but by His grace He makes me clean. His final triumph will expose your impotence. You cruelly accuse me but He will absolve me. My sins are confessed. His promise is sure. His blood has availed. I proclaim His victory. The Christ who died now lives to plead for me. You can do what you will but Jesus is Lord and His Name must prevail.'

Restraint was gone. The fiend's vituperation raved madly on through all the lunging fury of his miming symbol. 'I hate Him!' cried Apollyon with frenzied voice, 'I hate His laws! I hate His Cross! I hate His people! I hate His Church! I hate His Word! I hate Him with an everlasting, unrelenting, burning hatred! I will devour you! I will bring every weapon from Fort Lust to consume you! I will possess you with a legion of spirits. I will ... I will ... I will ...'

'And will you?' cried Christian. 'Beware what you attempt, Apollyon. I am a pilgrim on the King's routings. You cannot molest me with impunity. My departure from House Beautiful will be wired to my next staging post. Failure to arrive will mean an immediate search by the airborne emissaries of heaven. They are on constant patrol to assist the heirs of salvation. The battle is not mine but God's. You are no match for Him. He has declared the decree "I will bruise Satan under your feet shortly".'

There was a moment's pause, then from the T.V. came a hissing sound as if Apollyon were fused with invective and about to explode. Suddenly it happened and the vilest blasphemy shattered the room. Simultaneously the monster's eyes dilated alarmingly and the fierce black pupils pierced Christian's mind with their hypnotic stare. This was his adversary come to devour him. Nearer and nearer drew the face. It seemed like a nightmare. To wake or to die were the only alternatives. He made one desperate strike at the set but panic proved no substitute for faith. 'Try to cut me off, would you?' taunted Apollyon. 'Just try it and see.' The challenge spurred him. Christian reached for the volume control. There was a blinding flash. The set was alive and he fell heavily to the ground, stunned by a death-dealing shock. 'It won't be long now,' gloated Apollyon and his voice blared on, growing louder and louder till the walls and windows shook. Christian, although somewhat numbed, felt intuitively for his briefing. Yes, it was there. He drew it out, held it tightly, then with one deft movement used it to depress the button on the T.V. panel. It was not the parchment he trusted, but the word of God contained within it. That, for sure, would not conduct Satanic power. A sullen click, then deathly silence. It was for a moment only. Ee-er! Ee-er! Ee-er! The A-POL Dragon Squad was on its way. Closer and closer came the sound, as the vehicles streaked along The Freeway. Christian was suddenly dynamic. Up to his feet he jumped, sprang to the Venetian blinds and with one zip of the cord, flashed them to the ceiling. The setting sun, shining obliquely from Immanuel's land, flooded the room with golden light. The cars drew up just beneath him but nothing could hold him now. The window lay loosely upon its catch and he flung it open. He stepped lightly on to the footwalk outside, then ran out past the lounge. People were drinking and music playing. Not a soul noticed him. On he went, past the place where Pilgrim's Rest merged with Motel Magnificent: only thirty yards to the footbridge now. Soon he was mounting it; over he went, four, eight, twelve, sixteen lanes. 'Broad is the way,' he thought, then reaching the farther side he merged into the landscape straight before him.

When the Dragon Squad burst into the room they found their

bird had flown. The premises were searched but without result. The walkie-talkie 'Satannae' picked up fresh instructions from their H.Q. Numerous calls awaited them along The Freeway. The men returned to their vehicles; not that Christian's case was abandoned. Apollyon had already radioed down the line. All agents had been alerted. Vanity Fair and Doubting Castle were well informed. A day or two, and attacks on this insolent pilgrim would be resumed. Meanwhile, there was enough to daunt him in between.

# CHAPTER ELEVEN

# TRAIL OF TERROR

IT was some considerable time before Christian felt able to slacken his pace. 'Shun youthful passions,' his briefing reminded him, and he felt it safer now to put as much distance as possible between himself and The Pilgrim's Rest. As the sun went down, he suddenly remembered his packed lunch. Thrusting his hand into his deep coat pocket he found it was still there, together with the little bottle of Salvation. If only he had remembered God's provision for the way, he would never have drunk what had proved to be 'the cup of demons'. His humiliation hurt his pride, but he had learned from experience now that indulgence, even in 'harmless' things, could in certain contexts lead to disaster. Whilst he unwrapped his 'piece', he noticed some words printed on the paper. They read 'No temptation has overtaken you that is not common to man. God is faithful and he will not let you be tempted beyond your strength, but with the temptation will also provide the way of escape, that you may be able to endure it.' 'Thank God!' he exclaimed; and as he ate the meat of His Lord's table and drank afresh the wine of heaven, his spirit revived. 'He restores my soul!' he cried. 'I will forget what lies behind and straining forward to all that lies ahead, press on toward the goal for the prize of the upward call of God in Christ Jesus.' Spurred by the recollection of these words, he took courage and walked on into the night, singing to himself the song of David, 'Though I walk through the valley of the shadow of death, I will fear no evil, for Thou art with me.' And such songs he needed for that valley of the shadow lay right in his path.

As the light faded, he became conscious of a drastic change in the countryside. He was entering what is commonly called a thermal region, though to the pilgrim it proved, more properly, an infernal region. The choice of epithet depended largely on whether he thought on the physical features of the terrain, or the invisible terrors of which they spoke. On every hand the landscape bore the scars of volcanic action. The soil was an ashen grey devoid of vegetation. From craters and fissures rose columns of steam, and the entire atmosphere reeked of sulphur. The path grew narrower and narrower, until on the one side lay a precipitous gully down which coursed a torrent of water, whilst on the other extended a wide area of boiling mud, where uncouth bubbles rose and fell within the seething slime, emitting, as they burst, the croaking sound of some monstrous reptile. Christian wondered which death would prove the more fearful: to drop like a stone into the rock strewn river, or to be swallowed alive in the gurgling morass of hot black mire. It was pitch dark now and he could only grope his hazardous way, haunted at every turn by unearthly sounds, and certain that every step would be his last. After what seemed an age, the face of the moon began to glisten through a veil of clouds, clothing the wreaths of steam with an eerie light. The very spirits, it seemed, became incarnate. His heart beat louder and faster. This was a world of things undreamt of, each with its fears. He strained his eyes for a way of escape but found none. Then out of the night came a blood-curdling scream. He stiffened with dread. Two wild and tattered figures raced swiftly towards him. 'Death! Death! Nothing but death!' they cried. 'Turn back! Turn back!' He watched them with apprehension as they hurtled madly on. Their eyes were vacant, looking weirdly before them; their voices frantic and high pitched, but growing fainter and fainter, the further they ran. Then their shouting ceased, suddenly silenced. Christian shuddered. No doubt the maelstrom or the mud had claimed them. Unnerved, he cried yet again to His God, and though shaking all over, he tramped doggedly on. Not far below, the restless cauldron seethed and turned, mounting at times as if to engulf him. The rocky path grew worse. The crevices increased, until the countless columns of rising steam became, in the silver moonlight, a swirling host of ghostly beings, rising and falling, writhing and calling, through all that arid canyon of no return.

At times some vaporous pillar would resemble an acquaintance long since departed. There it would linger, holding his gaze, till the uncanny likeness sent a chill right through him. Then just as quickly the shade would change, and others emerge to startle him. How long must the valley be? How long the night? Would all the dead of all the years come forth to greet him? He halted, transfixed with horror. He could see his young workmate, just a wisp of a lad; the one who had died in the furnace. They had been on the same shift all that month, tipping at the kilnhead, when his foot had caught and down he had gone. It was only seconds till the flesh was consumed, and all he could see was a round bare skull, glowing white in the pulsing inferno. The impression passed but another arose. This time it was the girl just down the street. Only eighteen at the time, she was, hoping to get married to a fine young boy. He'd known them since childhood.

Then she fell ill and no one knew her complaint, though often he'd wondered. Could he ever forget the agony, when he stood that night on the step with her father? One word, that was all. 'Cancer!' he'd groaned. Then the door had closed and he'd walked down the street with tears in his eyes. For ten long weeks she wasted, till the bright young face was lost in the wan and sunken features. He thought of the flowers on the grave, so fresh and beautiful, just like herself when her boy first met her. Now she was there; there in front of him. Would she touch him, that cancerous touch? But the likeness was gone and only the coiling cadaverous steam clasped at his face and caressed his cheek.

A whole company of spectres now swept into view, so human, so true to life; but their faces were blue, that ugly night-shade of bodies lying long in the water. Then he remembered them, and the day in the park when the ice gave way. There must have been hundreds skating; and thy laid them on the footpath, stiff and cold, still in their coats and anoraks, and their skates on their feet. Catastrophe, disaster, tragedy—their sordid memories thronged him. How could it be, this reverie of hurt and heartbreak? And there was the child, its very face! What a crash at the corner! Just yards from their door, it was. And they'd run straight out to where the cars lay twisted and found the blood on the road and the broken glass of the shattered windscreen. And the little one wouldn't move. He'd been sitting on his mother's lap, or so it appeared. He was dead when they lifted him, and on his feet were those little white socks and such smart little brand new shoes. As Christian's emotions choked him, a tiny column of soft warm steam seemed to flow through his fingers. Yes, it was warm, warm as that head and its golden curls that terrible day.

The mounting pressure of sorrow and fear, suspense and encounter was well nigh unbearable. Was this the valley of the shadow of death, the dark domain of man's last foe? Oh what an enemy! Where could he go, where find oblivion, in all the turmoil and the groaning of the night? Back, back his mind would trace, as if the total quota of his dead must still be marshalled, as if all hell must meet him at his coming. Then came that haggard face, so black and grey. One inch, that's all it was, the measured distance marking life from death. The neighbours sensed the silence, but in the end it was the police who found him, hanging in the dust and darkness of the loft. 'There's no foul play,' they said—but why, Oh why did he do it?—his uncle, always so kind and so thoughtful, with his liquorice allsorts for the children? What is it that comes over a man? The absence of motive had frightened him and the sight of the corpse had stalked his thinking for months. He peered through the mist and the rock loomed above him. There was the likeness, strangely persuasive, drawing the eye to the grotesque formation. One moment of time, or ten millions of years? How long had it hung there? Again the earth tremored. The mountain was shifting. A crack split the silence. The stalactite fell and Christian dropped low. He was dazed by the impact. The dark line of severance had circled the limestone. His hands reached to grasp it. 'Get it off!' he was muttering. 'Oh loosen it! Loosen it!' And back from the cliff his voice echoed coldly, a lone mocking echo in the empty ravine.

All at once a series of violent detonations rocked the chasm. A blast swept through the area, leaving him heaving at the chest. Avalanches crashed into the valley and scattered rock descended around him. It seemed as if the whole area must explode by force of hidden fires. 'Oh, not again! No! Not again!' he shouted. 'Not the air raid and its flaming hours!' The landmine had fallen first and then came the incendiaries. But surely the war was past. He felt bewildered. What was this place? Now he was gasping and dust filled his lungs. Then he remembered. It was the morning after that he saw it, after the night in the underground station; and it was in the gutter that he found it. Just the palm of a hand, with a thumb and a girlish fourth finger. It carried an engagement ring and the diamond glittered in the morning sunshine. He had picked it up when he came to it, but then had felt guilty, as if he had touched something sacred, something which could never be his; and he'd laid it down on the curbstone. Very gently he'd laid it down, then washed his hand in a puddle.

The air grew hotter and hotter, as once again he picked his way through the boulders. He was descending now, and at the foot of the defile, a stony floor broadened out into a large round crater. There before him the molten lava surged back and forth, its folds emerging, converging, devouring and being devoured. The lurid smoke lifted high in the night. It seemed like the 'blitz' again, with the city ablaze, and those days and nights of the burning cloud. He had not been mistaken. The sight of the fires spoke afresh of man's doom. He started to pray, not just for himself but for Christiana, the children, his nephew, and for Obstinate and Pliable. His heart so yearned for them. How could they face heaven's wrath in that day? Fresh lava spewed upward as Christian proceeded and skirted the crater. Like the tongue of a serpent it struck viciously at him. He cried out again, 'Deliver me, I beseech Thee, Oh Lord, for Thou only canst keep me from the paths of the destroyer.' This weapon, that never failed to repel the insurgent evil, Christian called 'All-Prayer'. So it was that the

Lord of the Hill kept the feet of his pilgrim and he passed on unharmed. This was a miracle, for at the last, no scent of fire was found on his person. Notwithstanding, the crackling echoes of the erupting volcano, the fierce hissing where countless streams ran down to the lava's edge and the strange sense of agonised voices falling on his ear, disturbed him greatly, all through the night. The fiery atmosphere around him felt like the breath of Gehenna and its weight and pressure, as the touch of fiends. From time to time he would shout some portion of his briefing into the populated air. Then his strength would come again. In the quieter pauses, however, when blasphemous voices echoed at his own, he would wonder whether he or Satan were the author of them. Such was the devil's design to neutralise his prayer to his Father.

Towards the dawn he heard another soul, crying out in the darkness the very words that had been his comfort. 'Though I walk through the valley of the shadow of death, I will fear no evil, for Thou art with me!' This lifted Christian quite out of his weakness. 'To think,' he said, 'that someone else is passing through this place of terror, and what is more, that God is with him. If God is with him—He's with me too. Praise be to Him who saves me from the horrible pit. I will go forward and seek the company of this faithful man.'

Then the day broke, and he came to higher ground. Now he could look back on all the way his God had led him; and being delivered from so great a death, resolved to trust Him still, who would yet deliver him. The devices of Satan, he realised, were formidable but not invincible. Exposed to the light of day, Christian viewed them in a new perspective. Had not his Master said, 'I have given thee power over *all* the power of the enemy'?

# CHAPTER TWELVE

# WALKING AND TALKING

At the furthest limit of The Valley of the Shadow of Death, the whole area was littered with human bones. There they lay, on all sides, white and gleaming in the sun. Christian stood mystified, but spying one of the residents (and there were many, both young and old on the fringe of that region), he sought from him an answer to the riddle. 'Oh,' said the resident, Half-Dead, by name, 'this land through which you are passing lives in fear of two man-eating tigers. Their lairs are in the hills of Tradition and Superstition. You will have heard of them, surely, in the City of Destruction, for their cruel attacks have often been reported in the press. One is known by her nickname, Pope, and the other by his surname, Pagan. They each used to keep to their own mountains, preying separately on the poor inhabitants, but, of late, some say they have mated and their raids have certainly slackened; but may God have mercy on us, once their offspring are born. There will be more mouths to fill, and honest pilgrims, with their warm-blooded faith, will be just the flesh for their cubs.'

As Christian continued on his way he came to a rise which much facilitated his vision and there, not far ahead, was another pilgrim. 'Hello!' cried Christian. 'Hold on a bit and I'll catch you up!' 'I'm not waiting for anyone!' came back the reply. 'Don't you know we're in tiger-country?' Stung to action by the rebuke, Christian doubled his pace and quickly caught up on the man before him.

It proved to be none other than Faithful, and with what joy they met. They had known each other in former days, in the City of Destruction. Now they were fellow-citizens of the City of God. Christian could hardly wait to hear the news. Faithful had left later than Christian but his progress had been faster, so they decided to exchange their experiences.

'Did you meet Mr. Worldly Wiseman in his big limousine?' asked Christian. 'No, the road over the moor was deserted when I came by, but I did see someone else. It looked as if folk were having a picnic on a grassy patch. It was a lovely day and they'd spread a cloth on the ground. There was a thermos flask, some plastic cups, rolls and butter, a jar of honey and some delicious fruit. As I came up to the spot—it was quite near the road side—I suddenly recognised my neighbour's wife. She'd poured out a cup of tea and was spreading some honey on the rolls. "Good afternoon, Mr. Faithful," she greeted me. "Out for a walk? First bit of fine weather for a while, isn't it? My husband was coming this way," she explained. "He has a business, you know, in Carnal Policy, so I thought we'd have a picnic. Being so nice, he dropped me off here. There was no point in my going into town, for he'll be occupied only an hour. Sit down a moment," she said. "Wouldn't you like something to drink?" So we got talking and one thing led to another. "You look tired, Mr. Faithful," she said, seeming quite concerned. "I've always said you city men go at it too hard. If it's not board meetings, then it's some club night, or failing that it's a Masonic do ... And as for the golf business— Relaxing? You're all so intense at it, you'd think every game was a tournament. Do you know, Mr. Faithful, you look that dead beat, you could just drop in your tracks. I don't know how far you expect to go hiking over the moors today, but if I were you, I'd just stretch out in the heather and take it easy. You might even get sunburnt." I sat silent for a minute or two, glad of the rest, then I seemed to catch her eye, and became very conscious of her looking at me. "I'll be going now," I butted in, perhaps rather rudely, "thanks for the tea." When I spoke she smiled, that was all; but as I walked away the golden sunlight lit up her face. I'd only gone a few steps, when she said courteously, "Have a nice walk, Mr. Faithful." I didn't want to turn. I was somehow afraid that something would happen, yet turn I did. You know how it is, Christian. And there we were, our eyes each held by the other's. In that moment of hesitation, she rose and walked quietly over to where I was and we stood together, those silent moments, in the deep purple heather. Somehow her hands found mine and she gazed up into my face with a pathetic, pleading beauty. "No one would see us here," she said. "He won't be back yet. It will be all right, I take the Pill ..." As I stood speechless and motionless, the words of your Book, Christian, came like a knife to my conscience. "Can a man take fire in his bosom, and his clothes not be burned? So he that goeth in to his neighbour's wife; whosoever toucheth her shall not be innocent. Lust not after her beauty in thine heart; neither let her take thee with her eyelids for by means of a whorish woman a man is brought to a piece of bread!"

"You are very thirsty, Wanton," I said, "but my Lord has said they that hunger and thirst after righteousness shall be filled." Then I broke away and she tried to hold me back but, thank God, I escaped with my life.

'As the drystone wall came into view and the ground ascended,

I could see, in the distance, her husband's car coming in from the direction of Carnal Policy. I had been just in time. It may seem absurd to you, Christian, but the old nursery rhyme came singing through my mind at that psychological moment.

> *The King was in his counting house,*
> *Counting out his money.*
> *The Queen was in the parlour*
> *Eating bread and honey.*

'How the sublime and the ridiculous weave together in our minds and yet it kind of made sense, Christian; and so it was I came to the gate. What do you think of it all?'

'It just goes to show there are many reasons for people turning from the way,' said Christian. 'Some are too brainy, some are too greedy and others too sexy. Give me knowledge! Give me cash! Give me a man! Give me a woman! It is the same old cry in all our hearts. We're a race of blood-suckers crying, Give! Give! But the saying of the Lord remains. "If thou knewest the gift of God ... thou wouldest have asked of Him and He would have given thee living water." '

'Yes,' said Faithful, 'and that's something we've proved by experience. It's a well within us springing up into everlasting life.'

'And what happened next?'

'Once through the gate, who should meet me but Old Man Adam and what a time I had with him. You remember how he has three daughters, called Lust of the Flesh, Lust of the Eyes and Pride of Life. Well, believe it or not, his sole purpose in waylaying me was to get me to marry them. Can you imagine it? Not just one of them but all three. Needless to say, I quickly "put him off" and made haste to The House of The Interpreter.'

'I should think you did,' said Christian, with something of a twinkle in his eye. 'They would have made you old before your time and brought your grey hairs with sorrow to the grave.'

'I met Moses, too, and got quite a surprise. I'd always understood he was the meekest man on earth but never, in your wildest dreams, could you have imagined how he assaulted me; but he desisted once my Lord of all grace showed His nail-pierced hands. I learned that what God's law demands, His grace provides; that the Law makes us sore, revealing our sin, but grace brings us healing through the blood of His cross. There were others I met too, everyone of them with their backs to the City, which you and I so long to enter. Maybe you also passed them. There was Discontent, then Pride, followed by Arrogancy, Self-deceit and

Worldly-glory. Each in turn had some suggestion, and offered to settle me this side of the wall, though short of Heaven's Gate. The hardest to shake off proved to be Shame. What a persistent fellow. Really, he seemed to have the wrong name altogether. The name he bears sounds self-effacing but anyone more audacious would be hard to find. As soon as he met me, he started on me. "A pitiful thing," he said, "to see a grown man like you fettered in conscience and bound hand and foot with religious graveclothes. You'll never be a full-orbed personality. Fancy hugging a guilt complex day in and day out. Nothing could be more crippling. How you expect to get on in business I don't know. Your outmoded morality will see you hamstrung every time. People just won't take it these days. You are committing financial suicide. And ideologically, why, the way you people talk, you'd think there was something spiritual about being medieval. You've had a decent education but you won't be rational about anything. It's an insult to your own intelligence, much less to other people's." I was naturally taken aback by such an onslaught and thought I would ignore him by walking on, but not a bit of it. He wouldn't let me go.

' "I thought you'd have been ashamed," he went on, "to be associated with the ignorant bunch of ne'er-do-wells opting out of society these days; pilgrims, tramps, beatniks and what have you. You're all the same to me, the way you hold aloof. Why, some of you won't even vote! Still, what can you expect. Most of you evangelical people come, anyway, from the less educated classes. Anyone worth his intellectual salt wouldn't wish to be seen, chanting the cant you do, or singing those silly little ditties you teach the kids in Sunday School. I consider it a disgrace that an intelligent human being should attend church and after being ticked off by some parson, go around moping all day, thinking about his sins. I believe in God, too, but not your nasty snooping little deity. Fancy being a slave to such notions when you're the master of your fate and born to be free!"'

Christian was very eager to hear how Faithful answered such a tirade. 'The first thing I told him,' said Faithful, 'was that those things highly esteemed amongst men are an abomination in the sight of the Lord. Secondly, I told him that he had everything to say about man but nothing about God and that he hadn't so much as quoted one word of Scripture to support his assertions. Thirdly, I informed him that on the Day of Judgement what would count would not be what he, a mere man, thought about Christians, but whether he had submitted himself to the Righteousness of God. "Finally," I concluded, "what God deems best *is* best. If God prefers a tender conscience then I prefer it. If God prefers a simple trust in Himself and a loyal confidence in His Word, then I prefer that too. If God says that those who make themselves fools for Christ's sake are the wisest, and those that make themselves poor for His Kingdom are the richest, then this is my verdict also." Looking him squarely in the face I said, "Get moving—Shame! I won't tolerate you a moment longer. You are the enemy of my salvation. I've more to do than listen to you, when right now I could be listening to my Lord. The things you despise, let it be known, are my glory. I'll not bite your bait, Shame. It's ragworm!" This seemed to finish him and he went off down the road to fish in other waters.'

By the time each had recounted his story, several hours had passed and they had begun to catch up with another traveller. Faithful spoke to him first and found his name to be Talkative. He was a tall handsome man, well dressed and possessed of an excellent flow of language. From the start, he exhibited a great interest in spiritual matters and Faithful was delighted to find a man so well acquainted with current affairs and so thoroughly versed in 'contemporary theology'. He turned to Christian to express appreciation of their new-found companion, but it so happened that Christian could recall his background. 'He's the son of Say-Well, you realise,' said Christian, 'and was brought up in Prating Row. He's very accomplished and passes well amongst strangers but what the neighbours say is another story. You know the old saying, "A saint abroad and a devil at home!" It's a pity to have to say it but that's the type of man he is.'

'Still, let's have another talk with him,' said Faithful, a little crestfallen at his lack of discernment after all he had said. 'Let's ask him a question.'

'I say, Talkative, will you answer me this? Once God has saved a man what evidence of God's work in his heart will be seen in his life?'

'That's a good enough question, Faithful, and I'll give you my answer, although it's obvious you are more concerned about the demonstration of God's power than the theology of His Person. First of all I would say that God's work in a man's heart results in that man denouncing evil. Secondly . . .'

'Hold on!' interrupted Faithful, 'one point at a time. Surely the better answer would have been that it results in the man *re*nouncing evil.'

'Oh, don't split hairs! What difference is there between denouncing and renouncing that you think so important?'

'All the difference in the world! It is one thing to criticise sin and deplore its existence but quite another, to brand it for what it is, judge it in one's own heart, and repent from it altogether. A person can decry a sin but be a long way from abhorring it and throwing it behind his back. Joseph's mistress brought the place down shouting out against sin, but she it was who desired it all the time. There's many a man in the pulpit who condemns sin most eloquently, but if the truth were known, butters his bread with it in secret.'

'So you're going to make me an offender for a word then?'

'No I'm not, but I can't let you get away with the blurring of such basic distinctions. Now what was the second thing?'

'Well, if God's grace is at work in a man's heart then he'll obviously have a clear grasp of the truth of the Gospel.'

'That's what many say but actually, the one can by no means be inferred from the other. The Bible tells us it's possible to have all knowledge and understand all mysteries, yet have nothing that counts with God. The Lord asked his disciples, "Do you know all these things?" They said, "Yes Lord," but Christ added "Blessed are ye if ye *do* them." The blessing was not in the knowing but in the doing. One of the Master's parables tells us it is possible to know God's will and still not do it. To know a thing may satisfy folk like yourself, who can talk intelligently, but obedience to the thing known, that is what pleases God. I don't want to be unkind, Talkative, but that's how the matter really stands. Is there anything you'd like to add to what you've already said?'

'What's the use of my speaking further? It's obvious we're not going to agree.'

'Well, if you'll listen to me, I'll give you my own answer to the question. All right?'

'Yes, but don't preach at me. Discussion and honest debate are what I appreciate, not brainwashing. I loathe conversations in which people get at one another.'

'To my mind,' began Faithful, 'the work of God's grace in the human heart is evidenced first to the person himself, and then to the folk around him. As far as the person himself is concerned, the grace of God brings him to a conviction of his sin in all its enormity before God. It leads him to sorrow over it and to repent from it, not just to bemoan it, but to reject it completely. God's grace causes a man to flee from the wrath that hangs over him and to find refuge in the arms of Christ, who bore the punishment which by rights was his due. God's grace begets in the person such a hunger and desire for God that he will never rest until he finds his all in Christ, who died for him and rose again.

As to the evidence before others, they will see a life completely transformed. There will be the confession of Christ as Lord on his lips, and the evidence of the fruits of the Spirit in all his attitudes and behaviour. Isn't this the answer, or have you some objections?'

'No, no objections,' replied Talkative, in a rather noncommittal tone of voice. 'If you've no objections,' pursued Faithful, 'tell me, have you tasted this in your experience?' Talkative was obviously embarrassed, and prevaricated strongly with the words, 'You're talking now, of course, not about theology, which is my forte, but about things to do with experience and conscience. This is really not my line. I just cannot permit myself to be catechised in this way by a person like yourself. Why you people can't be content to chat happily about divine things, I just don't know. Why must you always be so personal? It's really obnoxious.'

'I've not minced matters, Talkative, because it is a known fact in your native town, that your religion is nothing more than a lot of hot air. The life you are living denies the very faith you profess. One day you'll hunt with the hounds, the next you'll run with the hare. No doubt you become all things to all men and count it scriptural. To an Anglican you'll talk like an Anglican, to an R.C. you'll talk like an R.C., and to a non-conformist, you'll be a non-conformist. It may even be with a Communist you would chew the fat and give no offence. I just don't know.'

'I think your allegations are scandalous. You make me a man without principle but what's the good of talking. You've been listening to some slanderous back-chat about me; and if that's the kind of person you are, I've no more use for you!'

The termination of the conversation on this note seemed most disconcerting and unsatisfactory. Faithful rather felt he had gone too far, but Christian on the other hand was undismayed. 'There's far too little straight speaking nowadays. Anyone would think that ecumenical "soft-soap" was spiritual just because of the label it bears; that fundamentals don't matter as long as you can shake hands all round. It's folk like Talkative that make the Christian faith putrid in the eyes of the world at large. People can talk so glibly about Christ today. They deny His deity, slander His manhood, sneer at the atonement, discount his resurrection, laugh at His coming and debunk His judgement. They are prepared to blur every frontier the Church has known and which our forbears defended in blood. What is more they will do all this dressed up in robes and vestments, daring to represent the very God whose Truth they deny. Such wolves in the flock, such serpents in the grass, are nothing less than the instruments of Satan, talkers and deceivers ripe for destruction. To expose them for what they are is not pride of heart but safety for God's people. "Beware of dogs," says Paul, "beware of evil workers. To say the same thing all over again is not tedious for me, for I say it as a safe-guard, for you who are so easily deceived." '

As Talkative sheered off, feeling greatly insulted, who should come along the road but their old friend Evangelist.

'Great to see you both,' he said. 'In spite of every situation, I see you are victors still. I can't tell you how glad I am that the seed I sowed in your hearts is yielding its harvest. I've come to warn you, now, of the things that await you for "only through much hard-ship can you come to the full realisation of God's Kingdom." In every city, prison and death, torture and chains will confront you. The next place is one of the vilest. The scum of the earth they will call you, but what your Lord once said is valid still. "Be thou faithful unto death and I will give thee a crown of life." ' When the Pilgrims heard this they were much sobered but nevertheless went joyfully forward, glad at the prospect of suffering for their Master's sake.

# CHAPTER THIRTEEN

# THE FUN OF THE FAIR

THEN I saw in my dream that Christian and Faithful had sighted a large urban area away on the horizon. It was one of the so-called new towns, and was situated in a tongue of territory, long dominated by invading enemy forces. The policy of the alien authorities had always been to annexe the area as completely as possible. They had set up their administration and renamed the province Supersex. In the main plaza of the town was a grandiose supermarket, open night and day, and seven days a week. Originally it was called Vanity Fair, but sported now the ultra-contemporary name of Sexpo. These designations were selected because everything to do with the town was bigger and better than anywhere else. Superlatives were the only words countenanced in the promotion of its trade; and furthermore, nothing could be bought, sold or exchanged unless it were allied to a sex-symbol. The supermarket itself, whilst a more recent innovation, was actually built on a very ancient site. Business has been carried on there for thousands of years and countless pilgrims have passed through the area, all down the centuries. For this reason, Old Dragon Face (that being the affectionate title given by The Town Council to each succeeding trade-convener) deliberately maintains the shopping-centre astride the route taken by all persons emigrating from the Kingdom of Darkness to the Kingdom of God. By waylaying them with every knick-knack likely to take their fancy, some are dissuaded from proceeding further.

The great commercial centre is more popular today than ever before. The shopping precincts are continually extending and the variety of articles available to the public increases year by year. For an agreed consideration, you can acquire combines and corporations, machinery and men, estates and nations, appointments or disappointments, seats in parliament and a place in the sun. Once show your money and all is before you. There are contracts and verdicts, votes and intelligence, drug-trips and scholarships, and the 'right' to be free. There to be purchased are substitutes, prostitutes, gods and gold, sins and assassins, homosexuals, intellectuals, extortions, abortions, spies and lies, and of course, unfaithful wives on sale or return. Those more religious can buy masses and images, wholesale indulgences, charms for alarms; and by special arrangement, real holy water drawn straight from the 'frig'; not to speak of hand-shakes with popery and the best coffins anywhere this side of the river. To do justice to Sexpo it must be said there is nothing that money cannot buy, except eternal life; but as most pilgrims profess to have it and most other people never ask for it, there would be no demand worth speaking of, even if offered free.

Adjacent to the main plaza stands the huge Helliodrome, a vast arena devoted to all kinds of entertainment, in which the curtain never falls and the applause is indefinitely prolonged. It is difficult to tell, they say, whether those applauded, or those applauding, are the performers, so inebriated are they both with the deafening noise. Day and night a stream of professional actors drive up to the stage doors, maintaining a round-the-clock performance. There are the jugglers in finance and the tamers of 'bulls' and 'bears'. There are the political strip-tease artists, who never rest until they have divested each other of the last vestige of respect. There are the promoters, whose range of puppets include sportsmen, mannequins, models, singers and even pin-up preachers of the times. These able manipulators prove especially successful with Sexpo audiences for they not only make a 'nobody' seem a 'somebody', but do it at the expense and to the obvious delight of everybody! There are also the student-sponsored amateur theatricals but they always turn out the same; big mock battles with lots of shouting and 'sword-brandishing' aimed at putting the world right; but they are generally short sketches, and the players once they graduate, soon retire into obscurity, behind the affluence of their professions. The Betrayed Union movement, one of the biggest shows of all time, is essentially a snake-dance and a farce of the first order. Not that it was always so, but the snakes performing now tend to be pink ones and are terribly poisonous; though they seem attractive little creatures to many in the audience, expert as they are, in the mystique of the movement. The trouble generally starts when the tempo of the dance increases, and not infrequently the performance ends in a riot with the whole troupe, snakes and all, rampaging loose in the crowd. On these occasions ambulances and fire engines wait at the alert along the side streets near the Helliodrome. Police action, though, is little used to suppress such hooliganism, it being more gainfully employed against those motorists whose parking offences have reached 'criminal' proportions.

In addition to direct entertainment, all sorts of courtesans and partisans frolic on and off the stage, but no matter how vehement their word or graceful their posture, the proceedings inevitably conclude with everyone dancing to some current 'hit' struck up by the masses whether it be 'Roll out the Barrel', or 'The East is Red'.

The different celebrities, whatever their category, owe much to the mass media of modern communications. Lest their 'importance' to the community be under-estimated, they are continually advertised, televised, idolised and between commercials for beer, and yet more beer, are daily immortalised, until everyone laughs themselves sick, and like stupid dogs turn to their vomit again.

Another feature of the Fair, lending a cosmopolitan appeal to the whole enterprise, is the variety of pavilions that have been erected over the years. These are permanent structures for the most part, though frequently modified; and reflect the cultures of many nations each displaying their own particular vanities. The English, the Irish, the Scots and the Welsh are all there though lately eclipsed by their American and Russian counterparts. Some pavilions stand grouped together and others are more isolated. The French Pavilion was closed when Christian and Faithful passed through. This was in protest against the Sexpo market, in which they control special interests, being viewed as a World Fair. Then there was the Italian Pavilion, where you could hit the jackpot by buying and selling an old master. And as for excitement, the Spanish Pavilion was hard to beat. Three times a day, for a modest sum, you could watch a bullfight and afterwards spear a real live bull, that is, if you weren't too squeamish. This was a great favourite with the teenagers, some of whom liked to smear the blood on their hands and faces, and look real he-men to their group. Amongst the many others, mention should be made of the Roman Pavilion, where for a limited period all sorts of one-time expensive baubles were being sold at greatly reduced prices!

So deeply did the province of Supersex extend beyond the Frontier Wall that any travellers en route for The Celestial City were obliged to go through it. Such, too, was the system of new approach roads, that whereas in times past it was possible to skirt old Vanity Fair along a less frequented suburban route, every pilgrim now needed to go through the main plaza of the town. In the days when The Prince of Princes passed through the Fair, it was not so sophisticated, though its wares were just as seductive. Lucifer, the chief trade convenor at the time, escorted Him from street to street and invited him to invest in all manner of bogus ventures. He took Him to the 'Arcade of Every Nation Under Heaven' (that was before the present pavilions were in vogue) and extolled the glories of all their cultures. 'I'll make you the sole proprietor, if you'll but personally admit of my supremacy,' was his tempting word; but the Prince displayed a total disdain quoting with devastating force, that shrivelling word 'Thou shalt worship the Lord Thy God and Him only shalt thou serve'. Not one item did he purchase but went straight through doing good and healing all who were oppressed of the devil, for said He, 'I must be about my Father's business.' Thus did He take His triumphant way, untarnished and unmoved.

Now as Christian and Faithful appeared on the plaza, first one and then another turned to stare, until they were the focus of unnumbered eyes. This was primarily due to their multi-coloured coats, which showed the favour of their Father and were quite unobtainable at the Fair. To the crowds their clothes were 'out of this world' and a distinct challenge to the Marketing Board of Trade Associations. Backless dresses, sleeveless dresses and even topless dresses could be tolerated, or for that matter encouraged, by Fashion, the Mistress of the Fair, but the sheer quality of the material together with the divine workmanship of the pilgrims' clothes, irked the merchants of Sexpo, for it revealed their tawdry rubbish for what it was. Some folk gaped with curiosity, others glared in animosity and most called them a monstrosity. 'A sales gimmick by a foreign competitor', was the official comment of most businessmen. As Christian and Faithful talked to each other, they were surrounded by clamorous Sexpodians, all anxious to hear the language they were speaking. Finding them using strange expressions and a different dialect (for all heaven's pilgrims speak earth's tongue with a foreign accent), they felt even more outraged. Whilst many nationalities mingled on the plaza, yet there was a sense in which they all spoke the same language and looked at things from the same standpoint. 'Money talks' says the old proverb, and when it does, everybody understands what it says, thus communication was never a problem at Vanity Fair. Their alien speech, therefore, brought Christian and Faithful under the gravest suspicion. They were viewed from the beginning as interlopers, with a question-mark upon their heads. This prejudice of the local tradespeople was only accentuated when the pilgrims showed their total disinterest for every line of Sexpo's goods, however flamboyantly displayed. This, in addition to their upward look, so easily interpreted as arrogance, incensed the vending community beyond measure. Assistants were specially deployed to approach them with a view to soliciting their custom. 'Is there nothing you will buy?' they asked. 'Yes, we'll buy the Truth and sell it not!' came the unexpected reply. This only humiliated the salesmen, for the last thing any of them stocked was that unpopular commodity. As they continued to walk on, turning neither to the right or to the left, truculent youths began to taunt and abuse the pilgrims. Instead of restraining them, shopkeepers stood at their doors urging them on. Soon others joined them and articles began to be thrown until one and another struck the pilgrims in the face. Some even tried to tear their 'garments of salvation' from their backs. As the scene grew more ugly, the Sexpo Constabulary, observing that a breach of the peace was about to occur, suddenly stepped in and took the men into custody. They left in a black maria to the howls of a raging mob. It was, for them, the beginning of sorrows, with blacker days to come.

# CHAPTER FOURTEEN

# THE JUDGE AND THE JURY

THEIR first cross-examination was held under the direction of the Police Superintendent of the Sexpo Metropolitan Area. He conducted the interrogation with the utmost rigour, insisting they divulge, in fullest terms, their place of origin, their ultimate destination and their real purpose in traversing the plaza in a way calculated to incite the public to an unlawful and violent assembly. To this they answered with an alacrity and spirit which staggered him. 'We wear no other clothes than those pertaining to our own country and it was thence we were travelling, when molested by the rabble in the square. Had you been for order, you would have arrested our attackers rather than ourselves, but we have long since heard that your overlord is the author of confusion and by it, deliberately retains the masses in his grasp. As to our business, we are under no obligation to purchase your merchandise, which we neither require nor desire. Were Truth to be bought, we would pay the highest prices but your traders have never once handled it, and deny its worth altogether. It was for envy and no other reason that they set their men against us. Nettles only have to be touched to sting, so our coming has revealed what you are.'

The superintendent, though startled at first by their temerity, showed no genuine interest in the pilgrims' answers and they felt they were being subjected to a procedure, the outcome of which was already decided. What followed only confirmed their misgivings. 'A disturbance of such dimension is attributable, of course,' insisted their interrogator, 'to other causes than you have chosen to mention. You have concealed your true mission. We are in no doubt of that. Whatever occurred, or did not occur on the plaza, you were already liable for arrest, for we have copious files on your past history. This brief and initial enquiry was only to test your honesty. Seeing from the start, however, you have elected to deceive the authorities, it will be necessary for you to undergo special preparation, prior to the commencement of your trial. You will, of course, receive justice. We represent a great government and administer its law with impartiality, not I might say like the Despot in your country, who has already prepared a lake of fire for people who as yet have not even stood for trial.'

But that was too much for Christian and he blurted out, 'The truth of the matter is this, "He that believes on the Son has eternal life: and he who does not obey the Son shall not see life: but the wrath of God rests upon him." Yes, in this sense, "he who does not believe is condemned already because he has not believed in the name of the only begotten Son of God." God will not hold you guiltless if you blaspheme His Name.' 'Quiet,' bawled the superintendent, 'this is a police office, not a Mission Hall. We won't have that stuff here!'

They were not left long in doubt as to what it meant to be prepared for trial. The superintendent pressed a bell on his desk and in came two hulking brutes of men, with loose limbs and long ape-like hands. Their bloated faces absorbed their features and encroached upon their shifting beady eyes. 'These highly intelligent gentlemen will help you through the first part of your course,' he explained. 'I hope you do well, Mr. Christian and Mr. Faithful.'

'By God's grace,' said Faithful with deliberation, 'we shall do better than you imagine.'

'Silence!' snapped a voice and the two pilgrims were frog-marched bodily out of the room.

Along the railings which surrounded the Police Headquarters, the crowd, who had witnessed the arrest of Christian and Faithful, now gathered in force. Others had joined them and they must have been, already, several hundred strong. In the open courtyard, visible from the road, was an area marked out for parking but beyond this was an enclosure in which there were several iron posts placed in the ground. This was a public flogging area, where enemies of the State were beaten, whenever such action was deemed conducive to the education of the common people. On occasions, the proceedings would even be televised. To this place Christian and Faithful were now brought, like chimpanzees to a tea party, where juvenile faces gape through the fence. With hands tied above their head, the two men were mercilessly attacked. At the sight the crowd became animated. Feeding time had arrived and their sadism would be satiated at least for a while. All manner of catcalls and blasphemous abuse was now hurled at the prisoners. Soon the men sagged at their posts and the bestial guards slashed the ropes and dragged the pilgrims, like sacks of offal, to a trap door in the courtyard. There they unceremoniously bundled them into the darkness and slammed the flap over them.

Out in the street there was a bit of a scuffle going on. 'Good riddance to bad rubbish!' shouted one. 'Say what you like,' shouted another, 'It's a downright disgrace thrashing two visitors like that. It could ruin our tourist trade, once the news gets round!' 'But they were spies, not tourists,' someone insisted. 'That's what *you* say!' rounded his neighbour. 'And are you a spy too?' came the answer tartly. 'You tie the hands of the police and you wouldn't know who was infiltrating the Fair. After all they know the facts. They wouldn't arrest anybody without reason.' 'Not likely,' said someone sarcastically. 'Nice fellows, all of them!' And with such remarks beginning to fly, things got more and more out of hand. 'You're just jealous of them, that's all,' cried another bravely. 'If some of you people with the big talk were half the men they were, Sexpo might be worth living in, whereas it's getting more of a hell on earth every day.' 'Grab that fellow,' cried another and with that, fighting broke out, and it was only when a hundred police armed with tear gas, hoses and truncheons ploughed into the crowd that 'order' was restored.

Six months elapsed before Christian and Faithful were brought to trial. By that time the heat was out of the situation and the authorities knew they could handle the trial in a fairly public way without too much difficulty. After being deliberately debilitated, the two men, when the day came, were but a shadow of their former selves. Notwithstanding, they were given a special shave, haircut and a hot bath on the morning concerned, and told to brush their clothes and look spruce for 'His Justice'. The latter order was largely unnecessary because the texture of their garments was such that the dust of the earth found great difficulty in clinging to it. Even so, it was their desire to keep themselves unspotted from the world and for this reason alone they complied. The purpose of the authorities was naturally to present the prisoners with a fair physical appearance, though psychologically weakened for the trial.

When Christian and Faithful were led into the court, there was quite a scurry, as T.V. cameramen, journalists and photographers all jockeyed for position. The trial was obviously going to be used as a propaganda piece but the pilgrims determined to make it an arena of witness. The words of their Master inwardly strengthened them. 'When they deliver you up, do not be anxious how you are to speak, or what you are to say; for what you are to say will be given to you in that hour; for it is not you who speak, but the Spirit of your Father speaking through you.'

The Judge appointed to the case was none other than Lord Hategood, renowned for his impartial judgement in the interests of the Fair. The court was now assembled and called to order. Preliminary formalities were officiously dealt with, then in a deathly atmosphere the indictment was at last read. The long retention in custody had been hard for the pilgrims to bear but now they were elated that their moment of witness had come. They listened therefore, intently, as the charges were made. In brief, they were as follows:

1. That the accused, known on arrest as residents of the City of Destruction (though absconding therefrom), did, on the afternoon of Doomsday last, notwithstanding their cognisance of the customs and decorum of Vanity Fair, conduct themselves wilfully, and of design, in a way calculated to prejudice good order in the public area of the Sexpo precinct.

2. That the accused on the aforementioned day did, without prior application or receipt of permit, illicitly display articles of clothing manufactured in a realm hostile to this State; that they did on their own person and with prior intent advertise same, all with a view to intruding said commodities on the Sexpo market; and inasmuch as such goods are, under the orders of the Minister for Merchandise, prohibited, either of sampling or of sale in Supersex, the accused in consequence, did commit a breach of the aforementioned regulations and thereby did violate the rights of the legally constituted, and government authorised Free Traders' Association of Sexpo.

3. That the accused did introduce by word of mouth and act of life, a code and spirit of conduct which are not lawful for us to observe, being Sexpodians. That by so doing they inaugurated a movement seditious in character, whose aims are the destruction of the very principles upholding the policies of the State.

4. That the accused by reason of their insidious teaching and pernicious example, subverted and then converted certain politically unstable and weak-minded elements to their cause, inciting such to assemble for harmful purposes such as Bible-reading and prayer-contact with our arch enemy, all calculated to issue in acts of riotous behaviour and foster those conditions conducive to a more general insurrection against the Satanic authority by which the reputation of Vanity Fair is universally upheld.

Faithful was the first to enter the dock. He stood erect and spoke with dignity and feeling. 'I have set myself,' he began, 'against no personage, no teaching, no trade and no authority, except in the degree that any such persons or things have set themselves against Him who is higher than the highest. As for a breach of the peace or an incitement to outrage—I am a man of peace and totally innocent of all such allegations. If any have chosen to stand with us in this place, it is of their own volition, and consequent on their seeing your own base handling of our case.

Their choice is surely a wise one, for who would not turn from the worse to the better. As to our actions being branded "subversive", let it be known to everyone present that we Christians have no secrets, but openly defy all things and persons opposing Jesus Christ, our Lord. The existence of the province Supersex is, in itself, a usurpation of His territory. Your court is, therefore, unconstitutional and you who serve under this devilish regime will answer at the last day to that King whose subject I am and whose interests I gladly serve.'

Faithful's statement being completed, he was made to stand down. 'Call the first witness for the prosecution,' said the Judge, in a commanding voice. A tall thin man with pince-nez glasses stood up, dressed from head to foot in black cloth. 'State your identity, and then proceed with your evidence,' instructed his Lordship.

'My name is Mr. Envy, your honour, and my present appointment is Minister of The Conformed Church of Supersex, and Representative for Religious Affairs on the Town Council of Sexpo.' His plausible voice halted a moment, as if to allow the weight of his office to sink into the minds of the hearers; then he continued, 'As one who has spent many years studying, not only theology and Church history but the development of human society, I am thankful to those benign cosmic forces at the heart of the Universe, and to their every manifestation in the progressive company here present (the accused excepted), that I have lived to see so prosperous a community brought into being as Supersex. I feel it, therefore, a matter of duty to expose the insidious work of these secret agents in our midst. This man, Faithful, in spite of his affable appearance and high sounding name, is unquestionably a most dangerous figure to have loose in our province. May I say that I personally witnessed the unfortunate breach of the peace referred to in the indictment. On that lamentable occasion, the accused, far from withdrawing from the commotion which his own presence had precipitated, took, on the contrary, every opportunity to thrust his propaganda down the throats of the curious crowds that were gathering. Being an enemy alien, this was nothing less than a political aggression carried on under the cloak of commerce and religion. It is hardly needful to reiterate that the ideological welfare of the citizens of Supersex is *not*, I repeat is *not*, the affair of all and sundry persons who imagine themselves preachers and advisers of the public, especially so in the case of the accused; but is the responsibility of the district priest approved by the secular authority. Only such persons, having attended the appropriate courses in sociology made available by the kind arrangement of the Satanic authority, are capable of teaching the essentials of true citizenship today. My bureau, as you are all aware, is attached to the Shoppers' Community Chapel situated in the main plaza. You may judge of the motives of this intruder, when I tell you, that at no time did he contact me, but from the moment of his arrival, proceeded with independence and arrogance, to indoctrinate all with whom he came in contact. Were there a grain of good-will towards our people, he would have exhibited at least a modicum of interest in what is already being done on a large scale in our town to benefit the thought life of the masses. I submit that there is every evidence in his mode of infiltration to suggest the presence of more sinister motives. Here is a serpent, if ever there was one. I trust this court will uphold its long tradition of justice today, justice not only to the prisoner, but justice to *true* religion, and above all justice to the people of Supersex, some of whom this man of ill-repute has already perverted and defiled.' Mr. Envy stood for a few moments in silence scanning the court over his pince-nez spectacles. The brief pause was most effective and he sat down conscious of a great impression being left upon all—all, that is, except Christian and Faithful, who looked steadfastly at him with the clear eye of innocence, so much so that he took off his glasses and wiped them rather ostentatiously with a great big handkerchief, which was blue on one side and red on the other.

Mr. Superstition was the second witness and was now called to the box. 'My Lord,' he began, 'I cannot profess to have a close acquaintance with the accused but I do have first-hand knowledge of his beliefs, for he spoke with me a full five minutes on the plaza on the day of the crime. What I found so appalling was that he said all the church-going in the world could not make a man right with God; and what's more, that all the charities organised by our citizens counted for nothing with Him. And you will remember, your honour, that the traders of Sexpo contributed no less than a small fortune for the relief of the under-privileged in The City of Destruction. Yet here's a man that dismisses the whole thing with a wave of his hand. I've never heard such heresy against good religion or such attacks on social welfare. Good in this life surely means good in the next. If helping others doesn't please God, I don't know what will! But there you are, this man would tear down the lot of us, yes he would, and from what he said, the big crucifix in St. Lucifer's into the bargain! He's an iconoclast! That's what he is!'

Mr. Pickthank now followed. He was viewed as one of the loyalest citizens of Supersex and particular attention was given by all present to what he had to say. His evidence was very personal. 'I have heard this man speak in the most derogatory and seditious manner concerning the mayor and the members of the Town Council. He has slandered the very noblest amongst us and cast a smear on those personalities who have most selflessly served the community. I am willing to publicly state the names of those he has so wickedly maligned. Amongst others, I mention the following: our good friends, Lord Old Man, Lord Carnal Delight, Lord Luxurious, Lord Desire of Vain Glory, not to speak of old Lord Lechery and dear Sir Having Greedy. His assertion was that these honoured gentlemen are corrupt and scheming characters, unfit for office; and that if he had his way, all would be sacked and sent into exile. My last, though by no means least, item of evidence is that even you my Lord,' and at this he lowered his voice in reverential horror, 'have been personally vilified. He says, and sir I hardly like to mention it in your presence, that you are a godless rogue!'

With this the evidence for the prosecution was concluded, the commercial, religious and political implications of the pilgrims' conduct having been set before the court by chosen witnesses, albeit all of them suborned men.

The Judge, Lord Hategood, now permitted Faithful to speak for himself. Point by point, he answered his accusers. Christian was thrilled to listen and marvelled at the wisdom and courage given to Faithful as he spoke.

'Your lordship and all gentlemen here present, I would ask you to listen carefully to my defence. My contention is this, that everything contrary to the Word of God is of necessity diametrically opposed to true Christianity. I challenge you. Is there one member of your Town Council, or a single member of this court, who upholds the integrity and veracity of The Word of God?' There was an awkward silence as Faithful's eyes scanned their scowling faces.

'Continue your defence,' blared the judge, 'and don't waste the Court's time staring about.'

'Your silence is enough. I know you are deeply opposed to the Bible and all that's in it. You have even passed legislation to prohibit its instruction and your entire radio and T.V. network takes every opportunity to ridicule and discredit it. Am I therefore doing you an injustice or committing a slander when I say that your policies are opposed to the Christian Gospel? Is it not the truth, and if I speak the truth, why am I tried as a criminal?'

Then turning to the first witness for the prosecution, Faithful said, 'Mr. Envy, you profess to speak in God's interests but you are a catspaw of the State. There are more than we two men on trial today. Verdicts on earth are not by any means the edicts of Heaven. You shall answer for your words before the bar of God. Yet if I pleased men, I should not be the servant of Christ. And as for you, Mr. Superstition, you deliberately confuse my statements. You infer that I oppose all social welfare but this is just a smoke-screen to evade the issue. It's with man's standing before God we are dealing. No one denies, least of all ourselves, that we should care for our fellow-men, but do you think their poverty can be our stepping-stone to Heaven. Far from it. The faith that saves is not a faith in what we do, but in the work God's Son has done. Faith's virtue lies not in itself but in the object of its trust. Ritualism and philanthropy, rooted so often in the aesthetic and the sentimental, cannot expunge the sin that separates from God. Christ gave His life for each of us and rose again to be our Lord. He met heaven's claims, so faith in the Saviour is the faith that saves. He is the Rock on which I build—the only ground on which I stand. But the religious floorboards of your city, let me warn you, are riddled with the dry-rot of pride and complacency, and once they give way they'll drop you, and all your neon paradise, into the pit of hell.

'Finally I would say to you, Mr. Pickthank, if slander is speaking the truth about "the establishment" to the benefit of the people, and if libel is the exposing of hypocrisy in the seats of judgement, then let my "slander" and my "libel" abound, for this is a place where all that is good is made evil and all that is bitter, called sweet. I would assert, though it may be my last word on earth, that the mayor, the council and the judicial officers of this place stand guilty before God; and in their perversion, cruelty and unbelief are better fitted for the Divine Burnings than to litter the offices of this doomed earth with their wine-filled carcases.'

The Judge glowered ferociously at Faithful and called the jury to attention. 'Gentlemen of the jury,' he boomed again, 'I call upon you now to give your mature reflections on the accused, who has occasioned such a furore in the town. You have heard the witnesses for the prosecution and his own defence, which he has personally conducted. The verdict now lies with you. If it is "guilty" then the sentence must be the direst penalty known to a law. If it is "not guilty" then his life is spared, but before you retire, I would summarise the case in your hearing and give you the salient factors necessary to enable you to reach a sound decision.

'First you must have regard to the various Acts passed in our history. Some of these go back to great antiquity but are by no means to be disregarded. In the days of King Pharaoh, one of the early founders of our great Society, an Act was passed authorising the drowning of all male descendants of those persons holding a religion contrary to the State belief. This was a wise piece of legislation, as it ensured that the families of the deluded sector of the public would not multiply, thus precluding the perpetuation of pernicious ideas through their posterity. A more recent example of this was the action of Hitler, who sent even Jewish children to the gas-chambers, so concerned was he that his race might be pure and the State uncorrupted. Then later on, the great Nebuchadnezzar passed an Act legalising execution by burning in the State Furnace of all those who refused to bow to his image, symbolic of the proper interests of the State. Concerning this you have no better example than Mao's revolution. Just think what he has done for China. And how would it have been possible had he not purged all disruptive elements, both in the party and amongst the people. After Nebuchadnezzar, one, King Darius by name, passed an Act which precluded the conducting of religious exercises, whether in private or in public without the express permission of the State, the penalty for violation being execution in the State den at the mouths of the State lions. We have therefore all the adequate machinery of law and precedent at our disposal. These Acts are upheld and applied in varying degrees in both East and West today. It would be a serious thing, therefore, to show weakness when progressive forces are gaining such victories across the world.

'Lest you should be swayed by your natural emotions rather than by the high interests of a State, which ever has the wellbeing of its people at heart, I must point out to you that each of these Acts has been contravened, at least in principle, by the accused.

'Firstly, the Act of King Pharaoh. In relation to this Act, you must understand that should the accused be permitted to continue his activities in this town, it is more than likely he will marry one of those deluded females whose sympathies he has already aroused. Then very soon we shall have children nurtured from infancy to give loyalty to our arch enemy, and that in our very midst. At such an advanced stage of corruption, it might prove necessary to enforce the Act and eliminate the offspring for the good of all. Better surely, and more just by far, to exact the penalty on the accused now, before such a crisis arises. His action merits it. That much is certain, so do not fear.

'Secondly, the Act of King Nebuchadnezzar the Great. Let it be said that the accused by entering this town and illegally advertising his goods, in what was nothing less than a masculine manne-

quin parade, has unquestionably flaunted the authorities of
Sexpo and done despite to the image of our time-honoured Fair. It
is in essence an act of political aggression with commercial and
religious overtones. When unstable and unreliable elements in
this town are led to believe that the clothing so introduced is of
superior quality, they are then seduced further, to conclude that
the realm from which they come must of necessity be superior in
all else. So they are drawn not only to the goods they see but the
God who made them. It has, I deem, been adequately proven that
the accused has no intention of conforming to the standards and
customs of Sexpo. What you must particularly consider is this—
was it by chance that he and his accomplice came here, displayed
the wares they did, and disseminated the teaching they held, or was
it the planned activity of a higher mind? If so this must be con-
strued as a deliberate attempt to sabotage the spiritual and
economic life of Supersex.

'Thirdly, the Act of King Darius. It is known to you all, of
course, that religion in this province is not to be indulged in to
the inconvenience of the general public, nor is it to be foisted
upon the innocent and unsuspecting rank and file. Furthermore
it is also known that religion in this province is only permitted,
and therefore welcome, in the appointed places and at the
appointed times. The accused, be it noted, has not ceased night
and day and in the most public places to disseminate his doctrine.
For any of our citizens, heresy in the State doctrine marks the first
step towards treason. There is no doubt this alien teaching, left
unchecked, must lead, at last, to open insurrection.

'Your course, then, as a jury, responsible to the populace you
represent, is to fulfil your duty without prejudice and to uphold
the Satanic justice.'

The Jury then retired. They were a motley crowd, if ever there
was one and their names remarkably suited their varied disposi-
tions. There was Mr. Blind-man, the foreman; Mr. No-Good, Mr.
Malice, Mr. Love-lust, Mr. Live-loose, Mr. Heady, Mr. High-mind,
Mr. Enmity, Mr. Liar, Mr. Cruelty, Mr. Hate-light and Mr. Implacable. In the seclusion of the room appointed for their deliberation, each one in turn gave his vote against the accused.
Their comments, inspired by Lord Hategood's instructions, gave
every evidence of their loyalty to the Supersex regime. How very
safe 'democracy' is when exercised by the State-appointed repre-
sentatives of the people! Mr. Blind-man spoke first, 'He's a
heretic,' he said. 'Exterminate him!' shouted Mr. No-Good. 'He's
vermin,' declared Mr. Malice; 'I hate the sight of him.' 'I can't
stand the fellow,' grunted Mr. Love-lust. 'Nor can I,' said Mr.

Live-loose. 'Scum of the earth,' said Mr. High-mind. 'I'd tear him limb from limb,' cried Mr. Enmity. 'A rogue of the first water,' piped up Mr. Liar. 'A bullet's too good for him,' maintained Mr. Cruelty. 'Let's be done with him,' proposed Mr. Hate-light. Then said Mr. Implacable, 'Give me the moon and I still couldn't do with him!'

With deepest solemnity Mr. Blind-man led in the jury, and with even deeper solemnity Lord Hategood looked for the verdict. All bore the greatest air of impartiality and exhibited the ardent desire that not only should justice be done but that it should be seen to be done. 'Guilty, my Lord,' pronounced Mr. Blind-man gravely. The ritual of the black cap then commenced, without which the justice arrived at by so great a machinery could not be fulfilled. The black cap being properly placed, Judge Hategood, without the slightest indication of feeling, for he probably felt nothing, passed the death sentence, adding the dread proviso that, in view of the seriousness of the crime, the extreme penalty was to be carried out by the newly installed atomiser at Fort Lust. This machine was the refinement of all tortures. According to the setting, it could either kill instantaneously or over an indefinite period, the body and mind just wasting away under the bombardment of the nerve centres. It was customary for other prisoners with suspended death sentences to be made to watch the process in its different stages. This had in view the recovering of their minds and wills for Satanic service. Progress in repentance, it should be noted, during this probation period, could lead to the alternative outcome of life-labour. Many are still re-educated in this way rather than endure such destruction of the flesh.

As Faithful's spirit left his mutilated body, for those with eyes to see, there was such spiritual transport available as could take him at once to the gates of the Celestial City. Thus his affliction endured for a moment but his glory for ever.

Meanwhile Christian was remanded in custody, strengthened now by Faithful's unflinching stand and ready, he felt, to face anything; but God is gracious, He knows us better than we know ourselves. Some weeks slipped by, then suddenly, without warning and for no apparent reason, Christian was released and given an hour in which to leave the province. So it transpires that one, through faith, perishes by the edge of the sword, whilst another, by faith, escapes the edge of the sword, and in all this the pilgrim learns that whatever befalls him, the Most High God still rules in the kingdoms of men.

# CHAPTER FIFTEEN

# GODS OF GOLD

CHRISTIAN felt the loss of Faithful very keenly and on the day of his release he longed more than ever before for someone to walk with him towards the Celestial City. He was so glad to be free, yet a sense of depression dogged his steps and more than once he looked back over his shoulder, expecting to see some spectre from his recent trials pursuing his track.

The road leading from Vanity Fair was lined with all manner of cafés, bars, cabarets, night clubs, boutiques and caravan sites. Paradise Boulevard it was called; and he had to watch his step as the cars slewed in and out of the parking areas. Some patrons stepped from the latest models immaculate in dress and coiffure; others returned to their 'wrecks' lurching along the pavement, mouthing their fish and chips from greasy newspaper, and at intervals wolfishly whistling the girls. On ahead, Christian could see a grotesque 'pieman' advertising the biggest hamburger ever, vied by a baneful billboard hailing 'the best buy in beer'; whilst overhead, a museum-piece of a plane trailed an advert of a revue called 'The Naked Truth'. Christian felt sick in his stomach; not that he was any better than the carnival crowd around him, he knew that now, but there was something about the whole set-up that was so nonsensical and he felt just nauseated by the deathly odour of such a fatuous, godless society.

In sheer desperation he prayed, and almost before he asked, God gave him his heart's desire. 'Can I go with you?' a voice said pleadingly. 'Must you walk alone? Don't think that Faithful died in vain. Others will follow soon. From the ashes of His martyrs, God's new recruits arise. I am one of them. My name is Hopeful.' The face of Christian, so pale and thin after his harsh treatment, lit up with a smile. The two men gripped each other's hands. Their eyes searched deeply to the other's depths. It was enough. Falling in step they walked together towards the light, talking of all the wonders of God's mercy as they went.

They had not gone far before they overtook another traveller. He was a man, well groomed and of handsome appearance. When they first saw him he had just emerged from a road-house called The Drift Inn, but seeing him go on foot down the road (and steady at that), they concluded he might be one of the pilgrims.

'Good morning!' said Christian, acknowledging him cheerily, 'are you going our way?'

'By the look of you both,' he replied, 'I should say I was. I'm en route from the City of Fairspeech to the City of God.'

'Without wishing to be personal,' said Christian, 'I rather feel you move with nobility.'

'Maybe I do,' he replied, 'but you're bound to be familiar with some of our notables, if you come from the City of Destruction. They were always hobnobbing with your crowd, what with being on the same committees for the improvement of the urban and rural amenities. Lord Turn-about, Lord Time-server, and Lord Fair-speech, founder members of our community, were household words in your city for many years, being co-pioneers of the New Society. I expect you've heard of the current bigwigs, Mr. Smooth-man, Mr. Facing-bothways and Mr. Two-tongues. They are incredibly active people and when they've done their bit, I guess they'll each get a peerage too. That's one thing about our City, we always give praise where praise is due. By the way, speaking of Mr. Two-tongues, perhaps I should tell you he's my uncle on my mother's side. She, of course, is Lady Feigning's daughter. It's through her I really stake my claim to the aristocracy.' He paused for a moment, his eyes harbouring a knowing look, then continued, 'To be fair, though, my grandfather was no more than a game-keeper to Lord Turnabout. They say that the site of the new disposal area, before it reached its present proportions, was a fine stretch of open water, where fish could be pulled in three at a time. As a young fellow he used to propel his Lordship around what is now the Slough of Despond, looking one way and rowing another; and some people,' he added laconically, 'say our family's been doing the same ever since.'

'You're a family man then?' probed Christian.

'Of course! Whoever heard of an aristocrat without a family? And in great respect we are held, too, especially by the religious community; and little wonder, for we're not like some people I could mention, who are for ever putting others right. We never set our sails against the current feeling, or the tide of opinion. The kind of religion we foster doesn't disturb or embarrass anyone but fosters a proper appreciation of all those who further the welfare of mankind. We like to get on with people, not antagonise them. That's our faith if you want it in a nutshell.'

Christian looked doubtfully at Hopeful and whispered, 'You know, I'm of the opinion this man is the fellow they call By-ends.* The way he speaks, you'd think butter wouldn't melt in

* i.e. Crafty.

his mouth, but if I remember rightly, he's as slippery a customer as we'll find on the road. He'll hold to nothing. You wait and see.' Picking up with the stranger again, Christian popped the question to him quite unexpectedly.

'Your name's By-ends, isn't it?' He was rather taken aback but put a good face on it. 'Nick-name would be nearer the truth,' he said. 'It's what my critics call me. One of the penalties, I suppose, of being a writer, for that's my profession. The only time I ever deserved it, though, was when I had articles in two papers at once, each with a different political viewpoint. One article was entitled "The Welfare State", and the other, "The Farewell State". And just because I collected a fiver for each of them, they called me By-ends. But what's wrong with earning your living, I can work with anyone, so long as they keep me out of the red.'

'Sounds as if the name suits you, By-ends,' said Christian. 'I don't think we'll be long together before we part company. If you come with us you'll have to be game for all weathers and there'll be no one on the side lines to pay you for doing it. Let Christ be loved but for Himself alone, that's our faith.'

Very soon By-ends began to slacken his pace. He loathed arguments about religion and would sooner walk alone than be disciplined and stimulated by the thoughts of others. Why couldn't people accept him as he was? He was willing to accept them as they were. As he walked along, feeling very hard done by, three men appeared, each riding his own high horse and trailing another. Their steeds cantered imperiously along the dirt track at the roadside and as soon as they approached, By-ends recognised them as three of his former school pals. They proved to be none other than old playboy, Hold-the-world, little titch Money-love, and Scroogy, whose real name was Save-all. By-ends hadn't seen them for years. The sight of them took him back to their boyhood days, when they were all at school under their wily headmaster, Mr. Gripeman. This seat of learning, located in Love-gain of the shire of Coveting, had made its mark in history and to this day many famous names are carved on the gnarled and antiquated desks. 'We owe a lot to old Gripey,' mused By-ends. 'Talk about comprehensive education, he was a man before his time. He didn't waste his breath talking about 1066 and all that. Think of a number and double it, that was his maxim for any problem; then he would show us the means to an end, and how the end could justify it. Clever fellow, he was, and all so practical too. If it were a question of permutations and combinations, then he had us doing practical work on football pools. If it were an I.Q. test, then he'd try us out on Housey-Housey. If it were biology, then he had us studying horses and what we didn't know about horses by the time he'd finished wasn't worth knowing. Studying "form" he called it. He taught us things that would really count when we grew up. The ways and means of making money, that's what he majored in. And today there's hardly a successful business man who wasn't educated at Love-gain.'

The old friends greeted each other with much fraternal back-slapping and loud-speaking. 'The old school tie goes a long way yet,' laughed Hold-the-world. 'Where's your horse these days?' asked Money-love. 'Mortgaged to pay my bets,' said By-ends. 'A pound in your pocket's worth two on the favourite,' grunted Scroogy-Save-all. 'Oh, you were always like that,' answered By-ends. 'Nothing venture, nothing gain.' 'What are you doing any-way?' they began to ask. 'I'm on a pilgrimage,' said By-ends a bit sheepishly. 'On what?' they exclaimed. 'Oh, it's a kind of walk-ing tour for the good of my health,' he explained. 'Thought there was a catch in it,' said Money-love. 'You'd have to get something out of it, that goes without saying. Who are those guys on ahead?' 'Oh, they're pilgrims too,' said By-ends. 'And you're all so high and mighty you can't even walk together?' twitted Hold-the-world, who was a particularly sociable character. 'We tried it,' replied By-ends, 'but they were too narrow-minded, the fanatical type you know, willing to sacrifice everything on the altar of their own inflexible ideas. Quite impossible people, I would say. Unless they're lying on a bed of nails, they don't feel spiritual. It's the old, old story—they can't be happy unless they are being miser-able. They'll be martyrs one day, but what good will that do anybody. Give me my faith in peace and plenty. There's nothing dishonourable in that, and anyway it puts you in a position to really help people.'

'You never spoke a truer word,' applauded Hold-the-world. 'Isn't there a Bible verse which says, "Make hay while the sun shines"? Perhaps it's in Shakespeare after all, I forget, but it's a wise outlook anyway. Fancy losing in sacrifice what you could handle in stewardship. Let's be thankful for God's blessings and God's sunshine; time enough to face His rain when it comes. Didn't Abraham and Solomon get rich through their religion? And Job maintained quite openly that "a good man shall lay up gold as the dust". God's given us all things richly to enjoy, what's the good of courting hardship for the sake of being called faith-ful!'

'I'm with you there,' cried Save-all. 'If I thought this pilgrimage business would cause me the slightest inconvenience I'd be dis-mounting right here in Paradise Boulevard.'

Finding themselves supported with such a consensus of opinion, By-ends began to feel that the four of them could prove more than a match for the simple-minded evangelicals foot-slogging it some way ahead. He began to lay his plan. 'Gentlemen,' he said, 'I'd like your opinion on a certain matter. Take now, for instance, a minister of very moderate means, or for that matter an ordinary tradesman. If they had an opportunity to better themselves financially by acquiring a larger living or a wider round of customers, would you say they were morally wrong, if at least for a while they talked the religious views and political outlook of those people whose patronage they sought to procure?'

'I see what you're getting at,' said Money-love. 'Some people, of course, would call it "playing to the gallery" and others "a bit of back-scratching" but I don't think we should judge another man's servant. If he has a call to these people (speaking of the ministerial profession that is), then he has got to make contact with them somehow and the fact that he even has the opportunity to do so, surely is an act of Providence and not merely fortuitous. Such a situation is bound to exact more from him mentally and nervously. He will have to study more deeply and work more diligently, and this itself will result in his being more industrious. This is surely commendable when one thinks of those country parishes where a man will give one sermon a week to half a dozen people, and apart from an odd funeral and an infrequent wedding, spend the rest of his days with his pipe and his roses. I would say, if a man can get a wider opportunity for his gifts, then he's worth the money, and I myself would not be so hyper-critical as to call him covetous.

As for the tradesman, I guess most are irreligious in the first place, so to become more religious, whatever the reason, I would have thought, was better than being an infidel. Then who can tell, in espousing religion, he may acquire contact with a good family. Surely, he who becomes religious gets a good thing and if by this good acquisition he eventually gets a good wife from a good background, and these good connections result in good custom, isn't it to the good all round? I've not forgotten the wisdom of old Gripey during our Love-gain days, "Look at the end and you'll soon stop worrying about the means." '

'I didn't know you had it in you, Money-love,' they all cried euphorically. 'Now,' said By-ends, 'let's go and tackle the two upstarts before us.' He said this with some confidence and no little satisfaction, smarting as he was under the snub of their 'ill-informed' profession. His friends motioned him to jump in the saddle of the fourth horse, and at a sharp gallop they careered down the dirt-walk, whirling past Christian and Hopeful, with a crack of their whips, then reining their mounts to confront the pilgrims.

By-ends gave a nod to Hold-the-world and with this cue, he put the prearranged question, but Hold-the-world somehow failed to make the question sound so powerful as he did a few moments before.

'Are you serious?' said Christian incredulously, for even a babe in Christ would dismiss such a suggestion. 'If it wasn't right to follow Christ for the loaves and fishes, how contemptible it is to think of making the ministry of His Gospel, a stalking-horse for personal enrichment. This is the outlook of pagans, hypocrites, devils and sorcerers.' They were rather startled at Christian's violent reaction but By-ends looked knowingly at his friends, as much as to say, 'I told you so.'

Christian now went into the attack. 'First of all I said *pagans* because Hamor and Shechem, in the days of Jacob, were willing to be circumcised and adopt Jacob's religion, but there was only one reason behind it, namely that Hamor might get Dinah for himself.

'Then I said *hypocrites* because Christ tells us that the Pharisees only made long prayers and put on solemn faces so that people would count them holy men. In this way they gained the confidence of wealthy widows, obtained their money and at the last left them penniless.

'As for *devils*, you've only to think of Judas. He was religious enough to look at, always going around with Jesus, but he'd got his eye on one thing and that was "the bag" and all that was in it. And you know what happened to him at the last—suicide in time and perdition in eternity.

'Lastly I mentioned *sorcerers*. I was thinking of Simon in the Acts, who said he wanted the Holy Ghost and tried to purchase the power of God to further his influence in the witchcraft business, but Peter gave him short shrift and named him for what he was.

'My conclusion quite simply is this, that if a man will take up religion for what the world can give him, he will, for the same reasons, be ready to abandon it. Judas is the classic example. For money he followed Christ and for money he sold him.'

When Christian finished there was a prolonged and embarrassing silence. The four men still sitting on their high horses were chagrined and speechless. Then Christian turned to Hopeful and said in their presence, 'If these people cannot stand before the sentence of men what will they do before the sentence of God? If they are silenced by vessels of clay what shall they do before flames of fire?'

Leaving them standing, Christian and Hopeful went on their way, which for a short distance continued over a small plain called Ease. This however quickly receded and they made their way into a more mountainous area, scarred by industrial workings. The territory immediately before them had long been disputed by the Satanic authorities, and the mining district they were entering, was really an exploitation of resources annexed, in part, by an agency in Supersex. Christian was thus much on his guard, for they sought to reach the Delectable Mountains and Immanuel's Land without further entanglement or malicious assault. As the road began to mount again, they saw an imposing gateway and, beyond it, well laid-out grounds leading into a vast complex of futuristic installations. The large board at the gate proclaimed the name of the organisation controlling the operation. It was D.E.M.A.S. which was the designation of the venture known as 'The Department for the Extension of Man, the Atom and Society.' Underneath there was a long rigmarole regarding the purposes and aims of the institution, and an invitation to invest capital in the project. The prospects seemed fabulous and Hopeful became thoroughly fascinated with its contents. Even the smallest investment was guaranteed the most astronomical return. Hopeful still had a wad of notes he had brought out of Vanity Fair and he lingered a long while at the notice.

'Don't you realise this is the hill called Lucre,' said Christian, 'and whilst these installations look like the year two thousand, remember, mining has gone on here for centuries and countless workers have lost their lives in the hope of gain. Statistics are no longer kept but the disasters attending their labours are simply horrific. Do you want to join them?' At this Hopeful felt ashamed and wished even the wad of notes he'd retained could be dispensed with, but he held them still. 'Whatever shall I do with this cash?' he groaned. 'Ask your Lord,' replied Christian; but Hopeful hadn't thought of that. 'Don't you remember the words of Paul. *Demas* has forsaken me having loved this present world. Is it only coincidence that his name stands before you?'

Not long after, By-ends and his friends came trotting up to the gate. Whether or not they ever intended going further is open to question, but one perusal of the announcement on the D.E.M.A.S. notice board and they gave the matter of pilgrimage no more thought.

'I have heard something about this concern in the Supersex Finance Bulletins,' said Money-love, 'but I had not realised until now its great potential. I think it might be worth while seeking an interview with one of the directors to get more detailed information. It's the first time I've ridden over this way. I'm generally in the car and take the freeway in the valley.'

'What interests one,' said Save-all, 'is not only the enormous potential on the financial side but the amazing future opening up to those in authority on the anthropological side. Did you read that about the androids, recently. The population explosion is so tremendous that it's going to be quite impossible for everyone to enjoy a high standard of living; yet as man is today, it is equally impossible to expect the "have-nots" to knuckle under and let the "haves" get it all their own way. This is true, of course, whether it be a question of material wealth or political power. The D.E.M.A.S. organisation, however, opens up the possibility of a two-tier humanity. The problems of those who have the burden of wielding wealth and power can be solved by introducing specific antibiotics into the food and water of certain sections of world population, rather like the chlorinating and fluoridising of drinking water now. These new antibiotics, however, would simultaneously sterilise and tranquilise such peoples, so that they would become willing, though not unhappy, workers for the regime. For instance one drug has already shown that, when used on animals, it will permit it to put in an efficient day's work, yet prevent it building up a permanent body of experiences, memories and abilities. Properly modified for the human species this would mean, for instance, that the black population of America would forget their resentments and become amicable to working day by day for The Great Society; or the rank and file in Russia and China would not have to spend time on being indoctrinated but could be induced to work for their political overlords with great docility. Thus instead of wasting energies on all manner of ideological controversy, these energies could be concentrated on the physical tasks of the day. What a labour force! What an efficiency!'

'Yes but if their memories were affected how could they do their job the next day,' By-ends asked. 'I guess it would depend on the dosage,' replied Money-love rather nonchalantly. 'Anyway I'm prepared to put everything I've got into this concern for the development of Man and Society,' and with this, they tethered their horses and walked into the forbidden area. They were immediately halted by a guard, but after a few moments went with him towards the main building. They were really quite excited. 'I'm glad I've saved all,' said Scroogy. 'I'm glad I've set my affections on the right things,' said Hold-the-world. 'I'm delighted I've held to my financial principles,' laughed Money-love. 'Keep the right end in view,' chuckled By-ends, 'and you'll get to the end all right!'

The last Christian and Hopeful saw of them was when they passed through the swing-doors with the guard behind them. As far as is known, the four men never emerged again. They were taken for spies and, it has been said, they became experimental material for 'the android project', which is quite likely, seeing how men with the love of money are so amenable to forgetting all else.

As the pilgrims continued they saw what at first sight looked like a war-memorial but it was a statue of a woman, white as a ghost, standing stiffly in the noonday sun. They paused to read the inscription. 'Remember Lot's wife!' it said. 'A fitting warning,' remarked Christian, remembering Calvary, 'to every pilgrim who covets Sodom's gold.'

# CHAPTER SIXTEEN

# THE GIANT AND THE GAOL

As the hill Lucre faded into the distance, Christian and **Hopeful** began to relax. They were occupied now with the beauty of creation around them, and things that neither had noticed before gripped their attention and filled them with joy. At last they came to a broad sweep of a river, clear as crystal, known to David as 'the river of God' and to John the apostle as 'the water of life'. There they stooped and drank to their heart's content, an elixir indeed, to their tired bodies. They ate, also, of the luscious fruits hanging in great profusion from the trees along its banks. For nights and days they encamped by this living stream until their spirits grew stronger, nourished by the vitamins of heaven. The birds' song in the dawning and every lily of the field spoke of the loving kindness of their Lord. With what ease the flowers grew and blossomed at their feet. Then they remembered the Master's word, 'They toil not, neither do they spin, yet Solomon in all his glory was not arrayed like one of these.' How the lustre of life excels the splendour of office, and the humblest daisy shows more of God than all earth's diadems. Back in the dull grey streets of their unregenerate days, their faces were as listless as the pavements but now God's love and life had brought His radiance to their eyes.

One day as they came to another bend in the river, they saw a little stile by the roadside, with a footpath stretching beyond it into the open country. They surmised from its general direction that at some point it must emerge again to the river. It therefore presented itself as a permissible short-cut to their destination. They felt more especially disposed to take it, as the river overflowed its banks in places, making the going more demanding on certain parts of the road. 'What shall we do?' they asked each other. Christian thought the alternative route held real possibilities. Hopeful, on the other hand, pointed out very logically that if they kept to the river, hard though it might prove, they would at least be able to drink of its waters and, what was more, be sure of reaching their goal, for did not the river of life proceed out of the Throne of God and the Lamb. 'I perfectly agree with you,' said Christian, 'but in this case, I think the situation is just a bit different, because, after all, you can almost see where the footpath comes out. I don't think it would take us more than an hour at the most, so shouldn't we try it?' Hopeful, being just as anxious as Christian to shorten the road, agreed they should. After all, it seemed reasonable enough and if things came to the worst, they could always return to the stile and little or nothing would be lost.

It was already well on in the afternoon when the two men turned into By-Path Meadow, but as they climbed the stile they did not notice that all through the trees and brushwood, both to the right and left, was interwoven a mesh of thick wire netting. In certain places great umbrellas of bamboo foliage dropped low, until the wire and the hard cane stems made an impenetrable curtain. It was only at the stile that it was possible to pass from the river to the meadow. Christian and Hopeful walked blithely on across the open grassland, observed by the unseen eyes of frontier guards stationed in the forest nearby. With each step, the path descended lower and lower until it was well below the level of the river. The ground became marshy and stagnant and the mud clung to their feet in heavy clods. Valuable time was lost as they picked their way slowly from tuft to tuft, and when night fell they found themselves far from the river, and entering on heavily wooded country. It was at this stage, when feeling most despondent, that they saw a faint light in the distance. They went forward as fast as they could and soon caught up with a fellow-traveller, who bore the name Vain-Confidence. In his hand he held a torch which looked as if it needed a new battery.

'Are you going the same way as we are?' enquired Christian. 'Of course,' said Vain-Confidence. 'I would have thought that was self-evident. All progressives, when it comes to it, have the same end in view.' 'But we are going to The Celestial City. Where are you going?' 'Well, I wouldn't exactly use that terminology but I have no doubt we're all heading for the same place. You see at one end of the scale you've got Christianity and at the other end of the scale you've got Communism but our ultimate goal, whether you call it "The Kingdom of God" or "The Classless Society", is, as far as I am concerned, all one and the same thing. I myself am a humanist and have every confidence that man by one means or another will achieve his noble ambitions. You may not concur with me at this stage of the journey but even so, I have met some churchmen who wouldn't disagree with me. In fact they've written books about it.' Sensing no response from Christian and Hopeful, Vain-Confidence looked quite disconcerted.

'You're not fundamentalists, are you?' he asked suspiciously. 'I took it for granted that you must be more liberal than that.

Didn't the frontier officials interview you, before they let you through this area?' Christian and Hopeful looked at each other, shocked beyond measure, but in the light of the torch, now almost out, they could hardly see each other's faces. 'Will your battery last till we get to the river?' asked Christian in anxious tones. 'Oh yes,' said Vain-Confidence, 'it's been like that a long while now. They are long-lasting batteries. Mind you, I get them recharged sometimes and on occasions even get fresh ones. Most philosophic agencies can supply me.' Vain-Confidence went ahead waving his torch for the pilgrims to see the path, but in actual fact showing them nothing and only landing them deeper in the mire of his own confusion. Suddenly a shot rang out in the night. There was a brief cry and Vain-Confidence fell face downward in the mud, his flickering torch marking the place where he fell. He had been murdered by the very people to whom he had pandered. They had used him and now they had done with him. Almost simultaneously a loud-speaker blared through the trees. 'Stand where you are! You are under arrest!' The words of Jeremiah flashed into Christian's mind. 'Set thine heart towards the highway, even the way which thou wentest ... turn again ... turn again!'

'We must get out of here,' he whispered to Hopeful but even as they ran, disaster met them. Running headlong in flight, they fell straight into a forest pool, then from all sides little men with red eyes closed in upon them, pulled them from the water and led them away cold, wet and dispirited, to they knew not where. Although Christian and Hopeful could see nothing, their captors marched them through the dense trees with the greatest facility. Eventually they reached a broad open space and could see the stars. Their friendly twinkle cheered the crestfallen pilgrims, urged on as they were, by the hard muzzles of the guns at their backs. Looming before them was a large cube-like building with no windows and no doors. Still surrounded by red eyes they were hustled down a ramp and at the foot of the decline, confronted with a sheet of steel. It lifted like a portcullis, just for a matter of seconds, then once the party was inside, it closed noiselessly behind them.

For weeks on end, Christian and Hopeful sat in the darkness of a tiny cell. Twice a day the door would open to reveal a pair of red eyes. Two dog biscuits would then be thrown to them and break to pieces, as they fell on the floor. There was also a can of water. After each visit the men would spend the next hour crawling around the tiny room trying to locate the fragments, and feeling the floor for every crumb. Had it not been that in recent days they had been so nourished by the fruit at the river, they would have barely survived their fresh privations. How often the cry escaped their lips, 'As the heart longs for flowing streams, so longs my soul for Thee, O God. My soul thirsts for God, for the living God. When shall I come and behold God's face?' 'It's all my fault,' moaned Christian, 'I led you astray. Oh, Hopeful, what can I say?' 'I don't blame you,' comforted Hopeful, 'I should have stood firm. Now we must stand together. God is able to deliver us. The darkest pit, the fiercest flame are all within the compass of His powers.' 'I'd like to think so,' said Christian, the odours of unbelief beginning to asphyxiate the breathings of his prayers. From the moment they had fallen into the pool in the forest, hardly an hour had passed when they had not been engaged in this kind of conversation, but talking solved no problems. Their dilemma remained the same. By now all sense of day and night had slipped away. The dog biscuits came at irregular intervals and they had no means whereby they could measure the time. They did not even know in whose hands they were held. All was black, and all was hopeless.

Then unexpectedly the door opened and numerous red eyes moved hypnotically around them. Some coarse calico was bound securely round their heads and they felt themselves being led out to another place. They entered what seemed like an elevator and went up several floors. Propelled forward once again, they were finally made to stand completely still. In one swift movement the calico was whipped away. For a moment their eyes were dazzled for they were surrounded by a searing scarlet glow, a kind of vibrating incandescence. 'It's like being in an X-ray machine,' thought Christian and apart from the colour he was not far wrong. They closed their eyes again but everything went green and they recalled those wonderful days when they camped in the deep lush grass along the river. It all seemed so long ago, and now this lurid, hellish glow enveloped them. 'Look at me!' The voice belonged to a big podgy figure of a man dressed in denims. He sat with arms akimbo and rolled up shirt sleeves, as much as to say, 'We're here to deal with you, and we mean business!' Slowly the size of the man dawned on the pilgrims. The red glow had distorted their perspective. They realised there must be fully twenty feet between them and their adversary, not six as they first thought. The person, whoever he was, must be a colossus. All around the wall were pictures of human faces, each larger than life, and gaping on the pilgrims with staring, accusing eyes. They were drawn from various nationalities yet somehow bore a resemblance to each other. Christian tried to think where he had seen the look before. In a flash it came to him—the leer of Apollyon, on that miming puppet in Motel Magnificent. 'Welcome,' said the denimed figure, 'to the State of Despair. As you may know, this is one of the outlying dependencies of the world dominion of our Chairman Satan. This fortress is none other than the world famous Doubting Castle. It is situated in the depths of Despair. Many brilliant scholars, including eminent psychiatrists, have sought to fathom the mystery of this place but have only succeeded in becoming prisoners themselves within its walls. Perhaps I should introduce myself. I am a very great personage. I need no regal robes to sustain my office. My own strength upholds me. I work night and day and at one time or another affect all persons living in the earth. I reign also in part of Hades, filling the thoughts of spirits there. I am Giant Despair, Governor of Doubting Castle and administrator of the whole realm this side of Supersex.' Behind his head ran a big slogan in heavy black letters.

> I submit to no man,
> but
> all men submit to me.

He now continued his speech. 'During these last few weeks you have been incarcerated in this fortress consequent on your being apprehended in our frontier region. You will receive no trial here. Things are quite different in The State of Despair. In Supersex you could have a jury and conduct your own defence, but here there is no defence. We just deal with you as we think fit and whatever you say, and however much you yearn for freedom, makes no difference. Everything there was public but the State of Despair conducts all things in camera. No one sees you here, and you yourselves will see nothing beyond this institution. You are, I repeat, in the depths of Despair. As to this place there is a way in, but there is no way out. You have not been brought here today to open your case. It will never be opened and that means, of course, it will never be closed. We felt it was time you should know your position. The first cell in which you have been existing—I won't say living—is situated in our "Hope Deferred Wing". We have your files from the City of Destruction, Fort Lust and Supersex. All have been forwarded. Vain-Confidence was shot for trying to break the blackout in the dehumanised zone. We used him to trap you, that was all, and you in your own conceits walked right into our clutches. Your only "hope" now is to join the ranks of the hopeless. When you have been long enough in the State of Despair, you will diminish in stature and your eyes, too, will turn that bloodshot hue. Then if you yield to us, you can become one of our little men, who run in the dark forest and lure other deserters into our hands. Would you like to make a gesture in our favour or must I pass you on to our second wing, "Hope dismayed"?' Christian and Hopeful stood resolute. 'We will not give place to you, no, not for an hour,' they cried. The giant-sized man did not argue with them but rose from his seat and left the room. The red glare faded, until the blackness closed around them. Silent and alone they stood. Then the red eyes came and strong hands grasped them. Back, back, they went, as if traversing the long and twisting corridors of the mind. Down and down they stumbled through 'labyrinthine ways' until they sat again in the darkness of the cell. It was a long time before either of them spoke. Was there anything to say?

Following the initial session with the prisoners, Giant Despair reported, together with his officials, to the head of The Satanic Advisory Bureau, resident in the State. In the overall Satanic administration, the dependencies, of course, were always subject to direction from the central policy-making body. Thus for all that Giant Despair might say of himself, he was controlled behind the scenes by the local agents of the Central Government.

Only in this way could the Satanic concepts be implemented at all levels of society and through all the dominions. Without such a system of control, local civil servants, especially those stationed near the river of God, might be influenced by the powerful forces at their door to act contrary to Central Government policy. Giant Despair was the big official who administered this particular State but he was secretly briefed and indeed controlled, when it came to it, by the Satanic agents. They were, so to speak, 'his nagging wife' behind the scenes and ruled the roost.

At the committee meeting, Giant Despair came under fire. He had to give a full account regarding the circumstances of the pilgrim's arrest and the nature of their incursion. The trap had worked, but whether or not he should have disposed of Vain-Confidence at that stage was brought into question. He could have been used again before that became necessary. However, that was a small matter and he had done well to capture two such determined pilgrims as Christian and Hopeful. Up to this point everything was basically satisfactory. The big deficiency was the absence of progress in the thought-condition of the prisoners. It looked as if they would need some help before they abandoned their faith. The trouble with physical violence was that it tended, with certain types, to stiffen resistance and hinder reform. If applied, it must be done unofficially. On this note the meeting closed. Giant Despair, following his instructions, consulted now with the Chief Warder. 'Leave it to me, sir. No trouble at all,' was the ominous reply.

The next thing the pilgrims knew was their cell flooded with light. At the same instant, four men armed with truncheons charged in upon them. Being unaccustomed to such brilliance, the two men screwed up their eyes. 'Don't make faces at me,' shouted the leader. 'I'm not making faces at anyone, it's the light,' replied Christian. 'What's wrong with the light? Thought you liked the light! Isn't our Chairman sometimes called an angel of light? Anyway what are you grinning at? Funny is it? We'll soon fetch the smile off your face.' With that, one of the men swore and the two pilgrims fell to the ground beneath a hail of blows. Three days later, when Christian and Hopeful once again appeared before Giant Despair, they could hardly stand.

'Well,' he began, 'now you've had three restful days to think things over, I trust your deferred hopes are making you sick enough to be sensible. It is so absurd to insist on your convictions. Look at the faces of these men around you. They represent the combined wisdom of all the progressive forces in the world. Surely you don't think you know better than they what is best for humanity. Don't imagine for one moment that we can go on feeding you with the best of dog biscuits indefinitely. Dogs can be trained but if you lack even canine sense, we shall treat you like the worms you are.' The two men were sagging even as he spoke. 'Stand up,' shouted one of the red-eyed midgets. 'What's wrong with you?' asked the Giant. 'Your men almost beat us to death!' answered Christian. 'You lie!' roared the Giant. 'Our staff is more enlightened than to use corporal punishment. Anyway they wouldn't do it without my orders!' Christian extended his hands and arms to show the bruises and broken skin. Faced with the proof, Giant Despair passed the matter off, saying lightly, 'Hm, it looks as if they've had a go at you this time. What you non-persons must understand is that some of these warders have suffered a lot at the hands of your God. They feel they've been deceived and abandoned by Him, with the result when they get the chance, they take it out on people like you. The only thing I can suggest is that you make a bold decision about your future, then we can discuss what work you are going to do.'

Hopeful, stirred to the depths by this innuendo, looked the Giant squarely in the eyes and said, 'Giant Despair, in this matter you will despair before we will, for we rejoice in the hope of the glory of God.'

These words seemed to clinch the whole matter. 'Remove these prisoners to "Hope Dismayed",' ordered the Giant and within a minute of that command, they found themselves under guard, traversing the grounds of the strange institution. The fresh air on their cheeks gave a brief sense of escape from their four walls and filled them with new vigour but the exhilaration quickly passed. They looked up but there was no sun in the sky, only a weird twilight all around them. 'Is it dawn or dusk?' ventured Christian, to one of the guards. 'Nightfall,' he snapped back, 'always nightfall. There are no more daybreaks for people like you.' A large pyramid filled the sky to the east. 'Do you see that?' said the officer. 'Well that's the final wing if you survive in "Hope Dismayed".' 'And what do you call that?' asked Hopeful. '"Hope Destroyed,"' came the gruff reply. 'Take a good look at it. That's where your remains will come at the last,' he added cryptically. 'It is a monument to human progress.'

'But it's not finished,' remarked Christian, observantly. 'No, it's not finished. There's always more to achieve,' explained the official. 'Don't you mean that man is always falling short of his ambition?' said Hopeful. 'You'd better cut out the sarcasm,' cautioned the guard. 'The reason they don't finish it is because they are always widening the base.' 'Isn't the task hopeless then?' questioned Christian. 'Not at all. Once we get the proportions right it will automatically come to completion.' 'And what will those be?' 'Six by six by six,' he answered carefully. 'Then the top will reach to heaven.' 'Do you really think so?' asked Christian. 'The thoughts of our Chairman say so,' he replied convincingly, 'and is your thought a match for his? Look on your left now. There is the Acid Pool, or if you like the Acid Test. It is for those who refuse to conform with the Satanic mind in "Hope Dismayed". If men are not malleable, then they prove soluble. The precipitate is eventually dried and once it hardens, it becomes a kind of human coral. This is then cut into blocks and used in the building of the Pyramid of Culture you have just seen. Just as coral is a vast cemetery of creatures yet a thing of beauty, so the remains of what must be millions of reactionaries form the material of this great cultural edifice.' He paused a moment, then said proudly, 'Truly a lasting memorial to Satan's will for progress! Who could have conceived such a majestic project but our Chairman? If you were one of our citizens you would love him. His thought extends over the entire world and releases millions from their agelong bondage to a holy Creator. He would release you if you wished!' 'Your chairman was a murderer from the beginning,' flamed Christian. 'He is a liar and the father of it.

K 145

Whom he deceives will share his doom.' 'You speak very audaciously, prisoner,' warned the officer. 'And well we might,' added Hopeful, 'for we know in Whom we have believed.'

The party reached an enclosure, in which was located a huge plastic sphere, reminiscent of the barrage balloons of World War II. At the entrance they read the ominous words 'Hope Dismayed'. They were directed now through a flap in a cubicle situated at its base. It was apparently self-sealing and they waited a few moments wondering what would happen, but another flap opened before them and they stepped from the cubicle, which was an air-lock, into the interior of the sphere itself. It was an extraordinary sensation standing at the base of the giant globe, all alone in an empty world, without people, without things and, humanly speaking, without hope. The vast interior was suddenly filled with the sound of a single word. It came from a concealed loud-speaker. 'March!' said the voice, 'March!' Instinctively the pilgrims began to move, and as they did so, the vast sphere started to revolve around them. 'Faster! Faster!' shouted the voice. Nervously they quickened their pace, until the globe gathered momentum. 'Left turn,' commanded the voice. 'Left! Left! Always left! Now keep marching!' As they turned, the globe slipped under them on its new diameter but wherever they went and whatever they did, they remained where they were. Christian's mind went back to an old-fashioned mill he once visited on holiday at Sinking Sands. He remembered the donkey treading the waterwheel, hour after hour. Hopeful thought of Samson, minus his eyes, turning the millstone for his Philistine masters. Was this where disobedience had brought them? 'If you don't march, they'll trample you beneath their feet. In every land our men are marching, from Memphis to Moscow, from Paris to Peking, from Cairo to Capetown, from London to Los Angeles. Marching, marching, from city to city and nation to nation, the working men, the hungry men, the white men, the coloured men, the angry men, the lazy and the crazy men, the student and the prudent men, harnessed in action, geared to the wheels of the cortège of progress. You must move. Yes, move with the times and move with the masses. All is revolving, evolving, involving. You cannot stand still. You must hate, to create! Burn down, to build! Resist, to release! Kill, to renew! You must not hesitate. You must participate. It is the wheel of life. It is the cycle of existence. It is the vicious circle. March or you die!'

'Am I mad?' asked Christian of Hopeful, 'What are these voices?' 'I hear them too,' said Hopeful, 'and feel urged to obey them.' 'The air has changed,' remarked Christian. 'How right you are,' came the voice. 'This is our Atmos-Sphere. Hotter, colder, lighter, heavier, clearer or mistier, you'll change as we change it. This is our "man conditioner". Soon you'll be glad to march; to do what we say and think what we will, in your abject despair.' A chill of horror ran through the pilgrims. They tried desperately to slacken their pace but the great balloon-like world around them would not respond and they found their legs caught up in a terrifying acceleration. Again they tried but they lost their balance. The blood drained from their faces. 'It is the way to the pool,' moaned Christian. 'And the pyramid,' groaned Hopeful. Suddenly, as if from a world beyond the world, there came the sweet remembrance of that sentence on the Hill. It was the truth of the Shining Ones. 'Oh Hopeful,' cried Christian, 'I believe in miracles! All God's promises are woven through my pilgrim's coat and in the lining are the hidden weapons of His Word. See, here is one,' and he lifted a needle of truth, sharp as a two-edged sword. 'And what is more,' he shouted, 'I'm going to use it!' 'Oh, no, you won't!' blared a voice. 'Oh, yes, I will!' And in that Name no spirit can resist, he plunged it in the palpable texture of the Atmos-Sphere. A harsh and ragged tearing rent the fabric. God's own fresh air rushed in. The pilgrims' strength immediately revived, and in a flicker of an eyelid, out they ran, borne as on eagles' wings. At once they set their faces to the river, and as they went were astonished to see nothing but a small grey cube of stone on the ground. It bore an epitaph. 'Here lies the remains of one, Giant Despair, who exists for all who believe him but who dies to all who defy him.'

'Did we imagine it all?' asked Hopeful, 'those four dark walls, that vicious circle, that dread infernal triangle, that awful pyramid?' 'I don't know,' said Christian, 'but what I do know is that the devil is real and so are the promises of God. Look! There's the River,' and as they reached it, the sunshine broke upon the waters and all their shadows fled.

Ere they left the scene, they carved in the bark of a tree the following words:

*Beware of the Bypath—Beware! Beware!*
*The Dungeons of Doubt are the haunts of Despair.*

# CHAPTER SEVENTEEN

# HILLTOP AND SHEER DROP

EMERGING from their nightmare experience, it was especially invigorating to move forward in the fragrance and splendour of the early morning. Their way lay now through the uplands known as The Delectable Mountains and before their eyes stretched broad arable valleys filled with ripening crops and laden orchards. From the hillsides gushed sparkling springs and they hastened to wash themselves in the pure waters and slake their thirst from the healing streams. As they lifted their eyes to the hills, they could see, on the gentler slopes, large flocks of sheep grazing slowly through the grass and here and there were some shepherds, eyeing their charges, conversing together and looking away to the glorious vistas the heights afforded. When, after some hours, they reached the topmost point, they met a group of these faithful men and were glad to talk with them as they rested a while.

'We would like to know,' said the pilgrims, 'to whom these hills belong.' 'These mountains,' replied the shepherds, 'in their entire length, together with all their adjacent valleys, pertain to Immanuel's Land. On a fine day, from this very ridge you can glimpse the shining city, where He is both light and sun. The sheep are His also, purchased with His own blood, for as you must know, He gave His life for them.'

'Is it far then to the City?' enquired Christian.

'Far enough for those who reach it, but too far for those who fail,' came the strange reply.

'And what about the road? Is it good from now on?'

'Good enough for the good,' they answered, 'but bad enough for the bad.'

The words of these country people sounded quaint in the ears of townsfolk like Christian and Hopeful, but they carried their own wisdom and made them think. At last Christian said, 'There's just one other question we would like to ask. Is there any place across the mountains where we might spend the night?'

'Why certainly there is,' said the shepherds, 'our task is not only to tend the sheep on the hills but to care for all God's pilgrims passing through, for the one is the symbol of the other. "Be not forgetful to entertain strangers," Immanuel has told us. Perhaps we should introduce ourselves. Our names are Knowledge, Experience, Watchful and Sincere.'

The interest they showed in the pilgrims was so genuine that Christian and Hopeful were hard put to it, to answer all their questions concerning their adventures on the road. Their story brought smiles of approval to the kind faces of these shepherd-hearted men and, at times, expressions of praise to God escaped their lips. 'Surely He keepeth the feet of His Saints,' they said. 'Now you must come to our tents for it is already late,' and so they constrained the pilgrims to spend the night in their company and to refresh themselves with the food of the flock. 'Do you have many pilgrims pass this way?' enquired Hopeful. 'Oh yes,' they replied, 'especially young ones. They love to come to these parts. In the summer months as many as a hundred will pitch their tents beside ours and stay for a whole week. Then we spend time with them and have much fellowship together, as we focus their thoughts on the Lord of the Hill, and show them the beauties of Immanuel's Land and point them onward to the City of God. They always leave stronger than when they came.'

The day following, the shepherds asked the pilgrims whether they would like to walk with them on some of their high places. It was a breathtaking experience with far visions and great distances on all sides. First they were escorted to a pinnacle of rock, called Error. The further side of the cliff was most precipitous and the pilgrims looked down a sheer drop of at least a thousand feet. At the foot of the scree below were the skeletons of not a few who had fallen over the edge. 'The bones of Hymenaeus and Philetus are down there,' explained Knowledge. 'They erred on the doctrine of the resurrection, you remember. Their fate is a lasting warning to all who tread these crumbling cliffs, for though a man may stand high in his own opinion, in a moment he can be dashed to pieces.'

From this awesome promontory, they were taken on to another peak called Caution. From this new point of vantage the pilgrims could see a bend in the river which enclosed some open country stretching back into a hinterland of dense forest. As they scrutinised the landscape below them, they became sensitive to the fact that this was the scene of their experiences in The State of Despair, 'Do you see a kind of cemetery in that forest clearing?' said Experience. 'Yes, I do,' said Christian. 'And I think I see some people there too,' said Hopeful. 'They seem to be groping around as if trying to find a way out.' 'You're quite correct,' confirmed Experience. 'They are of that number whom Giant Despair keeps in the dark so long that they become blind. The result is that even when his pressure declines they still can't find their way to the river.' As the shepherd said these words, he looked Christian and Hopeful straight in the face, until their cheeks flushed with shame, and tears started in their eyes. They had not told the shepherds about *that* adventure. 'I understand,' said Experience, 'but God has been gracious to you; only remember His Word, "He that wandereth out of the way of understanding, shall remain in the congregation of the dead."'

They descended now into a deep canyon until they were brought to the brink of a crevice in the rock. They looked down into it and although they could see nothing, all the time the ground was shaking, and from the bowels of the earth came the noise of rumblings and the scent of fire. Christian grew apprehensive and would have left at once had not Sincere begun to speak. 'This,' he said quietly, 'is a direct route to the Lake of Fire which burns for ever. Many a hypocrite has slipped down there, to be lost for ever.' It sounded so terrible that Hopeful asked fearfully, 'But who do you mean?' 'Oh, people like Esau who sold his birthright for a bowl of soup and folk like Judas Iscariot who said he cared for the poor, then sold his Master for thirty pieces of silver. And many there are who will yet disappear down this fearful shaft and one reason is that, failing to acknowledge its existence, they are not careful to avoid it.' 'You mean this will happen to actual pilgrims?' 'No, not to pilgrims indeed, but of course it's possible to have the name of a pilgrim but the heart of a demon. God judges us for what we are, not what we say we are. No doubt you have heard that before.' At these words Christian and Hopeful were quite disturbed. 'But, ostensibly, these people of whom you speak were pilgrims like we are.' 'That's what it looks like,' said Sincere, 'but time has a way of proving reality.' 'But are such people lost eternally?' asked Hopeful. 'They unquestionably are,' replied Sincere, 'if the life of God is not in them. Did not James say that faith without works is dead?' Hopeful was quiet a moment then he said, 'We need the strength of Him who is stronger than the strong.' 'Yes,' said Sincere, 'and having received it, you ought to use it. But fear not, God has said, "They that trust Him shall *never* be desolate."'

'Oh, let us go forward,' said the pilgrims. 'And so you shall,' said the shepherds, 'but first you must come with us to the beacon called "Clear".' As they mounted to fresh heights, Watchful stepped forward and handed the pilgrims a telescope. 'Now,' he said, 'do you see that blaze of light on the horizon?' Christian took the telescope, focussed it carefully, then suddenly exclaimed, 'I see a gate, shining like gold in the sun. You have a look, Hopeful.' 'I see it too,' shouted Hopeful. 'It is the gate of Heaven itself,' said Watchful, 'and beyond it lies the City you seek.'

With these words the shepherds sent them on their way. Knowledge and Experience gave them fresh directions for the route and Watchful and Sincere warned them of the Flatterer. 'He's bound to meet you,' they said, 'and whatever you do, don't be caught napping on the Enchanted Ground.'

# CHAPTER EIGHTEEN

# IGNORANCE AND ARROGANCE

An hour or two on the road and they found themselves at the foot of The Delectable Mountains, only this time on the heavenward side. All the darkness of their earlier encounters was forgotten and they sped on with fresh enthusiasm towards their journey's end. They had not gone very far, however, before they became conscious of alien territory to their left, dominated by a town with numerous skyscrapers, all reaching for the clouds. It bore no relation whatever to the route they were following, but they did notice a small track joining the road and they wondered if this were some secret path, trodden illicitly by citizens of the township in an attempt to join the Pilgrim Way. It was just at this point they caught up with an energetic young man called Ignorance.

'And where have you come from?' asked Christian in astonishment.

'Oh, from the City of Conceit, over there,' replied Ignorance. 'It's a great place. Have you never visited it? A proud city if ever there was one! Why, everyone feels proud of everything, yes, even of "not being proud"! All the residents must have the best and if you ask them, most would say they *have* the best and *are* the best. They insist on the best scholarship, the best positions, the best houses, the best furniture, the best clothes, the best cars, the best schools, the best hotels and the best amusements. Yes, even the best churches and the best preachers. Nothing less than the best will do for the best people. It is a place where everyone is un-bettered, at least in their own minds. Once they *are* bettered though, they become embittered. Then they'll go in for the best opinions and what fights there are about that!'

'If it's a city full of the best people,' interrupted Christian, 'then surely it must be the best of cities?'

'So it is, for the most part,' hedged Ignorance, 'but as I've talked to people there, I get the feeling, to be quite frank with you, that it's not quite good enough for me.'

'And are you bound for the Celestial City?' enquired Christian.

'I am indeed,' replied Ignorance, 'for the best of earth can hardly compare with the best of heaven.'

'But do you think you'll get in? The city you've come from, you say, is not good enough for *you*, but think of the City to which you go. Are you good enough for *it*? Have you any credentials to show at the Gate?'

At this, Ignorance became rather aggressive and even more self-assertive.

'My answer will be, of course, coming from where I do, that I've done my best. After all, what more can the Almighty expect from me? I've lived a good life. I've paid twenty shillings in the pound. I've attended church and I've harmed no one; and in leaving my home-town of Conceit, surely I have aspirations over and above the best of men.'

'But you've failed to come here by way of the Cross. If you will not stoop in repentance and faith and enter by the little white gate in the wall, there is no hope of entering the gate of God's City,' explained Christian. 'The briefing we carry says, without question, it's "not by works of righteousness that we have done but by His own mercy, God saves us".'

'Gentlemen,' said Ignorance, with exaggerated courtesy. 'I haven't the slightest idea what you mean. It is obvious your religion is quite different from mine and I really don't appreciate interrogation by strangers. I suggest you go your way and I'll go mine. As for the gate in the wall, nothing would be more ridiculous than to start searching for it now. It must be miles from here. Anyway, from the City of Conceit we have this pleasant leafy lane that gives us access to this very road on which we're walking. If, having started later, I have yet preceded you, am I not your superior?' 'Sounds like Hypocrisy and his helicopter all over again,' thought Christian. 'The more ignorant people are, the more arrogantly they speak.' Seeing the man was wise in his own eyes, Christian breathed to Hopeful. 'You know, I honestly believe there is more hope for a fool than for him.' 'Perhaps one should not talk further with him just now,' suggested Hopeful, 'he really can't take it from us.' So the two pilgrims went on their way and Ignorance chose to walk some distance behind them.

As they went along, the path became shaded for a while by overhanging rocks and it was at this narrower point that they saw a band of seven youths coming towards them. They were a ferocious looking crowd, armed with iron bars, bicycle-chains, knives and sawn-off shotguns. With them was a man with his mouth gagged and his hands tied behind his back. 'We're going to the canyon,' shouted one with a foul leer on his face. 'This man here was a pilgrim but we've made him a comrade. He's one of our fellow-travellers now and where we go, he goes. If our hands weren't so full, we'd be grabbing you too.'

'That man was a pilgrim in name only, you desperate cut-throats,' shouted Christian defiantly. 'I know who your prisoner is, though he won't show his face. His name is Turn-away from the City of Apostasy. No wonder he's fallen among thieves!' As they watched them disappear down the road, they saw round the neck of the prisoner a placard bearing the words 'Wanton professor and damnable apostate'. 'Once we place ourselves beyond grace,' said Christian to Hopeful, 'we fall into the hands of the wicked. In fact, seeing that gang reminds me of what happened to Little Faith. Did you never hear the story?'

'No,' said Hopeful, 'but let's hear it now.' So Christian began. 'Sincere was the village where Little Faith lived, and not far from his home was a street called Dead Man's Lane. In actual fact, it turned into the village from Broadway Gate. It was in that lane he met one of these gangs, only there were no more than three men in it, as it so happened. Their names had already been published in the local press, so Little Faith knew who they were. The gang was made up of three brothers, Faint-Heart, Mistrust and Guilt. Anyway, when they met Little Faith that evening, the light was almost gone. I guess they thought they'd get away in the darkness. "Where's your wallet?" demanded Faint-Heart. Little Faith held back trying to gain time, but Mistrust darted his hand beneath his jacket and snatched it away. Then Little Faith shouted, "Thief! Thief! Stop Thief!" But Guilt gave him one club over the head with his cudgel and Little Faith fell flat in the road. In the goodness of God, Great Grace came marching into Dead Man's Lane that very moment and, hearing his footsteps, they made a run for it and got away. So it was they missed his real valuables which he kept sewn in his breast-pocket, close to his heart.'

'He'd be glad about that then,' said Hopeful.

'Well, you'd have thought so but you know, he was for ever brooding over what had happened to him. He just couldn't forget that they'd taken his wallet and gashed his head open and although it healed up perfectly, he was like a dog constantly licking his wounds. The result was, the inestimable value of what he still possessed never dawned on him all the rest of his pilgrimage.'

'I'm quite sure I'd have reacted differently from that,' said Hopeful with confidence, 'and as for that gang they wouldn't have found me such a sitting target. If I couldn't have tricked them, I'd have fought them tooth and nail.'

'Yes, we're all so strong until faced with our own weakness,' said Christian. 'David was a real warrior until one fine day he saw

Bathsheba on the rooftop, then his passion tore him to pieces. Hezekiah was outstanding in faith when the Assyrians besieged his city, but later, when the Babylonians came with a princely gift, he proudly showed them everything and that was the beginning of the end. As for Peter, he talked just like you. "Lord, I will lay down my life for your sake!" "Will you...?" said his Master, but the warning fell on deaf ears. It wasn't long before he was cursing and swearing in the firelight and all because a girl asked him a simple question about Jesus. Say what you like, Hopeful, I've been in too many a fight to talk about being a hero or sporting my manhood. Only the Manhood of my Master will make me victor now. Our ignorance, remember, can quickly turn to arrogance, too. God is no respecter of persons and those who exalt themselves he is able to abase.'

# CHAPTER NINETEEN

# THE WORLD OF WOLVES

CHRISTIAN and Hopeful's conversation was brought to an unexpected end, for they were both suddenly confronted with a large
and elaborate hoarding, standing astride the road. It was really a
most lavish affair, painted in black lacquer and brilliantly illuminated. Whoever had erected it was taking no chances. Every
pilgrim must see it who passed that way. At the particular point
where it stood, the road divided into two lanes, both going in the
same direction. The two men looked at the hoarding and then at
each other. In large attractive lettering the invitation was
blazoned before them:

THIS WAY FOR TRANQUIL—
FOR THE SUN-FILLED LIFE!
FOR THE NERVE-STILLED LIFE!
FOR THE FREE-WILLED LIFE
OF TRANQUIL!

'I don't think we can be far from heaven now,' said Hopeful.
'You're right,' agreed Christian, 'you'd think Paradise was just
round the corner from what that notice says.' Beneath the main
announcement ran the words:

A golden shore for the men who have more;
A haven secure for the men who endure.

'It certainly seems to refer to us, wouldn't you think so?'
queried Hopeful. 'Well you would,' said Christian, 'and the
direction is all the same, whichever lane you take.' So they quickened their pace and followed the arrow. The rest of the hoarding,
however, was devoted to certain captions announcing sundry
foods, beverages and journals. The pilgrims, having their minds
on higher things, did not particularly notice these, but had they
done so, their suspicions might well have been aroused.
One read: 'BETTER-FARE for the men who dare.'
Another: 'Treat yourself to A PILGRIM'S PINT—You deserve
it.'

And yet another: 'Superior people read THE SUPERIOR PEEP-HOLE—With Celestial News and Celestial Views—for Ex-Terres-trials.'

Whilst at the foot of the signboard ran the words:

TRANQUIL'S A MUST—
FOR THOSE WHO TRUST

But the pilgrims were well down the road by now and would have been happy enough had the road not developed a continuous curve. This made them uneasy for a time, but when at last they rounded a bank of flowers and saw an entrancing lakeside of golden sands and silver waters, all seemed well after all. 'What a magnificent place!' cried Hopeful. 'Not Paradise itself, I suppose, but surely the next best thing this side of heaven.' 'Yes, it's certainly beautiful,' said Christian, with equal surprise.

They now approached the sandy bay and a streamer fluttered across the road bearing the slogan: 'You owe it to yourself to rest a while.'

'There's no doubt about it,' they both concurred, 'we've come a long way, our legs are tired, and it will be just wonderful to have an hour on the beach before pressing on. At the entrance to the strand an elderly man, with a walrus-moustache and a commissionaire's uniform, approached them courteously. Apparently there was an admission charge, no doubt with a view to maintaining the atmosphere of the place. He clicked out two green-coloured tickets. Hopeful found some coins he still had over from Supersex, and paid what was asked. They were just about to go in, when the old man clicked out two more tickets, red ones this time. 'It's the service charge,' he casually explained, as if these words would solve all the doubts of his patrons. They were a bit perplexed but they could hardly refuse, having already purchased the green tickets, so they paid the extra, and in they went. They stood now on the open promenade. Everything was excellently kept; not one piece of litter on the ground. The sands were scrupulously clean and even the waves seemed to break at regular intervals! 'Let's go down on the shore,' said Christian with boyish enthusiasm. They approached the stone steps and were about to descend when another little man with a walrus-moustache and commissionaire's uniform came towards them. He spoke with great deference. 'You wish to visit the beach, gentlemen?' 'That's right,' said Hopeful. 'Then there's just a small charge we make,' he said. 'It keeps it from being too crowded, you know.' The pilgrims looked about. There was not a soul in sight. 'But your season's over now, isn't it?' asked Christian. 'Oh, no,' said the commissionaire, *'we* serve in all seasons.' 'But don't these red and green tickets admit us to the sands?' they remonstrated. 'Not really,' he replied, 'they have to do with admission to the general promenade area.' The pilgrims gasped but not wishing to cause a disturbance by arguing with the man, they paid what he asked and sunk gratefully into two luxurious deck chairs. Yes, everything was first class and now they would try to get a little sleep in the afternoon sunshine. Tranquil was like a dream. Palms flourished to the water's edge. Their long stems leaned gracefully towards the sparkling water, and their feathered fronds caressed the sands in the gentle breeze. No sooner had the pilgrims dropped off to sleep than they were awakened by a voice saying, 'Excuse me, gentlemen.' As they opened their eyes, they saw to their astonishment yet another old man with a walrus-moustache and a commissionaire's uniform. 'It's just the charge for the deck chairs, sir. So sorry to disturb you. The daily rate is...' 'But we're only here for an hour or two,' cut in Christian. 'I'm afraid it doesn't make any difference, sir. It's a flat rate for the day.' 'But that's preposterous!' 'You'll excuse me, sir, but I'm only obeying the orders of the management, if you have any complaints, I'll gladly...' 'Give him the money, Hopeful,' said Christian, resignedly. 'What can we do?' The old man trudged away across the sands and the pilgrims were soon fast asleep once more. It must only have been five minutes, though, before another voice awoke them. 'Excuse me, sirs...' 'Whatever can it be now,' grumbled Hopeful and turning towards the sound, said rather irritably, 'Yes, what is it?' 'I am just enquiring of our patrons,' said yet another old man with a walrus-moustache and commissionaire's uniform, 'as to whether they will require the afternoon tea, or high tea à la carte?' As he said this, he put into their hands an extravagantly produced menu card, which looked more like a brochure for a new car than the intimation of a meal. Christian gave it a cursory glance and noticing one course would cost them more than a refugee's food for a month, handed it back to the commissionaire, and said, 'Thank you very much but we shall not be taking tea. We need to get on our way.' 'Very good sir,' said the commissionaire, most dutifully, and plodded away through the sand. As Christian's eye followed him, unpleasant memories of The Pilgrim's Rest began to come over him. To make it worse, at that very moment the sun disappeared behind a cloud and a roll of distant thunder came somewhere from behind the palm trees. 'Looks as if it's going to be stormy after all,' said Christian. 'Oh I don't know,' said Hopeful, who was beginning to enjoy himself; but just then a gust of wind caught up the sand and sent it scurrying around their feet. 'Let's try and sit it out,' he said rather grimly, but a cold current of air came sweeping along the mysterious coast, and on the lake the calm waters already flecked with white, gave a sense of impending disaster. Without speaking, they rose simultaneously. Something was wrong and they had to be going. They reached the steps leading to the promenade and one of the old men was standing there, rather pathetically, with cap in hand. 'It's the kind of place,' said Christian, trying to forestall further expenditure, 'where you don't give gratuities; it's all included.' 'But how can we pass him?' whispered Hopeful. They were too close now to say any more. 'Trust you enjoyed your afternoon, gentlemen,' the commissionaire ventured, and his walrus-moustache drooped so mournfully that Hopeful just had to submit. He dropped his last coin into the man's cap, and they passed on.

At the turnstile the ubiquitous officials of this extraordinary establishment were still to be faced. 'Just before you leave, gentlemen,' said a commissionaire, 'may I see your tickets?' They fumbled for the green ones. 'No, the red ones,' he said patiently. 'So sorry to detain you.' But Hopeful could only find the yellow ones for the deck chairs. 'You should have had a blue one for the restaurant,' he said. 'They would have collected that and clipped the red one.' 'But we didn't take tea,' explained Christian, 'we needed to be on our way.' 'Very good, gentlemen, in that case there will be just the minimum charge.' 'You mean you want more money from us?' protested Hopeful. 'Surely not!' 'Well, of course not,' said the commissionaire good humouredly. 'It doesn't mean any more to me, but as employed here, I have to carry out my duty. Perhaps you didn't realise, but it's generally anticipated, that patrons will frequent the restaurant, though of course there's no obligation. Should this service not be required, however, there is still a minimum charge. It protects both the customers and ourselves. Otherwise people would just make a convenience of the place.'

'Well, we are not paying it,' said Christian bluntly. 'Then you will appreciate, sirs, I have no option but to call the manager.' The minutes ticked by and Christian grew desperate. Yes, he'd force the turnstile or jump it if necessary. He was just about to do so, when the manager arrived. He was a man with a 'boozy' face but dressed in an exceptionally well tailored suit. 'Well,' he said, 'and what's all the trouble about?' 'Your commissionaires have done nothing but ask us for money from the moment we came in,' shouted Christian rather abusively, 'and we've paid enough for one afternoon.' 'But Mr. Christian,' said the manager, 'this is the golden shore for those who have more. A man of your calibre surely appreciates that. But if there's going to be trouble and you want to be nasty, I'll need to call A-POL.' And he looked them straight in the face. The mention of A-POL so obviously affected Christian that the manager became suspicious and reached for the telephone.

'That's all right now,' spoke a clear voice from the other side of the turnstile and they all turned to see who it was. 'The matter's settled.' There was a ring of silver on the counter. The commissionaire somehow released the turnstile. The pilgrims slipped through, and the manager was left standing before he could take further action. 'A close shave,' breathed Christian. 'Yes, I have met the demands,' said the stranger of beatific splendour, as his gaze pierced their hearts. His eyes had love in them but flashed like a flame of fire. Unnerved by his powerful demeanour and overawed by their sudden deliverance from the mesh of their self-induced circumstances, they offered no resistance to his handling for he gripped them tightly, and led them forcibly back to the parting of the ways. Both were silent and inwardly pained. His relentless hold was inescapable, in fact almost brutal. Would he never let them go? He made them pause at the foot of the hoarding. The white lights had been extinguished and the flamboyant captions looked flat and uninteresting in their dull black framework. He pointed to one corner, where a tiny plate was fixed to the wood. It bore the inscription, 'This is the Property of The Flatterer's Advertising Company.'

'Were you not warned by the shepherds?' he asked. 'Yes, but we thought he was a person, not a hoarding!' 'Hoardings are erected by persons,' said the stranger. 'Beware of the great persuaders. There is death and money in them all. Maybe you do feel sore but if you would keep your hand in the hand of God, you wouldn't need to be gripped like this. Don't be surprised and don't be resentful. Have you forgotten His Word which says, "Whom the Lord loves, he chastens"? He would have you partakers of His holiness, not the helpless prey of a world of wolves. Did you not realise, on the Tranquil beach, that your backs were again towards Zion?'

They walked on a little further and after the stranger had arranged a night's lodging at one of the King's hostels, he bade them farewell, the unfeigned thanks of the pilgrims ringing in his ears.

# CHAPTER TWENTY

# FALL-OUT! FALL-IN!

THE next day everything seemed different. A fresh song rose in the hearts of the pilgrims. Earth's shores were receding. Heaven's Gate was beckoning. The old songs of the Church pulsed with fresh meaning and an unspeakable yearning drew their whole being out to God. As they slipped away from the hostel and set their face towards the sun-rising, all their song was of Him whose love had brought them thus far, and whose grace would yet bring them to glory.

> *Still, still with Thee, when purple morning breaketh,*
> *When the bird waketh, and the shadows flee;*
> *Fairer than morning, lovelier than daylight;*
> *Dawns the sweet consciousness, I am with Thee.*
>
> *So shall it be at last, in that bright morning,*
> *When the soul waketh, and life's shadows flee!*
> *Oh, in that hour, fairer than daylight dawning,*
> *Shall rise the glorious thought, I am with Thee.**

But even as they sang, they saw a man coming towards them.

'And where are you going, my friends, so early in the morning?' he asked in a jocular tone.

'Why, to Mount Zion,' they replied with great conviction.

'You don't mean to say so,' said the man, convulsed with laughter. 'That's a joke and a half, that is! How far have you come?'

'All the way from the City of Destruction,' answered Christian, 'and my friend here, from Sexpo of Supersex.'

'Well, you've a long way to go,' he said, 'for the place you seek has never existed.'

'You mean the world to come is a myth!' exclaimed Christian incredulously.

'That's right! I've been looking for it over thirty years and am no nearer finding it than when I began. Ask the astronauts. Have they spotted your Celestial City on their starry horizon? My dear fellows, I don't for one moment doubt your sincerity, but really, if you must have your heads in the clouds, do keep your feet on the

\* H. B. Stowe.

ground, because the only reality you'll ever find is this material world around us.'

'It's quite obvious,' said Christian, 'your name is Atheist, in which case the first thing I have to say is, we're not going to argue with you. If *you* haven't seen it, *we* have, and that by faith, from the Delectable Mountains. There is a God-given perception that pierces the things that are seen and lays hold of the things that are unseen. We *know* in whom we have believed. It is the "fool who has said in his heart, there is no God". Your whole understanding is blinded by the god of this world, but our God is the Living and True God and the rewarder of all those that diligently seek Him.' At this moment Hopeful, who had been listening to Christian's testimony, suddenly cried out with ecstatic abandon, 'And we see Jesus, crowned with glory and honour, even Jesus at the right hand of God. O Lord, Thou art the rejoicing of my heart and the hope of glory. *All* my springs are in Thee!'

The genuine spontaneity of this confession so disconcerted Atheist that he slunk away, a supercilious look on his face and a sadness in his eyes.

Two or three hours passed and the sun climbed ever higher above their heads. Was it the heat that was making them drowsy? They seemed to get more and more tired with every step, until they could just have thrown themselves on the grass, and gone fast asleep. Quite a distance away, some big white clouds were billowing up into the clear sky. At first they took no notice of them, but when they saw that the trees and grass by the roadside had taken on an ashen appearance they became alarmed. All the vegetation was bespeckled with a pale grey substance filtering down from above. 'Some kind of "fall-out",' commented Christian. 'And the air, too, seems laden with fumes,' said Hopeful. 'I know what this area is,' cried Christian excitedly, 'it's The Enchanted Ground.' 'Don't let's sleep, or we may never wake up. This fall-out's deadly, if you're exposed to it for any length of time.' 'But where does it come from?' asked Hopeful. 'I'd forgotten for the moment, but I remember now,' said Christian. 'It comes from the big Lament works run by the Corporation of Conceit. Practically all the Lament in the world is manufactured there. The furnaces are fired with Criticism, a very combustible substance, producing terrific heat. The smoke emitted is something dreadful, and with all the scientific advance today nothing has been found to eliminate it. The fall-out pollutes a very wide area, befogging people's minds and befouling their whole outlook and way of life. If you lie down to it, all strength goes from you and you become so sleepy you just don't want to do anything. I think the only answer is to keep moving forward. We can talk and pray together as we go on our way, and the more vigorous our fellowship in Christ, the less likely we are to be affected by the evil influence of the Lament works. Tell me now, Hopeful, how did you really decide to join me on this pilgrimage?'

'Well, you know what my home town was like. Even in my lifetime Vanity Fair had expanded a lot. I saw, for instance, the present day Sexpo, with its many precincts, rise out of little more than a shambles. The authorities there, in the past few decades, seem to have learned how to commercialise evil more than any before them. Once I grew older and was trusted with money, I fell in with a right set of tipplers and we'd carouse around the clubs and the West End bars night after night. We liked to think we were the talk of the town, but in actual fact, we were just a lewd, foul-mouthed, besotted bunch of wasters sponging on our people's money. It was the look on Faithful's face that first shook me. How can I put it? There was something so pure about it and I'd never seen anyone pure before. He was just radiant. And I can tell you, if I hadn't been gripped by that something which spoke of Christ, I'd have gone down to perdition like the traitor himself.

'From that day I could never escape the accusing finger of God. If a hearse went by, I would think about Him. How could I face Him? If I read in the paper about someone being hanged, I would wonder about my own defence before God. Soon I became a haunted soul. Haunted by my secrets and my sins; haunted by my past and by my future; haunted by that face of Faithful. Yes, and our people killed him and what was I supposed to say? That old Lord Hategood was a jolly good fellow? I became so unsociable. I packed in the night clubs, let the gang go their way and started reading the Bible. What an extraordinary book! I hardly knew a thing about it but I couldn't stop reading it and I'd go on into the early hours of the morning, reading and reading, until I fell asleep in the chair, but whatever I did, I couldn't get peace. The more I read, the worse I felt. Unclean? I felt despicable! If I tried to reform, then the Scriptures, themselves, would make me despair. "All our righteousnesses are as filthy rags", I read. "There is none righteous, no not one." "When ye shall have done all these things, say ye are unprofitable." It was like being head over heels in debt. Even if I paid my fresh commitments, my old liabilities would still see me in court. So I realised unless my sins could be blotted out, I'd never have peace and be right with God.'

'Well,' said Christian, 'what did you do?'

'I didn't know what to do but shortly before Faithful was arrested, I spoke to him that day in the street; and do you know what he told me? He said, "Unless you can come to God in the character of a man who never sinned, your case is hopeless." Well, I felt really down then, and said to him rather disconsolately, "And tell me, is there any man anywhere just like that?" "There certainly is," he said, "and His name is Jesus. He was born into this world at the town called Bethlehem, though his generation was from everlasting; and He lived and worked amongst the ordinary folk. For three years He preached and they loved to listen to Him but there were those who hated Him and wanted to get rid of Him. Then for envy they killed Him, but when He died, He died not for His own sin but for the men who slew Him, and for your sins and mine. That's what it teaches in the Bible. One sentence sums it all up, 'The Lord hath laid on Him the iniquity of us all and with His stripes we are healed'."

'What must I do, then, to be saved?' I asked. "Believe on the Lord Jesus Christ and thou shalt be saved," he quoted. And Christian, right there in the street I spoke to Him. "Jesus," I said, "I believe you died for me there on the Cross. I believe you rose up from the dead. Lord, I believe you! And with all my heart I receive you! Oh Lord, save me from the wrath to come! Oh save me now!" Then the police came and arrested you both. Perhaps you don't remember me in the crowd for we all got separated but I watched you being taken away. Then I went down to the police H.Q. and I saw that awful beating they gave you and I knew I was done with Sexpo. I could stay no longer. I was just finished with the whole vile set-up, that treated the best of men as the scum of the earth and lauded the worst to the skies. I felt if I stayed, the very blood of the martyrs would be on my hands, so when you were released I was ready to follow. That's how I came on my pilgrimage.'

A great calm seemed to settle over the two men as they walked along. Then Christian spoke again.

'Yes,' he said, 'God's grace *is* sufficient, sufficient for you and sufficient for me! And it is good to know it in our hearts.'

# CHAPTER TWENTY-ONE

# FAITH FOGBOUND

JUST then Hopeful glanced over his shoulder and saw that Ignorance was still blissfully wandering along the road behind them. He wondered how he had missed the hoarding of The Flatterer's advertising Company, but Ignorance, living in a world of his own, had failed to notice it. Still, he looked very drowsy as he came across the Enchanted Ground, and the two pilgrims decided a little more conversation might be to his benefit.

'Come along, Ignorance, don't straggle away behind us,' shouted Hopeful. 'Let's have another chat together. You're looking really sleepy!'

'No, I'd sooner walk alone,' he said, 'than talk with people like yourselves.'

'I thought that's how he'd be,' expressed Christian softly, 'but let's do our best. Come on, don't hold our words against us. Tell us what you think of things now.'

'And what do you mean by that,' he parried sourly.

'Very simply, how is it between you and your God?'

'All in order, I should hope,' he said, 'in spite of your interfering. You people are all so superior, but you can take it from me, I've just as much desire for God as you have!'

'I should sincerely hope you have,' replied Christian, 'for our desires for Him are weak enough; but when you say that, what are you trying to tell us?'

'I mean that thoughts about God and heaven come into my mind every day.'

'Well, you're not alone in that,' said Christian, 'because demons and unbelievers all think about God at some time or other, but thoughts in themselves have never brought a soul to heaven.'

'But my thoughts,' emphasised Ignorance, 'are actual desires, not mere philosophical ideas.'

'Maybe they are, but to desire a thing doesn't mean you'll obtain it. Don't you remember that Bible quotation, "the soul of the sluggard desireth and hath nothing"?'

'But the thoughts I have, and my desires for God, are all backed by self-sacrifice. I've left everything to realise them.'

'Have you really,' queried Christian, though not unkindly. 'And who may I ask, convinced you of that?'

'It's the conviction of my own heart,' answered Ignorance. 'Surely I don't have to have people tell me what I have left for God's sake, do I?'

'But doesn't Scripture state,' cautioned Christian, 'that he who trusts his own heart is a fool?'

'Certainly it does, but that verse refers to an evil heart, not to a heart like mine.'

'But man's heart, the Bible says, is deceitful above all things and desperately wicked. Didn't you know that our hearts will even hope, when hope is groundless?'

'But if the aspirations of my heart and my whole tenor of life correspond, isn't that reason enough for believing my hopes are well-founded?'

'Yes, but who says they correspond? You bear witness of yourself and if you bear witness of yourself, there is no real guarantee of its validity. Have you no other witnesses?'

Ignorance became impatient. 'I tell you my own heart tells me I'm all right and if I can't trust myself, then who can I trust?'

'What a man says about himself is no criterion of his character,' replied Christian. 'It's what God's Word says that really counts. Listen to the witness it gives about our hearts. "The imagination of man's heart," it tells us, "is evil from his youth."'

'Well,' said Ignorance, in an offhand way, 'You can say what you like and quote who you like, but I'll never believe my heart is as bad as that!'

'If that's the case,' said Christian with vehemence, 'I venture to say you've never had a right thought concerning yourself in your life. The Word of God accurately assesses the nature of the human heart and every thought and action proceeding from it. When our personal assessment of our hearts is in harmony with all that God says about them, then and only then have we right thoughts about ourselves.'

'Well, if that's what you call right thinking about ourselves, what, may I ask, are right thoughts about God?' pursued Ignorance.

'To have right thoughts about God is to agree with what God's Word says about Him. He is not to be defined by the petty categories of man's proud opinions. Let me put it like this. We have right thoughts about God when we acknowledge that He knows us better than we know ourselves; when we acknowledge that He sees sin in us, even when we are oblivious to it; and when we accept His verdict and say, "Yes, Lord, all my righteousness is as filthy rags and my imagined goodness but refuse in Thy sight."

When we admit that, and acknowledge that in our own strength we can never attain to Him, then right thoughts about God have begun!'

Ignorance now did some intellectual side-stepping and startled Christian by saying, 'And do you think I'm such a fool as to imagine I can stand before God in my own strength or impress Him with my own efforts?'

'Well, it sounded very much like it, but if not, what do you believe?'

'Why,' said Ignorance blithely, 'I believe in Christ, of course.'

'And when did you really come to believe in Him?' challenged Christian afresh. 'And what kind of faith in Christ is it, when you have no sense of your own sinful condition, your need of cleansing, or any interest in the forgiveness and righteousness He offers?'

'I don't know who you think you are!' replied Ignorance indignantly. 'You'd think I was a prisoner in the dock and you were the prosecuting counsel! Why should I explain everything to you? I believe in Christ and that's the end of it!'

'Now don't get upset,' coaxed Christian. 'Surely it's a good thing to examine ourselves as to our faith. Could you not tell us what your faith in Christ really involves?'

'It means, for me, that Christ died for sinners. And that he therefore expects us to do the best we can. Naturally our efforts will hardly be perfect, but I'm sure His merits will make our offerings and self-sacrifice acceptable to God and so we shall be justified in His sight and obtain an acceptance with Him.'

Christian now spoke lovingly, yet with firmness. 'Ignorance,' he said, 'there are several things I want to say to you. Let me analyse your outlook in the light of God's Word. First of all, the faith you describe is nothing more than a figment of your own imagination. It has no biblical foundation whatever. Secondly, it is utterly false because it views Christ's work on the Cross as something added to your own works, whereas His work alone is the ground of our acceptance before God. You need to know, and know before it is too late, that your own works are your condemnation, not the first step in your justification. Then thirdly, the kind of faith you describe makes Christ the justifier not of your person but of your works, which works He can never justify but only judge at the Last Day. By viewing Christ as a justifier of your works and, in some mysterious way, the upholder of your corrupt morality, you naïvely imagine you can stand before God. The whole suggestion is preposterous, impious and untrue. Finally, your faith is altogether corrupt because it leaves the sinner something in which he can boast before God, whereas God has specifically stated that "no flesh shall glory in His presence".

'True faith on the contrary, acknowledges the total bankruptcy of every individual in God's presence and calls for a true dependence on Christ, in what He did at the Cross for our justification; namely that there He bore, as one utterly devoid of any iniquity, the full judicial penalty which was our due, and that by reason of this, the salvation of God can be offered freely to all who repent and believe. Not that repentance and faith, either alone or together, are in themselves meritorious or in any way additional to Christ's work. They express the outstretched hands of a suppliant who, believing that salvation is proffered, receives it with thankfulness and joy. The man with such faith acknowledges that all he receives comes through his Benefactor and Him alone.'

Ignorance looked pensively at Christian, annoyance written all over his face. 'So you mean to say that a man's personal salvation has nothing to do with his own moral effort but rests on Christ and His substitutionary death *alone*?'

'Yes,' said Christian, 'our acceptance before God rests in His availing blood and nothing else.'

'If that's the case, then,' said Ignorance, 'all we have to do is to believe and be saved, and we can do what we like. We are made fit for heaven, but what happens afterwards is wholly irrelevant. Isn't that making the best of both worlds? I tell you, the more I hear of your teaching the less I like it!'

'Really, Ignorance,' chided Christian, 'you're even more ignorant than your name implies. From what you say, it is quite evident you know nothing of the righteousness of God received by faith, nor do you know anything of His Spirit working in your heart. The true results of saving faith are a burning love towards Christ for all He has done, a deep compassion for one's fellowmen and an insatiable desire for His Word, His Kingdom, and His Holiness—the very antithesis of all you so ignorantly propound.'

Hopeful, who had been listening carefully all the while, suddenly broke in and said to Ignorance, 'It would seem, Ignorance, that you have never had Christ revealed to you as Saviour at all.'

Although the truth of the Gospel had been clearly stated, Ignorance felt angry and bewildered. 'I just don't see it,' he said. 'Didn't I say it was hopeless talking with you sort of people. I'll say no more. And if you're starting on visions and revelations I don't know where we'll get to. I might as well leave it to you. If you've got some kind of religious mania, all I can say is, don't give it to me!'

'But Ignorance, Ignorance,' pleaded Christian, 'surely you realise if you want to know Christ as your Saviour, you need to have God reveal Him to you as such. That is why you are ignorant, because you will not seek Him or learn of Him, but pack your head full of your own ideas, all of which are contrary to His Word. The things we say should not make you impatient and abusive but lead you to Jesus' feet. Then you would learn what it is to be forgiven, and God would work a work of grace and power in your soul, but if you continue as you are, there'll be only God's judgement at the last.'

'I've listened to enough of it,' said Ignorance. 'Just you go on. There's no keeping pace with you.' And with that Ignorance fell behind, and the pilgrims saw him no more, until his fate was sealed.

# CHAPTER TWENTY-TWO

# THE ROAD TO THE RIVER

CHRISTIAN and Hopeful were moving rapidly now towards the territory which fringed the mystic river flowing before the ascent to the City. Their conversations with each other and with Ignorance had seen them well over the Enchanted Ground, and as they moved into the Land of Beulah they sought to clarify their thinking and prepare their hearts, so that with spiritual composure they might face the challenge of their passing.

'I'm sorry for people like Ignorance,' said Christian in a subdued tone of voice. 'It will be terrible for him at the last.'

'And he's not the only one,' added Hopeful. 'I can think of whole families and streets of people, back there where I come from. Tell me, Christian, what do you make of them?'

'The god of this world has blinded them that they should not see,' said Christian, 'and many today are wilfully ignorant of spiritual truth. They desperately fear the conviction of sin, so stifle God's voice as soon as He speaks. That's why we humans delight in our cliques and spawn our mutual admiration societies, as if to convince ourselves we're really a fine set of people in spite of all God says about us.'

'But fear is often most wholesome,' said Hopeful.

'Yes,' replied Christian, 'if it's the fear of the Lord; for that is the beginning of wisdom, but the fear of man brings a snare. The trouble with us, generally, is that we fear the wrong things and for the wrong reasons. Man fears bereavement, illness, unemployment; he fears slumps and inflation, or the hydrogen bomb. We will fear everything and everybody but Him who can destroy both soul and body in hell. And that doesn't make God an ogre. If people won't have Him in this life, how can they have Him in the next? They wouldn't even enjoy Him if they could! Talking of these things, you know, reminds me of a fellow I knew some years ago called Temporary.'

'You don't mean Temporary, who lived in Graceless, just two miles beyond Honesty, do you?'

'Yes, that's the man, and he lived next door to a vacillating character called Turn-Back.'

'It wasn't next door,' corrected Hopeful. 'It was in the same house!'

'I guess it was, now you come to mention it,' agreed Christian.

'I should have remembered that. Well, Temporary was spiritually convicted at one time. Hard to believe now, of course, but there was no doubt about it. He knew he had sinned and was acutely aware of the penalty involved. In fact, he would weep at times, and some even heard him calling out, "Lord, Lord!" From this it was presumed he would go on pilgrimage, but he got in with that infamous scoundrel, Save-self, with the result that he never talked about it again.'

'What do you think was the reason for his sudden change of mind?' asked Hopeful.

'I think there must have been several causes,' replied Christian. 'In the first place, I doubt very much whether the sense of guilt was either deep enough, or prolonged enough, to permanently influence his mind and will. Then I wouldn't be surprised if, once the fear of hell diminished, he began to worry what people would say about him. Thirdly, I believe he resented being dependent upon, and submissive to, Another. Once the sense of his need for salvation passed, his old self-reliance re-asserted itself. Finally, I think he found conviction of sin such a disagreeable experience that whenever it waned, he was glad to be eased of it, rather than seek God's remedy for it. So the opportunity receded and his heart was hardened.'

'That sounds a fair enough explanation,' said Hopeful. 'Many a person in the law-courts is like that. A thief in the dock is generally more concerned about the stiff sentence handed down than the evil of his crime, or the wrong done to his victims. Once let him go and he's back at his old game in no time.'

'Well, I've given you my thoughts on Temporary's turning from pilgrimage, perhaps you could suggest what course such a development would take.'

Hopeful thought for a moment, then he began. 'I would say that such people first lose interest by failing to think consistently on God, on death and on judgement. Their mind then easily wanders to other things, with the result that they cease from praying and stop seeking God's salvation. Losing interest in divine things, they soon absent themselves from Christian company and consequently hear less and less of God's Word. Then to support their absence, they criticise genuine pilgrims, and finding fault with them, make their shortcomings a reason for not going along with them. This leaves them open to seek their former godless friends. Thus sin is resumed, first in secret and then openly; and revealing themselves for what they are, they declare by their life that the Truth has never been rooted in their hearts.'

'Yes,' said Christian, 'and when you think of our own folly, all along the road, it is only the grace of God that keeps us from returning to the cities we've come from.'

'It certainly is,' affirmed Hopeful, 'it's a daily miracle how our feet are kept in the way they are.'

Beulah Land now stretched before them, and as they walked and talked, they became quite excited, for they realised the distance between them and their destination was narrowing rapidly. It was here they came to the hamlet of Come-and-Go. Many were the pilgrims who reached the Land of Beulah and found it to their liking. This was especially true of the more elderly pilgrims, who had good pensions, enjoyed fair health and had not, as yet, been widowed. They had such happy visits with their own particular friends, developed such a variety of interests, and went on holiday so frequently, that they were not at all anxious to dwell in the house of the Lord for ever. Thus in spite of coming so far they were loath to proceed. As for the village of Come-and-Go, it was well known for two reasons. For many centuries it had, on account of its proximity to the River of Death, been the home of certain boating families operating under the name of The Vain-hope Ferry Company. The other reason was of far more recent origin. Come-and-Go had now become the site of a new hospital especially devoted to Transplant Surgery. The magnificent campus, with its imposing buildings, did much to inspire confidence, especially in the upper age-groups. The grounds were beautifully laid out with well-cut lawns and flowering shrubs. The life of the hamlet had been changed from a Sleepy-Hollow existence to one of bustling importance. A large number of official residences had been built, together with several convalescent units and some delightful private hotels. Certain desirable plots had also been put on the market and it was possible to select a new house before having one's transplant, thus much had been done to accommodate those whose expectation of life had been extended. Where diseased pilgrims were anxious for a longer stay on earth, they enquired at The Hall of the Organs. This was a wing of the main building and a model of efficiency in glass, marble and concealed lighting. Here private consultations took place and prospective patients were permitted to view the organs currently available in the aseptic refrigeration department. This large unit was clinically immaculate, and housed various special-purpose containers, each like a large transparent refrigerator. There was the Lung Section, the Liver Section, the Heart Section and, more recently introduced, the Brain Section. Each exhibit available for selection was marked male or female, and the age of the donor was also indicated. In the case of the

Brain Section, the social and ideological background of each donor was declared in detail. Should there be a run on 'transplant stock', those desperately desirous might select organs of animal origin from a special 'bank' established for such contingencies. The euphemistic Latin legend beneath each item did much to allay the apprehensions of would-be patients.

On occasion the conversations were quite extraordinary. 'No,' said the doctor to the ageing lady, 'I don't recommend that fifty year old male heart there. It might run for twenty years and I guess you'd want to live to a hundred.' 'But that fifteen year old female one would do all right, wouldn't it?' she asked in a trembling voice. 'Just a bit strenuous, I would say,' replied the consultant. 'At ninety you might feel like running round the house but your poor old legs wouldn't carry you. Personally, I would suggest this forty year old female one here.' 'But how long has it been under refrigeration?' 'Oh, only six months.' 'Are you sure it will be all right?' 'At six months there is not the slightest possibility of any deterioration, madam. If there were I would tell you. My professional reputation is at stake.' 'You will do your best for me, won't you?' 'We do our best for everybody, whether people be private patients or coming to us under the State Health Service.' 'Thank you, doctor. When do you think I should have it done.' 'You better call at the office at the end of the corridor; the Almoner will see you, and fix it up at your convenience.' The old lady prepared to leave the room. 'You see, doctor, I've got a little bungalow on the go and I'd like to move in as soon as possible. There's so much to be said for Beulah Land this side of the river.'

The doctor bowed her out, watched her totter away, then lit a cigarette and said rather cynically, 'I guess I should keep a lung for myself. This business of fifty a day is useless. I'd throw myself in the River if I thought I had "it",' and he coughed uneasily, as he spat out the words, plus a salivary piece of tobacco.

When Christian and Hopeful passed through the village they had a look at the hospital notice board. It announced a policy of limitless expansion but failed to inform the public that people could only be made to live if other people died. No doubt this was taken as being self-evident, though it had long ceased to be so. It was Hopeful who spoke first and when he did, he came out with a very startling question. 'If Ignorance had a brain transplant from a true believer, do you think it would make any difference to him?'

'A difference to whom and to what?' asked Christian, somewhat perplexed. 'A difference to the brain of the believer, or the body of Ignorance? Who would the new being be? The true believer with a new body, or Ignorance with another brain? Surely the brain compared with the rest of the body is unique, and wholly crucial in the realm of personality. Once Ignorance lost his brain, the body itself could hardly be termed Ignorance. It would simply become the vehicle for the brain of the believer, transplanted to it. I suppose there are two ways of describing such an operation. Either it is the transplant of a body to a brain, or else it is the transplant of a brain to a body.'

'But isn't the brain part of the body?' protested Hopeful, 'surely you don't call the brain the person? I always thought the person was something distinct from the brain.'

'Yes, of course, but whilst the spirit is still in the body, it is dependent, very largely, on the proper physical functioning of the brain, both for the control of the body itself, and for communication beyond the body to other persons.'

'Would you say, then, in the case of a successful brain-transplant, there would be the possibility of sustaining the organic function of a body without the presence of personality?'

'That's quite a question too,' said Christian and walked on silently for a long time. Then suddenly he began to speak, obviously thinking aloud as he grappled with the problem. 'The believer's body,' he exclaimed emphatically, 'including the brain, is the temple of the Holy Ghost. What's more the Bible tells us that "he that is joined unto the Lord is one spirit". Obviously then, what we do with our bodies is of spiritual consequence both to God and to us. Now, I think you will agree, Hopeful, that every man's spirit has a distinct identity, but have you ever carried that thought to its logical conclusion? Surely it means that the God-given body pertaining to any man's spirit is God's own ordained vehicle for the self-expression of that spirit. It is common knowledge that every organ in a man's body is just as distinctive as his facial features and therefore, I would say, equally linked with his own peculiar personality. We may smile sometimes at the claims of the phrenologist but isn't it reasonable to insist that the visible body, its inward organs and the resident spirit of a man, are all inseparably related and interact upon each other in quite a special way. To put it succinctly, I believe that each body God forms, is made for a particular spirit, and that every spirit has its own particular body.'

'But have you any Scripture to prove it?' interjected Hopeful.

'I think so,' answered Christian thoughtfully, 'For instance, David's words in the Psalms, "Thou has covered me in my mother's womb ... I am fearfully and wonderfully made ... Thine eyes did see my substance, yet being unperfect and in Thy

Book *all my members were written,* which in continuance were fashioned, when as yet there was none of them." The thought I am trying to express is illustrated supremely in the incarnation of the Son of God. The Scripture says, "Sacrifice and offering Thou wouldst not but a body hast Thou prepared Me", that is to say, "fitted me". In the case of Adam, God first made the body, then put into it the spirit of his man; but in the case of Jesus Christ, His last Adam, there first existed the Spirit of His Son and the body he eventually occupied, was subsequently prepared. In both cases however, the point I am making is upheld, namely, that in normal manhood (that is man as God conceived him) a spirit and a body exist for each other, and are complimentary to each other, in a quite distinctive way.'

'That sounds convincing enough,' said Hopeful, 'but seeing we shall all pass from time into eternity one day, I don't know that we can attach too much significance to such an emphasis as regards transplant surgery.' But Christian was not going to let Hopeful gloss the implications.

'What I have just proved to you,' he went on, 'is true, not only in this world but the next. The believer in eternity is not going to be some disembodied spirit floating around in an ethereal vacuum. His Lord isn't in that condition, and neither will he be. Think of our Saviour once again. The body which came forth from the womb was that same body which came forth from the tomb. The child had grown to manhood and the man had passed through death but that resurrected body, for all the changes it had undergone, pertained to the same Jesus and by it, He was physically identifiable, not only to His immediate acquaintances but by over five hundred persons at once. The Bible asserts it was this very person who went bodily into heaven, and insists that it will be "this same Jesus" who will return again. And in case there should be any doubt about the meaning of the words, the Scripture asserts clearly that every eye shall see Him and they shall look on Him whom they pierced. So you see how the Spirit of Christ and the Body of Christ are inseparably linked, not only in this world but in the world to come.'

'That may be true of Christ Himself but is the body of the believer to be similarly identified with his spirit, following his death? I shall be surprised if you can really maintain that from Scripture,' challenged Hopeful.

'Well, the Bible's full of surprises,' smiled Christian. 'What we must always remember is that what happens to our Lord is a key to what happens to the believer. Just as Christ rose bodily from the grave, so we, who have received His spiritual life, will know a physical resurrection as glorious as His. Our bodies, though they are marred by sin and thus at death, are buried in a condition of corruption, will, notwithstanding, through the work of God's Spirit, be raised incorruptible. It sounds incredible but Paul gives clear reasons, not only why this shall be so but why it *must* be so. Christ, in shedding His blood for us, has purchased the right not only to our spirits and souls, but also to our bodies. Furthermore, He has placed His Holy Spirit in each believer as His personal seal of ownership, and in doing this has guaranteed that our body will not moulder indefinitely in the grave or be cast into the Lake of Fire but will be raised and glorified. This is what the Bible means by the redemption of the body. Then our bodies will be capable of expressing the new nature we have already received down here through the new birth.' But Hopeful was still not satisfied.

'Surely,' he said, 'what you are talking about now is a new body altogether, and if so, doesn't that undermine your contention of one spirit for one body, in this world and the next?'

'I don't want to split hairs,' replied Christian cautiously, 'nor do I want to join the doctrinal tight-rope walkers at the circus, but it's most vital to notice that the Bible never describes our future body as a new body. It is always viewed as a changed body and to me this is significant. You see, whilst it is true that our glorified body will bear the likeness of God's man in heaven, that is Christ; yet, just as certainly, it will in some way be identifiable with that body which bore the likeness of God's man on earth, namely Adam. With reference to our burial and resurrection, Paul shows that the "seed" sown will, as always, be recognised in the grain that follows. The original "corn" will die but through the inexorable laws of God, a body suited to the renewed life, and indeed produced by it, will undoubtedly emerge. So as a saint in heaven, clothed in a body like my Saviour's, I shall be identified as a particular sinner who was saved on earth. On the one hand, I shall be known for who I was, but on the other, known as the man God always meant me to be.'

'I see it now!' exclaimed Hopeful. 'What you are saying is this, that the spirit of a man stands in a particular relationship to his own body—like a glove if you like, which only one hand can fit. And secondly, that this relationship between a man's spirit and his body exists not only in this life but in the life to come.'

'Yes, and if that is so these concepts should govern all our thinking about transplant surgery,' added Christian.

'That sounds, though, as if you are against transplant surgery altogether,' concluded Hopeful.

'It may sound a bit like it but that's not, in actual fact, what I'm saying. My plea is that, when it comes to transplant surgery, God's truth concerning the human body should be acknowledged as defining its ethical frontiers. The body, whether it be yours, mine or anybody else's, is not ours to do what we like with. "What!" says Paul to the Corinthian believers, "Know ye not that your body is the temple of the Holy Ghost, who is in you, which ye have of God and ye are not your own?" And it's precisely because of this fact that he enjoins them to glorify God in their bodies and in their spirits, which are God's. From which statement, Hopeful, I would strongly aver that the union of the body and the spirit in a human being is both specific and unique; a relationship divinely conceived and divinely effected, and consequently to be divinely controlled. It is a sphere in which God's prerogatives are paramount and on no account to be violated. But when we have said all this we must not jump to hasty or extreme conclusions, or infer that every aspect of transplant surgery is inherently evil. Surgeons, after all, aren't witch-doctors, even if they are trained in the City of Destruction. Most skills in themselves are neither spiritual nor unspiritual; moral or immoral. It is the "how" and the "why" of their using that reveals the kind of people we are. To alleviate suffering and foster life is something to be lauded, not despised. It is not for nothing we read how the Galatians would have plucked out their eyes and given them to Paul in gratitude for his bringing them the Gospel. Had they possessed the equipment and techniques, they'd have done an eye-transplant on the spot! That at least was their desire and Paul does not discredit their intentions. Personally I don't think it's a question of laying down rules but of insisting that God's principles and God's perspectives govern the application of each new technological advance.

'The trouble today is that the professionally able are too often the spiritually blind, and this being so, it is possible that some will insist on the development of transplant surgery to the point where there is a total desecration of God's temple. My own feeling, Hopeful, is that transplant surgery, by its very nature, looks on to the ultimate of things. And what is the ultimate as far as man is concerned? Man as God envisages him, or man when science has finished with him? Although it seems incredible, the first brain-transplants are already being planned. After all, a heart transplant was only a dream thirty years ago. Whatever we may feel about the transplantation of the lesser organs, I believe that once brain-transplant operations have been performed, our mandate for the healing of the sick will have been exceeded. Whilst by means of the heart all organs are physically sustained, it is by the brain they are nervously controlled. The brain, therefore, with its myriad impressions, conditioned reflexes and countless impulses is, more than any other organ of the body, delicately linked with the activity of man's indestructible spirit and his real personality. A brain-transplant must, I feel, be open to the most serious ethical censure.'

'Don't you think we are getting a bit theoretical,' suggested Hopeful. 'Oughtn't we think of the problem in more practical terms?'

'I suppose we should,' said Christian. 'Let's take, for instance, a situation in which a person with a healthy brain has just died and the surgeons have in view the extraction of the brain from this dead person, and its immediate introduction into the cranium of a selected patient. Now the first thing we've got to recognise is that the patient's diseased brain must be removed before the healthy brain can be inserted. What I want to ask you, Hopeful, is this: once the diseased brain is severed from the patient, can the patient, in any sense of the term, be called "alive"?'

'It depends on what you mean by alive,' answered Hopeful. 'If no irreversible changes have taken place in the body, I think you would say he is at least clinically alive, whatever that might mean. At any rate, he wouldn't be viewed as clinically dead.'

'I know, in a way, what you're getting at,' said Christian. 'You mean the body on the operating table is not mere decaying flesh, as in the case of an unattended corpse.'

'Exactly,' agreed Hopeful. 'Maybe you've never followed the scientific journals but I often used to visit the library back in the City of Destruction and I recall reading what some authority wrote on the coming brain transplant. He said it might conceivably be done in stages, aided by techniques of deep hypothermia and extra-corporeal circulation, through a heart–lung machine. Don't think, though, Christian, because I'm quoting this, that I understand everything it involves, but it would seem that a brainless body could be preserved from irreversible changes, at least for a while. Although I must say,' he added grimly, 'it sounds worse than death itself!'

'But surely,' began Christian again, 'a man without a brain *must* be dead. Why, you can't even call him unconscious! Even though his body impulses are artificially maintained, these movements must still be just a reflection of an applied mechanical force. Do you honestly think they could ever be more?'

'I just don't know,' said Hopeful, 'but you'd hardly think so.'

'Well, if the patient is clinically alive, even though he's without a brain, can it genuinely be said that the patient, as a person, is still with us or must we say he's departed?'

'His body is still with us,' answered Hopeful, faltering somewhat.

'Yes, minus the brain,' replied Christian, 'but is *he* still with us? That's the question. Just you imagine the position if once the diseased brain has been removed from the patient, the healthy brain, through some mishap, should be no longer available. Why, the surgeons would be left with nothing but the gaping cranium of an artificially animated body. And what, may I ask, would be left to the patient's relatives? A living loved one, or just a warm but mutilated torso? When is it that death takes place? When the brain is removed or when the machines are switched off? Personally, I believe that once you remove a person's brain, then irrespective of the condition of the torso, that person has departed this life; the spirit has returned to Him who gave it! That's what the Bible would lead us to believe and it sounds perfectly logical to me. After all the patient's brain has been taken out and disposed of as diseased and unwanted!'

Hopeful looked more and more bewildered. 'I suppose what you say is reasonable enough but what if the brain-transplant were successful, wouldn't that make some sort of difference?'

'If the brain-transplant were successful the torso would simply have acquired a fresh brain, but to my mind *only* a brain. Certainly not a spirit, for the brain was taken from a deceased person. The Scripture is very clear on this point, for it says, "The body without the spirit is dead". Therefore the body of a dead person whether viewed in its entirety, or in its separate parts, must of necessity be minus its spirit. I don't see, therefore, how the transplanted brain of the dead donor could be accompanied by his spirit to the patient's torso, though some may wish to speculate along these lines.'

'But couldn't the departed spirit of the patient himself return, once the transplanted brain was suitably integrated with the patient's body and providing there were no rejection problems?' asked Hopeful.

'As I read the Bible, Hopeful, there is no chance of that. For the spirit is prohibited by God from returning to its erstwhile body unless specifically ordered by Him to do so. It is God who kills and makes alive. Of its own volition, it can do nothing. As David said of his dead child, "I shall go to him, but he shall not return to me".'

179

Hopeful's face was suddenly white and drawn. 'What do you mean?' he asked Christian.

'I'm not sure,' said Christian, 'but you asked me at the beginning, whether in the event of a successful brain-transplant it would be possible for such a body, with its "new" brain, to function organically without the presence of true personality? All I can say is that the more I consider the matter, the more I am convinced that the advent of the brain-transplant must bring us, in the end, to that kind of nightmare; that is, to a world where people are no longer real.'

'I follow your argument,' said Hopeful, 'but, of course, you may not be right.'

'But I may not be wrong,' replied Christian, 'and that's the dread possibility.'

After this Hopeful remained quiet for a long while, until Christian asked him what was the matter.

'I was thinking about spirits,' he said, 'evil spirits; spirits looking for bodies; looking for a "house" to live in like Jesus said, seven and eight at a time. Remember how a whole legion of them went into the pigs at Gadara. You don't think evil spirits would occupy a body on which a brain-transplant had been performed, do you?'

'Maybe I do,' said Christian. Then after a pause he added, 'And maybe I don't. But when I read in the Book of Revelation, and see those monstrous characters of the Last Days, when devilish personalities stalk the world in human guise, and resurrection itself seems to be in the hands of the devil, I begin to see why they are called beasts. Maybe they're neither human nor divine.' There was a moment's silence; then pensively, he whispered, 'And to think, that all the world will wonder after them, ere long...'

'My mind just reels at the thought of it,' cried Hopeful.

'Yes,' said Christian, 'and whoever he be who holds the scalpel should know in his heart that Christ holds the keys.'

'But what keys?' asked Hopeful.

'The keys of Death and of Hades,' said Christian; and the two men walked on towards the River.

# CHAPTER TWENTY-THREE

# THE CRISIS OF THE CROSSING

On leaving the hamlet of Come-and-Go, the pilgrims passed through a wide pastoral countryside on which the sun never set. At every turn, they had fresh glimpses of the City Glorious, and the lush verdure of the fields and the prolific foliage of the trees all witnessed to the mellow and equable climate of those lands lying near to the gates of Paradise. Each day found their hearts filled with joy and their mouths with singing. Even as they slept, the praises of God were upon their lips.

But now they must address themselves to the River. The approach to its agelong shores was marked by a maze of shifting dunes and as they descended to its broad swirling waters, the sand filled their shoes and slowed their pace so much, that the last stage of their journey seemed almost interminable. Yet there were moments when they glimpsed, through the clouds, the battlements of the City of the Most High. Then the words of their briefing would come again to their minds, 'there is peace within thy walls and prosperity within thy palaces', and they would fall to the counting of its towers and the glad admiring of its ramparts, until with exulting cries, they would lift their voices to the skies and sing, 'Our feet shall stand within thy gates O Jerusalem.' Towards the bank of the River they were met by two radiant beings, one of whom had delivered them from the wiles of The Flatterer, at Tranquil. This gave the pilgrims fresh confidence and quelled their rising apprehensions. 'Will you escort us to the brink?' they asked. 'As heirs of salvation,' they replied, 'we will gladly go with you, but understand, each pilgrim who runs the race must run it to a finish, looking only unto Jesus.' The way became more and more exacting, and Christian asked their escort the meaning of the dunes. 'These are The Sandhills of Senility,' they answered, 'where The Sands of Time run out to the River.'

As they passed onward they saw a pathetic looking couple engaged in a dreadful argument. The wife, with a haggard face crinkled like one of last summer's apples, was seated on a tuft of dry grass. Her husband, a poor shrunken little figure, was clearly anxious to get to the River but there she sat, morose and recalcitrant, refusing to move. 'We've lived together fifty years,' he complained bitterly, 'and now she won't even see me to my passing.'

The look on his face was so sad that Christian could have wept for him. 'She keeps telling me,' he went on, 'that all life's ahead of her, and talking about the girl friend and how they're getting married on April the first. They've rented a flat, she says, over a shop in Sexpo. She never talked like this before. It's only happened since she had that brain-transplant back there in Beulah. Whatever's come over her? Is she insane?'

'Oh no!' said a Shining One. 'You see it's not she who's speaking. Did they not tell you? There was a mistake in the operating theatre. She'd requested the brain of a twenty-one year old girl but they put in the brain of a twenty-one year old boy. The transplant was successful and I would say the young masculine brain was functioning normally. See how the hands lay hold on the withered breasts! It has a man's memory, although in the virtual absence of the male hormone, there is no corresponding urge in the body adopted. Naturally it fails to understand it. After all, how could it?* Reality, you know, has always stood guard at the River.' The old man turned away quite overcome, but after a moment or two, followed the Shining Ones to the water's edge, crying like a lost child all across the sands.

Aghast with horror, Hopeful said furtively to Christian, 'But who is *it*? The young man or the old woman?' Christian was so unnerved he could hardly speak. 'I suppose it's the man, if his spirit still clings to his brain: but the woman if her spirit still clings to her torso. But how that can be I cannot imagine.' They stood silent for what must have been a full minute, transfixed to the spot. Then Hopeful whispered, 'But what if each spirit clings to its own particular fragment, are both together in the composite body? Who is it, Christian? Have you nothing to say?'

'It might be neither,' mused Christian, 'if both their spirits crossed the River some months ago.'

'You mean a "non-person"?' ventured Hopeful. 'I've heard of them politically but I never thought we'd have them biologically. Surely, the end of all things is at hand!'

Then a solemn voice rang out on the desolate shore. 'The

---

* If a brain transplant ever takes place, it will presumably be performed using a brain to which the pituitary gland is still attached. The pituitary gland, it has been said, acts in regard to the endocrine glands (a category which includes the thyroid, the adrenals and the sex glands) rather like a conductor handling an orchestra. What effect a male pituitary gland would have on the endocrines of a female body into which it was planted, is difficult to foresee. The intention here is simply to raise some of the moral and spiritual problems involved in the development of transplant surgery and encourage the public to recognise how serious they are, especially in relation to the human crises of life, death and the hereafter.

spectres of life are become the spectres of death, it cried, but blessed are they who die in the Lord! Fear not! For you are summoned to stand before the King of all kings. Be glad in your God. The Master is come and is calling for you.' With these words their hearts grew calm and Hopeful exclaimed, 'The darkness is past and the true light now shineth!' And so it was they came to the River.

One can well imagine the concern of Christian and Hopeful, when they discovered they must ford the river without any appliance to assist them. They saw no bridge, no ferry, no brace-and-tackle, no hovercraft or helicopter but only the cold grey stones and the dark murky depths sweeping on to Eternity. All their strength seemed to ebb away at the thought of entering the eddying flow and Christian cried out in anguish, 'Surely, O Lord, Thou carriest man away as in a flood; but Hopeful was more composed and said to the Shining Ones, 'How is it in these days of scientific invention, more is not done to transport the traveller in ease and comfort to Death's farther side?' 'Death,' came the reply, 'remains what it always was, "the last enemy of man", for none has power to retain the spirit, or authority over the day of death; there is no discharge from that war. Each man must ford this stream for himself. Each soul must tread the depths alone.'

They came now to a promontory of rock, protruding like a tapering finger into the main stream. The further it extended, the more narrow it became, until the pilgrims were obliged to tread it single file. Step by step they picked their way, till the world behind grew dim and there was no returning. 'It is the final point,' said a Shining One, 'the last extremity along The Causeway of the Years.' The waters lashed fiercely now and lipped angrily over Christian's ankles. Soon they were to his knees.

'Is there no other way but this?' asked Christian, his eyes dilating with fear. 'Did not Enoch and Elijah escape the River?' he whimpered. 'Be comforted,' came the reply, 'the greatest of all pilgrims passed this way and though His footprints are not seen, His path still runs through all these waters. Your sense of their depth will be according as you trust in Him, for He it is who sits upon the waterfloods.' But the tide was rising and a lethal chill caught at the pilgrims' hearts making their breathing difficult. Then all at once the river-bed shelved steeply and they were almost swept away. 'I sink in deep mire,' cried Christian, 'where there is no standing. The waves and the billows go over me; the waters come in unto my soul.' 'Not so, Christian!' shouted Hopeful. 'For the Lord is on our side. He is our Shield and the lifter up of our heads and by His power shall these proud waves be stayed.'

Then with a loud voice he shouted again, 'Oh, Christian, I feel
the bottom and it is good'; but Christian sank deeper yet. 'The
sorrows of death compass me,' he groaned, 'a horror of great
darkness comes over me. Oh, how shall I come to the gate of the
City?'

His faith being thus assailed, the receding bank of the river
began to be haunted by memories of the past and the land ahead
peopled with future fears. Scanning the earthward shore, Christian could see Mr. Worldly Wiseman and his chauffeur Caiaphas.
They had driven the limousine right down to the beach. Its
headlights were full on and the horn screeching wildly. His
nephew was there too, with Obstinate and Pliable. He held a
transistor in his hand and its banal blare drifted out over the
water. A little further down he glimpsed Simple, Sloth and
Presumption lounging on the sands, hirsute and shoeless, all
sound asleep at the brink of the River.

'How can they do it?' thought Christian. 'Have they no fears?'
'They have slept through Time but will wake to Reality,' consoled Hopeful. 'That's the only factor which Hell and Heaven
have in common.' And Christian marvelled at Hopeful's presence
of mind. Then he saw a hotel van pull in through the dunes, the
letters MOTEL MAGNIFICENT written all over it. It came to an
abrupt halt and out bundled a suave-looking man with leonine
features, followed by a woman who, for all the world, looked like
Christiana. Then the words came back to him, 'It sounds as if
something's wrong with you, Christian. It's just ridiculous to expect me and the children to pack up and go on this mystery tour
to the Celestial City.' At that moment Apollyon spotted the pilgrims, adroitly pulled out a revolver, and fired six shots in quick
succession. His fiery missiles spluttered to impotence around their
heads. 'There's a price to pay,' cackled the strange woman, beginning to disrobe. 'I've led many to these waters.' And as her
words fell on his ears, wreaths of vapour twisted and turned before his eyes. 'Yes, she was like her, so like her,' he murmured.
Then the lions let out a roar which ruffled the surface of the
River, and struggling ever more violently, he cried, 'I remember
my iniquities this day!' But there came a voice above all the
voices of the enemy, and straight from the gate of heaven. 'Thy
sins and iniquities I remember no more. I have cast them behind
my back. They are plunged into the depths of the sea.' 'It is the
Lord,' said Hopeful. 'Think of His promises. "When thou passest
through the waters, I will be with thee and through the rivers,
they shall not overflow thee, for I am the Lord, your God, even
Thy Saviour,"' 'Christian,' cried Hopeful, 'I see the Gate and men

who wait for us,' 'For you, maybe, but how for me?' spoke Christian fearfully. 'Is it not my wickedness that gives me such pangs in death?' 'Why no,' replied Hopeful, 'it is only that you might trust Him fully at the last, whose goodness, love and mercy have followed you these many days of pilgrimage. As for the wicked, "There are no pangs in their death. Their strength is firm. They are not in trouble as other men are, nor are they plagued as other men. Hope thou in God! Christ Jesus makes thee whole!"' As Christian grasped these words, the voice of the Lord rang again from the Gate, the light of heaven filled his countenance and immediately they were at the land.

Once they had stepped from the waters, a host of ministrants, like those first seen at the Cross, surged out to meet them. In the twinkling of an eye the pilgrims found themselves caught up in their spiritual current, mounting as on eagles' wings and lifting air, to worlds unsullied and unthought. Their mortal chrysallis was shed and thus they soared unfettered, borne by celestial pinions to the many-splendoured realms of light. Higher and higher they rose, till stratosphere and ionosphere were all exceeded. Through all the heavens they passed, where Christ their Lord had pierced them, into that world unseen where the steeps of heaven look up at last to the gates of the City. 'We are come,' sang their escort, 'to Mount Zion and to the city of the Living God, the heavenly Jerusalem, and to innumerable angels in festal gathering and to the assembly of the first-born who are enrolled in heaven, and to a judge who is God of all, and to the spirits of just men made perfect, and to Jesus, the mediator of the new covenant and to the sprinkled blood that speaks more graciously than the blood of Abel.' 'You enter now,' they said, 'on the Paradise of God, where you will taste of the Tree of Life and eat for ever of its pleasant fruits with the King of all kings, yes, even all the days of eternity. The afflictions of earth shall touch you no more, for sorrow and pain, sickness and death, are all unknown. The former things are passed away. The God of all grace has made everything new.'

'And what shall be our occupation?' asked the pilgrims, 'in such a heaven as this.' To which they answered, 'You must receive comfort for your toil, joy for your sorrow and the fruit of your prayers. There you will reap of the truth you have sown and shall rest from your labours. There you shall gaze on the face of your Lord, even on Him who is altogether lovely. There, as a kingdom of priests you shall serve Him with praise and thanksgiving, whom you served with tears and infirmity on the earth. Those in Christ who have crossed the River shall greet you, and you will know them, not as in Adam, weak and defiled; but in Christ, flawless in splendour before God's throne. And those who enter on their glory after you, you also will receive, and together with them you shall put on majesty and be fitted to ride with the King of heaven when He goes forth to reign on the earth. Then shall be heard the sound of a trumpet and you shall ride on the wings of the wind. And when He sits on the Throne of His Judgement, you shall sit with Him; and when He passes sentence on all the workers of iniquity, your voice shall be heard because they were both His, and your enemies, in the days of the insurrection. And when He returns to the City and shall have rendered the Kingdom to the Father, then you shall be there and God shall be all in all.'

So upward and onward they fly, up through the shining firmament and its terrible crystal, which mirrors man's world to the world on high. Now they scan its uppermost edge, one sea of glass reflecting heaven's glory. They look in wonder on its shimmering beauty, then lift their eyes to the City itself. This is their moment. Emblazoned cohorts surge out to greet them and all their being leaps out to God. 'These men,' their escort declares, 'are of those who believe to their soul's salvation. See how they stand in the garments God gave them. Thus far have we brought them and by command from the Throne. Before mankind they witnessed a good confession but now are come to behold their Redeemer.' Then the heavenly hosts wheeled in their armour and with a shout that rang through the vast expanse, cried in their welcome, 'Blessed are they who are called unto the marriage supper of the Lamb.' So with trumpetings and ten thousand voices they entered upon the threshold of their bliss. And there above the portals of the City they saw in shining gold the proclamation of its gladness, 'Blessed are they that do His commandments, that they may have right to the Tree of Life and enter in through the gates of the City.' 'Call now at The Gate,' said the Shining Ones and on the battlements appeared the unnumbered heroes of the faith. 'These pilgrims,' they told them, 'come from the City of Destruction and for love of your King. His subjects they are by reason of grace and through faith in His promise.' And with this they presented their briefings, their proof of that Word received at the Cross. At once their credentials were sent to the Throne and when He who sat thereon had pondered them, He made enquiry, and said, 'Where are the men?' To which the Shining Ones gave answer, 'They stand before Thy gates, Thou King of Glory.' Then the King in majesty and mercy commanded, 'Fling wide the gates that the righteous nation which keeps faith may enter in.' Then as the gates swung open, Christian and Hopeful passed into His Presence and were transfigured before Him, whilst the City rang again with the glad acclamation, 'Enter ye into the joy of our Lord.' But in my dream, I heard another song, that sounded above all others and the words were these, 'Blessing, and honour, and glory, and power, be unto Him that sitteth upon the Throne and unto the Lamb for ever and ever.'

In that one brief moment when the gates swung open to admit the pilgrims, I looked in after them, and I saw that the City shone like the sun, that its streets were paved with gold; and that in them walked men with crowns on their heads and palms in their hands, and they sang a new song which only new men can sing. And there amongst them I saw not only Christian and Hopeful, but Faithful also, whose blood cries yet from the streets of Sexpo. There were glorious beings too, each with their wings who cried without ceasing, 'Holy, Holy, Holy is the Lord!' Then they shut to the gates and I was left outside, yearning that the day might come when I might also enter in.

# CHAPTER TWENTY-FOUR

# THE GULF AT THE GATE

Now after these things, I looked beneath me, and infinitely far below, I could see the River of Death snaking its way through the realms of men. Ignorance had arrived and was mingling with various people along its banks. Since spurning the company of Christian and Hopeful, he had felt much happier and things had turned out better than expected. In fact, he had made quite a fortune in Come-and-Go. Just how was a mystery, but one thing was certain—basking in the local admiration, his self-confidence had become even more insufferable. Moving in more affluent circles, he had changed his name by deed-poll to Arrogance, though the elite in Come-and-Go abhorred his disregard of convention and bemoaned the decline of true aristocracy.

I could see Ignorance quite clearly now, dressed rather casually, and guffawing expansively with all and sundry on the beach. His hair was awry, his stance aggressive and his face bore that defiant look which says to all, 'Being who I am, and having what I do, I intend to call the tune right up to the River.' Ignorant as always, he was quite unaware that the people around him had come to molest the pilgrims. He fondly assumed they were there to bid him farewell. So nothing daunted, he commenced to shake hands.

'It's nice to have met you, Wiseman, old boy,' began Ignorance. 'If it weren't for this appointment with His Majesty, I'd be coming for a ride in that car of yours. Looks to me like the latest Gehenna!'

'How right you are!' replied Mr. Worldly Wiseman, his calm aplomb somewhat affected.

'Well, so long for now,' breezed Ignorance, without waiting for the slightest reciprocation, and away he went down the beach to talk with the beatniks. After cracking some jokes, which they failed to appreciate, he walked over to the van and asked, with the utmost of good humour, for a brochure on Motel Magnificent. 'Not a patch on the accommodation where I'm going,' he remarked crudely. 'Puts your place in the shade, I should say.'

But Apollyon only leered at him. 'Where ignorance is bliss,' he muttered, ''tis folly to be wise!'

Now he approached the lions. He found them the most friendly of creatures, and patting their manes, gave them each an old

188

English humbug from a bag he kept in his pocket. They licked their lips most appreciatively, and grinned after him all the way to the River. Ignorance then took a last look round, just to ensure he had shaken everyone's hand, but all he saw was an old man with a walrus-moustache in a commissionaire's uniform. Being oblivious, however, to both flattery and criticism, he could not recall him and so gave him the go-by. A good time, then, having been had by all, he popped down to the River where, contrary to expectation, the Vain-Hope Ferry Company had laid on a special craft to carry him across. It had been manufactured in the City of Conceit and transported overland for the occasion. 'Money's no object,' that's what he'd told them, and true to their contract, they had delivered the goods! So Ignorance went on board and made himself comfortable. The water that day proved as calm as a millpond and to the purr of the engines, he quickly passed over.

But now his problems began. Although on the earthward shore his plans had worked perfectly, he had made no provision for his onward journey. He had felt no need. 'Most travellers are met,' he'd been told, 'and given an escort.' Now on arrival not a soul stirred to greet him. 'It's outrageous,' he grumbled, 'and I'm here by appointment!' But what could he do? The launch was away. There was no going back. Mists of darkness descended. The loneliness gripped him. He waited. He wondered. The silence grew ominous. Still nobody came. How long had he been there? But Time was no longer. It seemed like eternity. But this *was* Eternity. At the foot of the canyon he groped for direction whilst far, far above glowed a glimmer of light. What use was there lingering? In death as in life, he must reach for the highest. So finding a foothold, he started to climb.

Now the higher he mounted, the lower he seemed; and far though he went, the further he felt from that City he sought. Then, for an instant, he sighted the Gate, and frantically shouting, he signalled the sentries.

'But who may you be?' they sternly enquired. 'And from whence have you come?'

'I'm a friend of your King,' he presumed to inform them. 'He's bound to recall me, for we've eaten together and He's taught in our streets. You should know of my coming. I'm here by command!'

'But what of your briefing received at the Cross and the mark on your forehead that speaks of our Master?'

More disconcerted than he wished to admit, he ran his hands through his hair and then through his pockets, but all he could find was his cheque book and driving licence.

'Have you neither?' the voice demanded, but Ignorance stood speechless.

Then the King was advised but refused to come down, and giving word to His angels, they led him by force beyond the ramparts. So the Shining Ones, who to the pilgrims were as ministering spirits, became to Ignorance as flames of fire.

Then I saw in my dream how they took him, and through a crevice of rock by the Gate of the City hurled him headlong below, to the blazing deep. Downward, still downward he went, down through unfathomed depths; and all the time I was saying it, and saying it over and over again, 'So there's a way to hell from the gates of heaven as well as from the City of Destruction.' And all I could feel was a falling, falling; and nothing in heaven or earth could stop me. Terror took hold of me. The bottomless pit leapt up to devour me . . .

Then something hard struck my head and I woke with a scream in the rock-strewn crater . . . where the tall grey flats look upward and upward into the bright blue sky.